THE HEART REMEMBERS

Andrea didn't say anything as Hank walked her to her room.

They reached the doorway and looked at each other in the dimness.

"Dandy," he said.

The breath caught in her throat. That was John's name for her, and it felt so wonderful to hear it again.

"I want to call you Dandy," Hank said. "Because that's what you are. Did anyone ever think of that before?" He touched her cheek.

Her skin blazed beneath his finger. The way it always did.

"No one but you," she said.

His arms went around her and he held her and dropped kisses into her hair and let her soak his shoulder with her tears of gorgeous relief.

BROKEN-HEARTED

NANCY WEBER

PINNACLE BOOKS
WINDSOR PUBLISHING CORP.

PINNACLE BOOKS

are published by

Windsor Publishing Corp.
475 Park Avenue South
New York, NY 10016

First Pinnacle Books printing: July, 1990

Printed in the United States of America

For Bob and Rose and Albert,
who make my heart whole.

At the turn in life's game, I went astray
from my wonted course and woke to find myself
alone at a strange club. How could I play

nine holes there? I never saw so cruel,
so swampy and dark, a first tee.
Even a pro would call for winter rules.

Death taunted me: Shoot out of bounds!
But the Greenskeeper saved me, and with His help
it was my fortune to play a birdie round.

—John Malcolm Pearce
PIN HIGH

The
White
Course

When a ball lies in or touches a hazard or a water hazard, nothing shall be done which may in any way improve its lie.

—THE RULES OF GOLF

Chapter 1

On the third day of their honeymoon, Andrea and John ran out of milk. There were raspberries and croissants for a sentimental breakfast but nothing that would turn coffee into café au lait.

They were in Kent, Connecticut, in the old farmhouse Andrea had inherited from her grandparents on her mother's side. She'd spent summers there as a girl, learning to ride on a pony named Pudgy and pulling trout out of the Housatonic River, and it had remained her favorite place, her retreat from the wildness of New York. John had wanted to take their honeymoon in China — his next book would be about acupuncture, and he thought pleasure and work mixed just fine; but she'd wanted a week against a background so familiar it would fade away and they would only see each other, and he'd agreed that sounded even better.

So Kent now, the first week in January. In June, when the weather would be nicest, they would go to Beijing, unless she were pregnant.

Meanwhile, they needed milk, and they were just about snowed in. The world outside the kitchen window was a white blur. Snow had started falling as they'd driven across the Housatonic River on Saturday, and by the time they'd gotten up the hill to the house, big sticky flakes had been coming down steadily and they hadn't stopped.

If they never stopped, she wouldn't mind. She had John Malcolm Pearce and this house. If those were the borders of her world, it would still seem dazzlingly grand, almost too grand to be true. She had read a short story of his in *The New Yorker* when she was sixteen, sitting in this very kitchen. She'd imagined he had somehow construed her existence and had written "The One and Only" to reach her, and with that thought her life ambitions had formed. She would stay on in New York, not head for San Francisco, after college. She would be in the literary, not the legal, world. She would know him and make him know her. To her amazement, it had happened as she'd hoped and then some.

She had to turn and look at him. He was standing in front of the stove, focused on the glass coffee pot, ready to move as soon as the last of the water had dripped through the paper filter. The moment came and she smiled her satisfaction as he pounced. His intensity during ordinary acts sometimes brought dance to her mind, but that wasn't quite it. He wasn't artful or stylized so much as capital-T There, making her aware—she realized now, putting the thought together—that few other people were fully present in the moments of their lives.

He grasped the filter with his right hand and cupped his left hand underneath to catch any drops and carried it over to the sink; then he poured coffee into blue-and-yellow flower-patterned thin china mugs that had been there since her grandparents' day. He put the mugs on the round kitchen table, setting them just so. In a lesser man, and these days all other men were very much lesser, the precision might have seemed fussy. Not in John. He was muscular, healthy, earthy, available to big ideas, spiritually as well as physically robust. And it was for her, Andrea Olinger, an ordinary woman, that this paragon was making the coffee perfect.

"Sugar?"

Absurdly—but knowing it was didn't help—she was hurt. "You know I don't use sugar," she said. She turned back to the window and stared out. The snow had swallowed everything between the woodshed and infinity—the apple trees, the pond, the hills.

"Because you always have milk in the morning," he said.

She heard him calmly stirring sugar into his mug. He never took sugar when there was milk.

"You're the one who got me started," she said. "I only drank black coffee when we met."

"Well, maybe you knew what you were doing. This tastes fine. I think I'll convert to black in the morning. With a touch of sugar. The secret wisdom in the accidents of life, you see?"

She loved his voice. It was clear without being thin and muscular though it wasn't deep—an intelligent voice marbled with jokiness. When she'd first read his stories, she'd known how he should sound and probably wouldn't, but he did. That voice was inviting her to sit down, share the joke, drink coffee, touch, maybe go back to bed. Luckiest of Andreas. But a strange mood had hold of her, was egging her on about the damn milk. They'd had two crystalline days since driving up from New York. He'd discovered her all over again, pronouncing her perfect. He'd been so newly smitten, he'd followed her into the bathroom to watch her brush her teeth. Now, because of the quart that wasn't there, she felt flawed.

She turned around and faced him. "I suppose if

we'd gone to China, we'd be drinking green tea, and you wouldn't miss milk at all."

He put his mug down. "Andrea, what are you doing?"

He was rumpled and beddish in his red plaid robe. The dark blond hair he'd worn distinctly parted at the wedding drifted vaguely to the right. She'd asked him not to shave, and a two-day growth of coppery beard covered his cheeks. If he were a movie actor, he would be cast as Paul Newman's younger buddy, a hell-raiser but righteous, and he would get the girl.

Oh, how he'd gotten the girl. Though she hadn't had a bad time with men for someone who'd stayed single until twenty-eight, no one else had made her feel so — she'd arrived at the word a month after she'd met him — recognized. And he seemed to feel that she did the same thing for him; none of his details was wasted on her, he'd once said — cocky but a compliment, too. Would he always feel that way, though?

He smiled at her, the smile that said he'd caught her being silly and he loved her anyway, and her need to fight with him diminished, as if something actual and physical were draining out of her chest.

"What I'm doing," she said, "is being neurotic."

He nodded. "It's your house so it's your fault there isn't any milk. Even though I was the one who said at the XYZ that we only needed a quart."

"Even though."

He patted his knee. "Come."

She sat on his lap. He put his arms around her. She could feel the wool in his robe through the silk of hers.

" 'Even though' is a grudging, nasty little phrase, isn't it?" he said.

"It is, rather." She kissed his chin. It was a very nice chin and jaw, shaped like the base of a heart, somewhere between triangular and round, not one of those excessively geometric jaws yet not a bit too soft.

"Even though we're out of milk, I love you." He shook his head. "Love means never saying 'even though.'"

"Is this the trenchant thinker and literary stylist John Malcolm Pearce? We may be out of more than milk."

"Never you mind." He ran admiring fingers from one of her shoulders across to the other. "We'll videotape your collarbones and make a million dollars. Those lovely pulsing hollows."

He was teasing and serious at the same moment, a very John piece of business. She delighted in his capacity for small excitements, but sometimes she worried that he dwelled on elbows, ankles, collarbones, eyebrows, the crispness and gleam of her chestnut hair because her parts were better than the sum. "You're beautiful—to me," he liked to say, laughing and ducking as she balled her fists in mock (but was it?) fury.

He kissed her, soft hop-skip trails of nibbles across her neck. "I'm glad we came here, Dandy."

His special name—she'd never considered herself an Andy, and he thought Andrea too forbidding for tender moments—provoked a throb, a rush of heat. But the demon insecurity had hold of her, and instead of kissing him as she longed to she said, "Tell me you're not a teeny tiny bit bored."

"Come upstairs, and I'll show you how bored I'm not. And then I'll fire up the Jeep and drive into town for milk. Enough to bathe you in."

"See." She nuzzled his neck. "You want to get the papers. Admit it. You kept me from buying more milk so you'd have an excuse to go for the papers."

"You're right. I want to get the papers even though we're out of milk." She laughed, and he kissed her. "I love you outrageously much."

13

And the demon was routed, at least for the moment. She leaned against him and sighed her contentment. Impossible that the dream had come true, but it had, and she must learn to live at this level of happiness—accept it, John said, as her due. "You're conscious," he'd proclaimed an hour after they'd met, that glorious day when she'd interviewed the new Pulitzer Prize winner for the *Daily News*. He'd said the word with respect, even wonder, as though consciousness had been outlawed and he'd thought never to see it again. He'd invited her to dinner as she'd started, with plain reluctance, to put her cassette recorder back into her briefcase, and by the time they'd gotten to espresso, he'd proclaimed her kind funny clever pretty sexy, but the consciousness was what had caught him. Made him want to make her happy.

The demon materialized again. Would consciousness hold him forever? Would anything? He'd been divorced twice, and there had been lots of women in between, snazzy women. He hadn't wanted to have a child with anyone else, though, and he'd been saying for six months that he could hardly wait to have a family with her.

Now he closed his hand over her fingers. "Are we tying the knot again?"

She looked down and saw that she'd taken an end of the peach silk sash of her robe and had twisted it around his red plaid belt. "Just in case the other day wasn't absolute," she said lightly.

"It was as absolute as your nose"—kissing the nose she still thought too big though he called it her nose for news and claimed to adore it—"but let's do it again anyway." His eyes danced, and he said, "Every new knot-tying in Connecticut requires a new act of consummation. The most enlightened of the blue laws."

"You want consommé, I'll make you consommé."

14

"No, madame, I will make you consommé. In my upstairs galley." He slid her off his lap and stood and took her in his arms. "Do you have any idea how great we're going to be? And I don't mean just in the next half hour. We're what the whole wild business is about, do you realize that? We're going to do it all before we're finished."

"And would you be knowing when that will be?"

"Don't get your hopes up. You're stuck with me for a long, long time. Forever and twenty minutes."

"That might be almost long enough."

"I'd say I'm long enough for you."

"Oh ho. Such arrogance. Your heart is beating fast."

"Because your hair smells so good. Like a vanilla milkshake. Can you hear? It's talking to you."

She listened to his heart and she heard. *Dan-dy. Dan-dy. Sweet as. Can-dy. I love. Dan-dy.*

She tugged at the lapels of his robe, exposed the flesh over his heart, kissed it. "I love you, heart."

"And now for a message from another member of our broadcasting group."

She got down on her knees and listened. "Well, since you asked so nicely," she said. Up and down and around she traveled, warm wet mouth humming its friendly song.

"Oh," he said, and "ah," he said, his hands sifting through her hair. Then his legs began to tremble and he whispered her name with some urgency and said they'd better go to bed.

He scooped her up as if she were a bundle of fluff and carried her to the second floor. He laid her down on the pale peach sheets of the honeymoon bed. He arranged her arms, her legs, her hair, and stood over her smiling, shaking his head in delight. "My beauty."

"Your funny valentine," she said.

He kneeled beside her and kissed the words away.

"No more insecurity, Dandrea, do you hear? You've used up your quota for the year. I'm wild about you, and if that's crazy, I don't care. I don't want to be cured." He pulled at the lapels of her robe, exposing her breasts, making her feel more vulnerable, exquisitely vulnerable, than if she were naked altogether. "Admit it. You're a star."

She wasn't much of an actress, but she did her best at faking outraged honor. "No no. I'll never admit it. No matter what."

He untied the sash at her waist. His hands moved knowingly over her belly, pulling warm waves of sugary desire from deep inside.

"So sweet," she told him on a sigh. "Unbelievably sweet."

"That's it," he said, his fingertips on her thighs. "Dandy, my dessert."

"Not what I am," she protested. "What you make me feel. There. Yes. Dearest."

"You are what you feel," he said, and she laughed and said she gave up, she admitted it, she was great and glorious — she would admit anything as long as he went on doing what he was doing. Then she wanted more and he did too and they gave all they had to each other, shouting of a love that would never die.

Chapter 2

Margo quickly wheeled her wagon past the cheese counter at Cheese 'n' Stuff. A bouquet of aromas trailed after her and teased her nose — the earthy coolness of Wensleydale, the tang of Saint André (on special for $6.49 a pound), whiffs of sheep and goat and garlic and hickory smoke. Faster, Margo.

Really, it was too awfully unfair (except that it wasn't unfair at all) to come to this store every week, two or three times some weeks, and only buy "stuff," when cheese was her absolutely favorite food in the world after chocolate (also forbidden). She had to come here because it was the best source in greater Hartford of the food Hank had needed for his diet in the four years since the heart attack — low in fat, salt, and sugar, high in vitamins and fiber. She didn't buy cheese because Hank couldn't eat any, except for bland, gummy mockeries like hoop cheese that were sadder than no cheese at all, and what he couldn't eat she wouldn't eat. Anyway, she wanted Debbie and Skip to grow up thinking of cheese and red meat and eggs and butter the way she'd grown up thinking (wrongly) of bread, as food you stayed away from if you wanted to be slim and healthy.

Hurray for bread. She headed for aisle three and

started filling her wagon. Pritikin whole wheat English muffins, which when Nathan Pritikin had committed suicide had led Hank to say (though he'd truly mourned) that maybe the great strengthener of hearts had been unable to face another breakfast of his own English muffins. Bran for Life raisin bread (Skip called it Run for Your Life, but he ate it anyway when he was home—they all did). Whole wheat matzos— Moses could have wiped out Pharaoh with these. Unsalted rice cakes—"made from brown rice and absolutely nothing else," except maybe a little styrofoam.

Not complaining, darlings! she told the packages in her wagon, bending to pat the rice cakes and not caring who saw her. Just teasing a little, was all. She loved every life-sustaining crumb in the joint. If only she'd known about whole grains twenty years ago. If only her mother and Hank's mother had known. Those two loving women had thought a challah the finest of breads, with potato bread and rye bread (mostly white flour) close behind. And of course they'd pushed and pushed the eternal chicken soup, Jewish penicillin. One of Hank's doctors (a rabbi's son, so he could get away with it) had told her that chicken soup with all its saturated fat had probably killed more Jewish men than the Gestapo had.

But how could you criticize? The previous generation had thought of white bread and golden broth as symbols of prosperity and well-being, a fine leap from the coarse crusts and watery soups of their oppressed forebears. Someday Debbie and Skip would shake their heads as they did their marketing and would wonder why on earth their poor misguided mother had fed them—fill in the blank. Or maybe the next generation would discover that white bread and chicken soup were good for you after all.

18

Meanwhile, tofu and radish sprouts went into the basket. Water-washed decaffeinated mocha-java. Spanish onions, which maybe did, maybe didn't cut cholesterol—in either event, Hank loved them: they made up for the salt he still missed. First pressing olive oil (to be used a drop at a time) because margarine was unspeakable (except in baking), safflower oil possibly carcinogenic, and Margo had been impressed by a study she'd read linking the low incidence of heart attacks among Italian men to the use of olive oil.

I could write a book, she thought, as she got into line to pay. She'd contributed a recipe, Valentine Cake for a Broken Heart, to the Temple Sisterhood cookbook—no egg yolks, no salt, no shortening, and carob instead of chocolate. Delicious, too! She'd enjoyed the compliments from people she hardly knew, but not nearly as much as she enjoyed Hank's compliments every mealtime. Even if someone were to ask her to write a book about the care and feeding of heart patients, and offer her big money and tell her she could help a lot of people, she'd say no. A project like that might rob her of the strength that Hank and Debbie and Skip had first call on—a brimming reservoir of strength, knock wood, but no one could do everything.

Pleasantly weighted down by shopping bags, she squished through the slush in the parking lot to get to her car. Really, she was a very lucky woman. At forty-eight, she was at the tail end of the generation of women who could call themselves housewives and not feel demeaned. Of course she'd had a career for the last four years, virtually running Hank's insurance agency, but it was work she was doing because she was Hank's wife and he needed her help, not because she was searching for fulfillment. When Hank got his new heart, God willing, and was himself again, she would

19

happily hang up her briefcase and leave the business world to him.

She pulled her dark blue Chevrolet out onto Farmington Avenue and joined the slow procession toward West Hartford. The plows had done their best, but snow was still falling, though lightly now, and there was only one lane of traffic snaking in either direction. Twenty minutes to go a distance that normally took four or five, and then, just past Prospect Avenue, where there was a hill, traffic stopped moving altogether, and her throat got tight and dry. Don't panic, she instructed herself, but her hand ignored the order and nervously groped in her shoulderbag for her beeper. Yes, it was on. Yes, the battery was alive. Hank was alive.

She'd carried the beeper with her ever since Hank's heart attack, and a dozen times he'd gotten her home in a hurry because he was having angina pain. She would burst in and find him stretched out on the Barcalounger reading a mystery, looking sheepish because he'd managed to slip a nitroglycerine tablet under his tongue and wasn't dead. Each time she'd had to explain that his panic came with the territory, was part of the chemistry of the angina, and he wasn't weak, he was still her hero.

Traffic started moving. She breathed normally again.

Hank had his own beeper now that he was officially a candidate for a heart transplant at Downtown Medical Center. Some days he checked his beeper every hour, and you couldn't blame him.

They knew a kid in the program, Mike Weller— only twenty-three, he'd been felled by cardiomyopathy—who was at the top of the list in his category but hadn't gotten his heart because he'd gone to the movies not knowing the battery in his beeper had run down. Which gave you an idea of how long some people had to wait for their call. Though God moved in mysterious ways (as Mike Weller had said at clinic last week). Sam Mancuso had gotten the heart slated for Mike and he was having trouble breathing, and he was back on the transplant list. The heart might have worked for Mike. You never knew. So much you didn't know.

A dented Volkswagen with a green Vermont plate went into a skid ahead of her, and Margo expertly tapped on the brake to slow down. A headline flashed in her mind—WIFE KILLED IN CRASH, HEART GIVEN TO AILING HUSBAND. It couldn't really happen—she was the wrong size, five feet four and a hundred twelve pounds to Hank's six feet and a hundred eighty pounds—and anyway she wasn't about to let it happen.

When Hank was well, she was going to be there to start a new life with him. They would have a second honeymoon, and a third and fourth and fifth, beginning with a weekend at the Plaza in New York while he was still on restricted travel, and then on to Bermuda, Paris, the moon! And they would be happier than they'd been as newlyweds, than anyone could be as newlyweds, because they knew what love was about.

She turned right at Trout Brook Road. She hadn't seen this much snow in West Hartford since she was a little girl. The street was lined with drifts as high as the car. School had been called off for the second day in a row, and igloos and snowmen—snowpersons, Debbie would humorlessly correct her—had sprung up in front of nearly every house. Skip, who was mad about skiing, was probably wishing he'd gone to Dartmouth instead of New York University, which he'd picked to be near his other passion, musical theater.

Margo loved the snow too, but it scared her. Anything that might come between Hank and a new heart scared her. She'd been awake before dawn the last two mornings, listening for the plows.

She detoured up Albany Avenue to run into the Crown Market for a kosher chicken. She and Hank were Reform — they didn't observe the dietary laws — but there was something about a kosher chicken. Really, she should call Hank's Aunt Becky and invite her for dinner, but Hank said Becky was murder on the blood pressure. The old woman had screamed at Hank and Margo and the kids that a transplant violated Jewish law because it involved the mutilation of a corpse and therefore was forbidden, as autopsies were; and it had taken her own Orthodox rabbi, called by a frantic Margo, to convince her that transplants were in the Jewish tradition, which always favored life. Then Becky had started in: What if it isn't a Jewish heart? A kind heart? Are you sure a bypass wouldn't do it? Shouldn't you go to Pittsburgh, the transplantation center? I'll go with you.

"Cut up and skinned, Mrs. Corman?" The young red-haired butcher smiled. He always made her feel he was glad to see her, never mind her war on fat, demanding trimming and skinning.

"Please, Louie. And we don't need the innards, so if you have another use for them."

"Right-o. You have some shopping to do?"

"I really just came in for the bird, but I can go read cereal boxes if you're backed up."

"I'll have it for you in five minutes. Don't go anywhere, Mrs. C." He disappeared behind the swinging door.

She was dreaming in front of the briskets when Sally Letterman, in a blue and white Norwegian reindeer sweater and gleaming white ski pants, pushed her loaded wagon up to the meat counter. "Margo, honey"—swooping—"how are you?"

"Terrific, Sally. How's everything with you?"

Sally shook her dark helmet of hair. Sally had been urging the same style on Margo, telling her to grow out her layers—the urchin look was dead, and she should get rid of the gray while she was at it.

"Margo, you don't have to put on a brave face with me. We go back a long way. It's hell, isn't it? When my poor sweet Walter was on the way out"—her mouth turned down like a trout's—"there were moments when I longed for him to have the peace of that good night."

If it had been anyone but Sally, Margo might have gotten angry, but Sally was, well, Sally. And when Walter Hirsh, her older brother, a bachelor, probably homosexual only afraid to be, had been dying of cirrhosis, Sally had looked after him in her own home, as tender as she'd been when her children were babies.

"Hank's going to make it" was all Margo said. So sure of her words that they came out sounding almost offhand. Then, rushing, because her friend was looking so damn pitying, "Sally, you have no idea what a miracle these heart transplants are. A month after the surgery, Hank could be standing up there at the first tee swinging his driver like nothing ever happened."

"But the wires, the boxes. Is it worth it? Is it really living?" Sally picked up a shrink-wrapped package of chicken livers and put it down with a little shriek. "Look at that, they're green! Oh God, if you can't trust the Crown, what's left?"

"You're thinking of artificial hearts," Margo said. Amazing how many people confused the two procedures. "When you have a transplant, no one could ever tell from looking at you that you're not an ordinary guy with an ordinary heart. Which is what you are." She pictured Louie wrapping her chicken in butcher paper—he knew she didn't like plastic. Hurry, Louie. "You ought to come to clinic with us one week. See the people who've gotten their hearts. It's very inspiring."

Sally put her arms around Margo and hugged her. "You're the one who's inspiring. You're the bravest woman I know."

Louie came out with Margo's chicken. "There you go, Mrs. C. Drive carefully, okay?"

"Thanks, Louie. You, too. Bye, Sally, love."

"Louie," she heard Sally say behind her, "those livers are positively chartreuse."

"Just a little bit of bile, Mrs. Letterman. I'll trim it right off."

"Make me up a fresh package, would you, Louie? If you knew from liver like I know from liver, we'd both be vegetarians, right?"

Brave, Margo thought, as she brushed snow off her windshield. She hated brave. It was right up there with humble and noble in her pantheon of unwanted virtues. Because there couldn't be bravery unless there were fear, and fear was the worst of all emotions. Let them call her fearless, not brave. Even if it weren't true.

Sue McKay honked at her as she was waiting for the green light out of the parking lot. She honked back and grinned. Ever since Sue and Gar and their kids had come to a seder at the Cormans', Sue had had a thing for kosher chickens, and though she still pronounced the word as if it were spelled "kojzher," it was as a joke on herself for being a superWASP.

The two women had a great, giggly friendship, mostly over the telephone, in which they exchanged ethnic recipes—whole-meal scones for bagels, sorrel salad for borscht—and made dents in their otherness.

Debbie, who claimed she didn't know what religion her friends were, mocked Margo's frank pleasure in having a Christian as a friend. But in this town, where people played golf according to their God, Margo thought the connection signified something good. Anyway, Sue was terrific, and Gar McKay, a cardiologist at Downtown Medical Center, had sent them to see Dr. Fox before anyone else knew Downtown was starting a cardiac transplant program.

Margo let out a whoosh of relief as she turned into the driveway on Pocahontas Drive. She hadn't been gone two hours, but she felt as though an eternity had passed since she'd tiptoed out of the bedroom in which Hank had lain sleeping and headed into the snow.

Before she could hit the button to operate the garage door, the door started rolling up, and Debbie appeared, barefoot, on the steps that linked the garage with the laundry room, which in turn led to the kitchen. The Cormans had moved from their colonial to the one-level brick and glass house after Hank's attack, when it had become clear that he would never again be friends with stairs.

"Quick, Mom," Debbie said, as soon as the ignition was off.

"Daddy?" Margo tasted metal. She hurried around the car and up the steps.

"It's not an attack," Debbie said, "but he's very hot and he's got a rash."

Margo pulled off her boots. The toes of her kneesocks were wet, but she left them on. She dropped her tweed coat onto the clothes dryer. "Why didn't you beep me?"

"Daddy wouldn't let me." Debbie's eyes filled with tears. "He said he didn't want you driving nervously in this weather. I called Gar, and he's on his way, but he's taking forever."

Margo squeezed Debbie's hand. "Good work, honey."

"Should I have beeped you?" Debbie was thirteen, but her voice still had a little girl's tremulousness when she thought she'd displeased her parents.

"No. Daddy was right. I probably would have wrapped myself around a pole. It's a mess out there. Is he in bed?"

They were cutting through the dining room, the living room.

"He never got out of it," Debbie said. "At nine-thirty I went and knocked on the door. Was that okay?"

"Yes. Yes."

"He said to come in, and I asked him if he wanted o.j. or some decaf. He said no, he just wanted water, and he sounded awful, and I turned on the light and I saw how red he was, and I called Gar."

They got to Margo and Hank's bedroom. Margo kissed Debbie on the top of her head. She loved Debbie's hair, long and blue-black and glossy, as her own hair had once been, with a scent like mulling spice, and she often kissed her where the part was, just left of center. This time she was kissing her to say she had to go into the bedroom alone, and she smiled her appreciation as Debbie hung back.

"Hank?" She cut across the pale green carpet. His bed was on the far side of the room, nearer the bathroom. Changing from a double bed to the twins had hit her harder than giving up their old house for this one. Another necessity, though, because after the heart attack he'd woken if she'd so much as turned over.

"Hi, kid." There was a choky sound to his normally raspy voice, and she knew he was fighting terror.

She could feel the fever coming off him even before she put the back of her hand to his forehead. A hundred two, a hundred three. And his face all mottled. She swallowed her own terror. She sat down on the bed.

"What's this?" she said, in a voice dredged up from when the children were small — You're not sick, you can go to school. Hank had kicked back the top sheet and quilt, and she saw that his pajamas were soaked with sweat. "A little flu?"

He shook his head. She unbuttoned his pajama top. Blue-and-white stripes, very New England, the kids' present last Father's Day. His chest was all rashy, too. He looked the way Skip had looked with the measles, but it couldn't be measles — no one in West Hartford got measles anymore. If only she'd kissed him goodbye before she'd left, she would have known something was wrong, and Gar would be here by now. Holding back her kiss — and slipping out of the darkened room to dress in the guest room — was a daily un-act of love. So many un-acts of love.

If Gar didn't get there in five minutes, she'd call an ambulance. Meanwhile, call Mickie Ross, the coordinator for the cardiac transplant unit, who wanted to know if any of her patients so much as stubbed a toe. Don't call anyone yet, keep him calm, calm saved lives.

Hank put his hand on his chest. Liver-spotted hand on grayhaired chest, head rising off the pillow, the panic owning him now, cheeks sucked hollow, he looked a hundred years old. Hank, I love you so much, I'll be ancient with you, hold on.

"I can't breathe."

"Yes, you can, darling. Breathe with me. In, out. In, out. Gar will be here any second. In, out."

At least there weren't chest pains. Hurry, Gar. Portable oxygen in the closet, but the sight of it would make him fibrillate. She bridged her fingertips to his,

27

both hands, so her pulse rate would control his, a new-age party game she'd learned from one of Skip's girlfriends, nonsense that sometimes worked.

"In, out. In, out. Terrific. In, out. Maybe something you ate, honey, that's all. It's not your heart. Your heart is fine. In, out."

"Mom, Gar is here," Debbie said at the door.

Tall, spare, balding, brisk Gar needed all of thirty seconds. "A hundred to one it's a drug reaction, old boy. Probably the captopril. We'll straighten you out in no time."

"But he's been taking it for four years." Captopril controlled his blood pressure, let him live almost like a human being. One of their best friends. Couldn't betray them this way.

"Allergies are like that, Margo. Five minutes, five years—they can happen anytime."

"So we just find another medicine?"

Gar nodded but he didn't meet her eyes. He reached for the telephone. "Hank, I'll feel better if you're in the hospital. I'm calling an ambulance."

"You'll feel better?" Hank said. "What about me?"

Hank looked at Margo, and she smiled to say she loved him the more for joking. Hang on, hang on, any day they'll have a heart for you, I don't wish for someone's death, but someone please die and give my Hank your heart.

Chapter 3

Andrea lay in bed listening to the heavy sounds of the Jeep as John backed it out of the driveway and started down Sprague Road. He was a sports car person — they'd driven up from New York in the red Lamborghini — but he handled the clunky four-wheel-drive Jeep with grace, and that pleased her. Too many of the men she'd known in the old days had proven to be either/or people. There were city-dwellers who couldn't build fires and country boys who shriveled among tall buildings, brains who had no character and nice guys without any wit, men who wanted sex or friendship, health or fun. John was a both/and person, someone who refused to see limits or contradictions where there weren't any, and this unsimplicity promised a life in which wonders would happen.

He'd proposed to her in Juan-les-Pins on their trip last summer, the day he'd acquired the Lamborghini, a day of roller-coaster ups and downs before joy held sway. The car deal had been clinched over breakfast, and then they'd gone off to do separate errands until lunch, which they'd set for one-thirty at La Maison des Pêcheurs. At two o'clock he hadn't come and hadn't called, and she'd been frantic. He was like a little boy with his new car, making *vroom vroom* noises as he revved up, dragging other sports cars at intersections, and her mind had been full of such calamitous pictures that when he'd arrived at two-fifteen, not particularly contrite, she'd yelled and hammered him with her fists. He'd laughed, he'd caught her up, he'd said he wanted to marry her. She'd said yes, oh yes, if he promised not to make her a widow.

She thought she could hear him shifting down to take the curve at the top of the hill, but the thick falling snow was muffling and distorting everything and she'd probably imagined the sound. For a moment she indulged in the old game — agony followed by sweet relief — of telling herself she'd imagined him altogether. She buried her face in his pillow, hunting for the lime and rum of his spice, and found it and inhaled it; and she lay back and let the John-ness of her life suffuse her. The cool side of her nature, what John called her coefficient of cucumbers, proclaimed her behavior excessive, even for a bride, and she came to.

She got out of bed and tugged the sheets and quilt into order and then went into the bathroom and turned on the water in the tub. The room was huge — it had three windows — and John had offered to buy a hot tub, but she'd chosen to keep the modest claw-foot tub in which her grandparents had bathed. She'd changed the house as little as possible, and when she'd replaced a lamp, a chair, a toaster, the rug in the dining room, she'd shopped as if Grand'Anna and Papa Sam were still alive.

She threw a handful of dried home-grown lavender and pennyroyal into the bath. The burst of fragrance carried her backward through time, and she saw herself at age ten and Anna at seventy, in twin wide-brimmed hats and heavy gloves, down on their hands and knees working to breathlessness in the kitchen garden — Anna's idea of the perfect therapy for a child

30

whose parents had just gotten divorced. That should have been a miserable summer. Andrea's mother, Kitty, had been off in Europe hunting for a second husband, and Frank Olinger had been too busy orchestrating his second bankruptcy to take care of a little girl. Having her grandparents to herself had been bliss, though. Her one frustration these days was that John would never know them. They more than anyone else had helped her become the person he'd chosen as his wife.

Anna and Samuel Sprague had loved her the way she'd wanted her parents to love her, even when it was inconvenient. They'd loved each other the way she'd longed for her parents to love each other, unconditionally. As long as they both did live.

At seventy-eight and eighty-four, they'd died in a plane crash off the coast of Maine. The grown-up mourners had called it a poetic ending to a rich life — the two of them going together and so quickly — but Andrea, eighteen, had simply pined. Grand'Anna and Papa Sam hadn't been ready to die. They'd wanted to see her graduate from college, know her husband, hold her babies.

She got into the tub. The hot scented water soothed her and focused her at the same time. In New York there rarely was time for baths. The one major addition she and John had made to the co-op they'd bought on Twelfth Street was a double shower off the master bedroom. With luck the shower would be finished and the plumbers and tilers departed before the Pearces returned to New York.

She hoped the new apartment would have the vibrant warmth of the Kent house, which was full of quilts and samplers and hand-painted early New England furniture, though of course it would look very different, with its gaudy view of downtown New York and the Hudson River and books in every room. The furniture they'd bought or culled from her old studio on Jane Street—John was keeping his apartment to work in—was either notably comfortable (her prized leather couches) or jokey pieces they'd picked up in SoHo. And they had good art, a Leland Bell oil of three figures and R. S. Cahn's exploded lines, and two aurelia trees, with sensuously curved branches, because they both loved green but hated pathetic city plants. It would be a marvelous home, a setting worthy of their love.

She heard a grinding sound, maybe the Jeep coming up the hill, and she strained toward it. John should be getting back about now. One stop, at Hodges' Market, for milk and whatever papers had come in, then home.

The sound faded away. She got out of the bath and reached for a towel bearing the nuptial monogram, a sans-serif P flanked by A and J.

Andrea Pearce. Andrea Sprague Olinger Pearce. The possibilities still tasted strange in her mouth, a schoolgirl's fantasy covertly tested on lined paper.

She would have kept her name but John's two other wives had kept theirs. She really was the first Mrs. John Married Pearce.

She sat at the old-fashioned kidney-shaped vanity in the bedroom and brushed her hair. When she was small, she'd hidden beneath the polished cotton skirt of the table—it had smelled powdery and full of secrets, and you might find a hairpin or a button there. She was a woman and a wife now. The secrets were hers to scatter.

Shiny white bikini panties with rosebuds, raspberry silk shirt that John loved to touch, six-year-old Levis worn to velvet, a single strand of seed pearls. The watch that had been Grand'Anna's, a delicate octagonal face. Maybe he'd stopped to gossip with Gary

Hodges at the market. Or he'd gone two doors down to Mrs. Goode's bakery for cranberry bread.

She'd declined to live with him before they got married. She'd wanted lines of demarcation, sharp new feelings. But they'd spent many weekends in Kent, had been there for two Thanksgivings. The people in town were beginning to know him. Books Unlimited had a John Malcolm Pearce shelf. His fame could have kept him more an outsider, but he wore it well—not too modest, not too shrill—and he had an at-home look wherever he was.

He'd been gone an hour and ten minutes. She went into the kitchen and put up water for fresh coffee.

Her father had never been accepted in Kent. Such a New Yorker, he didn't look right in sweaters. Too preoccupied with money to talk about the weather at Hodges' Market.

The coffee had dripped through. An hour and a half.

She thought about John's ability to work through wars and clogging colds and brand-new love, and she rustled up a legal pad and a fine-point green felt marker. She'd spent four years as a feature writer for the *Daily News,* composing her first drafts (often there were no second drafts) at a keyboard; now, at John's urging and with his financial backing, she was going to craft something bigger, a novel. The subject was one of the mythic heroines of her childhood, a suffragist great-aunt of Grand'Anna's, Leonora Whittlesey, a loving wife and mother of four who had disguised herself as a man to penetrate the world forbidden to women. "Both/and," Andrea wrote on her pad and underlined it, but that made her think of John and she looked at the clock. An hour and three quarters.

She called Hodges' Market, hoping Gary wouldn't be the one to answer. He'd always had a way of knowing what was on her mind, and if he heard her rising panic and reflected it, she'd panic for sure.

Gary answered. "The bride," he said lightly, when he heard her voice. "What can I do you for?"

He played the hayseed around her sometimes, teasing her or testing her—she wasn't sure which, and right now she didn't care.

"Has John come by yet?" she said. "I just remembered, we need vanilla." A lie, and a silly one. No one bought vanilla from Gary except the elderly ladies who were daunted by supermarkets.

"Haven't seen him, Andrea. Maybe he went to the IGA. Going to make snow pudding? It's the day for it."

"I wouldn't mind some blue sky." Her treacherous voice cracked.

"Coast Guard says it's clear in New Haven and down to flurries in Hartford. Relax. He'll be okay. You two have a fight?"

She looked out the window. Snow was blowing off the roof in little swirls, colliding with the falling flakes. She fingered the yellow-and-white striped wallpaper behind the phone. When she'd been fifteen and wild about Gary, she'd tried telling her grandmother that he was a shaman disguised as the grocer's unprepossessing son. Grand'Anna hadn't bought a word; the attraction was inverse snobbery, she'd said, coupled with a teenage need to rebel. The shaman would grow up to sell cold cuts, and Andrea wasn't to do anything foolish.

"We never fight," she said. "And don't tell me that isn't possible because really we don't. We ran out of milk. And he wants the papers."

"I'll save him a *Times*. If I were on a honeymoon with you, I wouldn't read anything but the Kama Sutra."

"In the hands of the right man, the *Times* is the

34

Kama Sutra," she said—a Gary-like pronouncement that would have felt satisfying if she weren't battling panic. "Say hi to Comfort for me."

She heard the sound of the cash register ringing up a sale.

"I will. I wanted to tell you, I hope you'll be very happy. I mean that."

"Thank you. I know you do. I'll see you, Gary."

Dearest John, where are you?

I'm going to town for milk, he'd said. Going to town meant going to Kent Market or Hodges' Market, and the Spragues had always gone to Hodges'. If he'd been heading for the IGA on Kent Green, he would have used their private babble and said he was going to the VCR or the IBM or something. No reason to shop at the IGA with its supermarket blahness and its lines. And they didn't have *The New York Times*.

At least he wasn't in the Lamborghini. The roads so snowy but the Jeep so sturdy. The Jeep so sturdy but the roads so snowy.

Two hours. A twenty-minute round trip in good weather. Forty-five minutes today.

She imagined the raw-faced embarrassed young state trooper standing on her doorstep twisting his hat in his hands. Ma'am, I'm afraid I have some bad news.

Is he alive? I have to know. Is he alive?

The trooper looked down at his snow-covered boots. It's our honeymoon. No. You can't.

She heard a distant siren.

The telephone rang.

Chapter 4

"Am I going to lose him?" Margo said.

Gar McKay, cardiologist and friend, pushed thinning reddish hair back from his freckled forehead. "He's stabilized, Margo. We've got the pressure under control. You know, that guy of yours has a tremendous will to live."

They were standing outside the intensive care unit at Downtown Medical Center. Hank was in the second cubicle from the door, and Margo could see his legs. Hank had great legs, better than hers. He was the only man she knew whose legs were remarkable. When they went to the pool at Rumblestream, she was always aware of people eyeing the long, supple calves, the sculpted thighs. If he hadn't also owned a hairy, barrel-shaped chest, the legs might have been too much.

From here his legs were a torture to look at, though. The ICU was two rows of indecent legs.

Self-control, honed to brilliance these last four years, was quickly muddying. She pictured his blood pressure building and building until his veins exploded and geysers shot forth through his skull.

"How long can you keep him stable? Please, I have to know."

"Long enough," Gar said, but he said it too quickly, and Margo turned away in frustration. Mostly he talked as their friend. Sometimes—now—he was all

36

doctor, and she didn't know what to believe.

And here came Mickie Ross, hurrying down the hallway, black hair bouncing. She always wore red under her hospital coat, the color of life she said — today a loopy turtleneck sweater. She was smiling. Margo started toward her, daring to feel a flutter of excitement. Mickie was the coordinator of the cardiac transplant program, the one who would deliver the word she was waiting for.

"News?" Margo said.

"Bobby's got a girlfriend," Mickie said. "A musician at Hartt College."

Bobby Cline, an eighteen-year-old, had been the second heart recipient at Downtown. He was the youngest person in the program, everybody's pet. He'd sailed through half a dozen rejection episodes, lamenting only, at every clinic, that the life-saving steroid prednisone was clobbering his social life. A moon face and pot belly came with high doses.

Margo tried to look thrilled for Bobby. Mickie, a sixty-year-old widow who'd never had children, demanded a family spirit of her brood.

"So my friend Hank's feeling out of sorts?" Mickie finally said, releasing Margo from her strained smile.

"He's on a respirator. He looks like hell. I thought he could hold out forever, but his color's from another planet." Her voice was spiraling, awful — she sounded like the shrill kind of wife she hated, but who cared? This wasn't the Crown Market. Debbie was down in the cafeteria, safely out of earshot. She didn't have to be brave. "Mickie, I think he's dying." Tears started flowing, a blessed relief. "Do something, dammit!"

Mickie waved a dismissive hand. "Of course he's dying. He wouldn't be in the transplant program if he hadn't signed a piece of paper that says, quote unquote, I acknowledge that my heart has suffered terminal injury and I therefore seek the procedure of last resort. And you signed it too, Margo. Isn't that right, Dr. McKay?"

Gar nodded solemnly. Margo wanted to scream. If she were at Mount Sinai, the Jewish hospital, she would scream. At Saint Francis, the Catholic hospital, screams were probably also okay. But Mount Sinai and Saint Francis didn't have cardiac transplant programs. And at Downtown Medical Center, where science was God, screams would be a violation.

She settled on saying weakly, "Come on, guys, give it to me straight."

"I've given it to you straight," Gar said. "Sure, I'd like to see a heart come waltzing in for him. But I've felt that way for a year now."

"Right now I'm more worried about you than about Hank," Mickie said. "I've got some jokes I've been saving for a special occasion"—she made mischief with her eyebrows—"and I'm going to try them out on Mr. Henry Corman. You scoot down to the cafeteria and get yourself a load of carbohydrates."

Margo looked from one of them to the other. She defiantly wiped her eyes. "Should I call Skip and tell him to come home?"

Gar's lips compressed. "Dammit, Margo, I almost wish I could tell you yes, and you could finally shed all your tears. I know it's been hell for you. Believe me, I know. There's my father with Alzheimer's"—he turned his hands palms-up in the eternal gesture of helplessness—"ain't it grand? That's what modern medicine's done for us." He tracked two teenage girls who came sobbing out of the ICU. He inhaled deeply. "Hank could go tonight. Or hang on for God knows how long."

His words brought her home to herself.

"It hasn't been hell. I don't want you thinking that. Hell is life without Hank. Keep him alive until that

38

heart comes in with his number on it — do you hear me, Gar?"

Mickie Ross applauded.

Margo went to the cafeteria and considered chocolate cake, but chocolate would be cheating on Hank, admitting despair. She had a bran muffin, no butter, and a cup of decaf, and thought ahead to the taste of champagne in their infinite bed at the Plaza.

Chapter 5

She raced to the mud room. She stuck her bare feet into boots and grabbed John's red hunting parka from its hook and burst out into the wildness of the snow. The cops were on their way to pick her up. She could hear the siren coming closer, but she could move faster than anything on earth. She would cut through the woods and meet them coming up the hill, get to her dearest dearest dearest a minute sooner.

An accident. The bridge. We don't know. Pretty bad. The words screamed through her head, and she thought she would choke on the snow, and she begged her mind to pretend it was pretending, but she knew the breathless stabbing pain was real.

She waved down the white-shrouded cop car, and it skidded to a stop in the middle of the road, which was all the road there was. A big soft clucking moustached person bundled her into the back and helped to fasten her seatbelt as if she were five years old on the Ferris wheel — her father had actually done that once.

"Is he alive?" she said, as the driver spun a dizzying U-turn. "I have to know. Is he alive?"

The moustached cop looked around. "Those Jeeps are built like tanks, so you have a prayer." He handed her a piece of paper towel. "Your nose is bleeding there. Happens to my wife in the cold. The membranes shrink, the doc says." She nodded and tried to smile be-

40

cause he loved his wife—they were members of the same club—but she knew it wasn't a matter of membranes for her. What was shriveling and bleeding was her heart.

The Jeep had smashed through a white wooden guard rail and plunged thirty feet to the ice-crusted rocks of the river, landing underside-up beneath the stately snowy pines. She had never seen a wronger picture. The overturned Jeep was a grotesque dog playing dead on a fine white carpet, its obscene belly exposed, desecrating all.

Nothing was what it was. The firemen in dull black rubber and the emergency medical technicians in bright orange were alien bugs swarming over the dog. The white ambulance was some urgent ice cream bringer she'd dreaded in a hundred nightmares.

She strained toward the awfulness, but the cop with the wife held her back—he said there was nothing she could do to help, she would only get in the way. She shook with chills in his soft grasp, she burned and boiled. She was going to vomit the way she hadn't vomited since the first day of kindergarten, over everything, the jumpseat in the taxi, her mother's shoes, the shopping bags full of things they couldn't afford from Bergdorf's. She was desperate to vomit. But—we don't do that, Andrea, we rise above, you must promise never to disgrace me again.

"Hang on, Andrea. They'll have him out of there in a sec."

She looked up through the slanting snow. Somehow it was Gary Hodges.

"Oh, Gary, do you believe this? I guess you were the last one to see him. Tell me everything he said."

He put an awkward arm around her, squeezed her shoulder. "He never made it to town, not if he went over on this side."

41

"Then he's been there nearly two hours. My God." She stared blankly into the whiteness, aching for him to come bounding out from behind a tree, ashamed of his joke but brilliantly alive. Promise you'll never do that again, sweetie. You can't imagine the scare you gave me.

Down below on the frozen river, one of the firemen shouted as he wrenched open the door on the driver's side. Two medics raced around with their stretcher.

"If you'd like to wait in the pickup," Gary said. "You must be cold."

His hair was hidden by his pile-lined hooded parka. He looked bald and tired. The summer she was fifteen, the summer of Andrea and Gary, her grandmother had said, "He'll wear out before you do, honey. Say a real goodbye on Labor Day. Next summer we'll go to Maine." And they had.

"I'm fine, Gary, thanks. How are Comfort and the kids?"

A young redheaded state trooper materialized with a thermos of coffee. "Mrs. Pearce? You could probably use some of this. Light and sweet."

"Thanks so much, but we only drink it black." To her horror, she started to giggle. "We'll look back on this summer and laugh," she said.

They got a medic over to her. She shook her head when he offered something to calm her down.

"I need up, not down," she said. She took some coffee. She bummed a cigarette from Gary, the first she'd had in nine years. The pain in her back as she inhaled blasted away the clouds. She dropped the cigarette into the snow and broke from the cops and Gary, scrambling down the rocks toward the motionless form being loaded onto the stretcher.

Face so wrong and everywhere blood like poppies in the snow, and an exultant cry rose in her throat — It isn't

42

John, they got the wrong guy! But he moaned, and in that dreadful music she recognized his voice, and her heart squeezed like a fist and then opened again because the moan meant he was alive.

"I'm here, dearest love," she crooned, as the men in orange started up the hill. "We'll have you fixed up in no time. Never mind about the milk, we'll get it on the way home. Gary is saving you a paper."

Strong arms lifted her into the ambulance. The medics let her hold John's hand while they stuck a tube down his throat and mopped gore off his forehead.

"This is John Malcolm Pearce," she said to the pale young medic who was pinching John's nose to stop the bleeding. "He wrote *To Save a Life: The Story of a Kidney Transplant.* That's what won him the Pulitzer Prize. He would want me to take notes, but I left the house without a pen. Do you think I'll remember?"

"If I were you, my friend, I'd pray for a little amnesia. Hit the gas there, Whitey, will you?"

The ambulance flew and she closed her eyes and held tight to him the way she did in turbulent planes, afraid not so much of crashing as of being hurtled away from him. The siren went on and she knew they were in New Milford. Seconds to the hospital. Into the pristine emergency room with its pale blue walls and hurrying men in green.

The triage nurse was Elizabeth Sky. Andrea knew her from tennis at Lake Waramaug. Elizabeth ordered X rays.

"He's got a fractured skull, Andrea. A clot on the temporal bone. I've sent for Phil Porter, the neurosurgeon. You couldn't have anyone better. Is there someone you can call to wait with you?"

She thought of the happy, affectionate faces at the wedding: Sukie, her great pal since college, back in London now; Mark, John's agent, at home in New

York with his uncomfortably pregnant wife. She couldn't call them, not yet, not until she could tell them he was safely through surgery. Couldn't call them because they'd be too upset and couldn't call her mother because she wouldn't be upset enough.

They told her to try to eat. A nurse walked her out to the lobby. Chairs around a table deep in magazines. An alcove with vending machines. Miniature cans of soup.

A completely pregnant woman dusted with snow stood laughing in front of the U-shape admitting desk while her husband filled in forms. "The little devil. He would pick tonight. Hurry, hon, I need a bathroom."

Andrea touched her belly. They'd ceremoniously thrown out her diaphragm the night before their wedding. Maybe she was pregnant. They could all wake up together.

Elizabeth Sky brought over a tall man, dark, pared-down thin, with an air of controlled tension, coiled energy, that made her think of soldiers on their way to battle, at least the way they were in movies.

"Andrea, this is Dr. Philip Porter."

She was in the movie too. She held out her hand. "I can't tell you how grateful I am for all that you've done. May I bring him home, or do you want to observe him overnight?"

"My water!" the pregnant woman yelped.

"Mrs. Pearce, I'm about to take your husband into surgery. We'll be four or five hours. Someone can take you back to your place, or we'll find a bed for you to stretch out on."

She wasn't sure she had said her important line. "Is he alive? I have to know. Is he alive?"

Philip Porter blinked twice. "He's got a shot, Mrs. Pearce. We'll give it our all."

"It's our honeymoon, you see. He wanted to go to China but I insisted on Kent. Oh God, do you think he

44

was trying to get there? But he wouldn't have gone without me. He hasn't given me one bad moment, not even when I deserved it, except that day in Juan-les-Pins, and look how wonderfully that turned out. We're having a double shower put in on Twelfth Street. We like doing everything together. Please" — she caught hold of Dr. Porter's sleeve — "take me in with him and cut me open. You might need a kidney or something. He wrote the book on transplants — that's what won him the Pulitzer — so I know all about how it works."

"If you calm down and have something to eat, we'll let you give blood," Dr. Porter said. He touched her shoulder and hurried toward the elevator.

She stood watching him until the elevator swallowed him, and she went on standing there, staring, not knowing what to do; even breathing the air seemed impossibly wrong in so foreign a place. Elizabeth Sky put an arm around her and urged her back to the couch.

"Is this really happening?" she said to Elizabeth. Her voice seemed to come from someone else, far away. "Just because we ran out of milk?"

Elizabeth shook her head in commiseration, pushed back strands of pale hair. "Accidents are never fair. Never make sense. I feel terrible for you, Andrea, but we've got Phil, and that's a huge plus for your John."

Her John. Hers. All hers, only hers, everything she had. She reached out her arms until they ached and still she stretched, trying to encompass the planet, rewind it three days, such a small piece of editing it had to be possible, John and Andrea at Hodges' Market on the way up from New York and this time they buy a half gallon of LitchFarms Homogenized Milk, one dollar and seven cents, and head on home through the falling snow and start their married life, and the bridge and the river are their friends: It's a take, print it.

Chapter 6

Margo had become a commuter within the walls of Downtown Medical Center, shuttling between the main-floor cafeteria and the fourth-floor surgical cardiac intensive care unit for the five precious minutes each hour she was allowed to spend with her very sick husband. The texture of the hospital had suffused her. She'd told Debbie, had told her twice because she was exhausted though she kept saying she wasn't, that she felt like one of those women totally caught up in a soap opera, its cast of characters and physical details the realest reality.

Three minutes before twelve noon, and she stood in front of the bank of elevators on main hoping the left or right car would come first. There was no light behind the fourth floor selector button on the middle elevator, and she so disliked touching the button—it was such clear evidence of the frailty of all things mechanical here in the temple of healing—that she sometimes waited for another elevator rather than deal with it.

The middle car came first, its silvery doors sliding open to disgorge the usual mix. So many stories, Hank! See the way those two women doctors wear their stethoscopes instead of stuffing them in their pockets the way the men doctors do? It's so no one will mistake them for nurses, right? Will you look at the expression on that nurse's face, the pale girl? She thinks she's terrific because she's joking with the black orderlies, but they're not fooled for a minute. That family with the matching down vests, I think they've been visiting someone in the ICU. They're eager to be out in the air and they feel guilty—why? You've always been so smart about hating guilt, darling. You would tell them you're eager too! The woman in the wheelchair with the man carrying her suitcase, I think she came in here convinced she would never leave alive. The way she's blinking, she still doesn't quite believe it. Like hijacking hostages when freedom comes.

The elevator emptied. She hesitated for an instant, then allowed the momentum of the small crowd around her to press her forward. A dark, heavy man in a shiny red stormcoat with a plush collar stationed himself by the floor selector panel, assuming the captaincy.

"Call 'em out," he said. "Take a number, any number."

People were smiling. Margo told him four. She looked away from the unlit button. She was embarrassed at her relief at not having to touch it.

She had never been mystical. Events and objects had always seemed themselves, not harbingers or symbols. Coincidences were exactly that. She believed in God, a mostly merciful God (but He disliked being taken for granted), and also in luck, good and bad but really more good than bad—wasn't existence itself a stroke of the greatest fortune? Someone at a party had told her the Talmud said a single question would be put to new arrivals at the gates of heaven: "Did you enjoy life?" That had sounded just right. Unhappiness had always felt like sin to her.

She knew she had changed in the last few days. The

47

bounce was still there, but something had been added — the extra anxiety — and she had a new need to make sense of things. She found herself looking for what Skip at one stage had called "connections," always saying the word in an important voice. The change frightened her because it felt like the sort of turn of mind people take in an attempt to cope with death. She didn't want to believe that Hank was dying, not just in danger of death like all other transplant candidates but actively deteriorating, because if she believed that, he might die. Which thought in itself was scarily foreign. Though she gave credence to the power of love, to a link between good spirits and good health, she had always given medicine and diet 99 percent of the credit for keeping Hank — everyone — alive.

Now here she was, unnerved by a fourth-floor button that didn't light (but worked just fine). And earlier in the morning she had stared obsessively at the patterning in the tattersall curtains that hung from curved rods between the beds in the surgical cardiac intensive care unit, separating Hank from Mr. Lombardy on this side and an empty bed on that side, a rhythmic blue-green-brown meshing of thin and thick lines that created sets of nine small squares within larger squares. Hank had once owned a shirt in the identical pattern. Which meant — ? That he'd been destined to come here? He'd never liked the shirt, which had a button-down collar he thought looked skimpy with sweaters, and he'd asked her to give it to Elgar Mason, husband of their faithful Amanda and sometime handyman around the Corman house. Would Elgar (who chainsmoked and drank a little) end up in the SCICU?

Four.

She got off the elevator and turned right. She had

quickly become known and liked on the floor, and all along the corridor people called out her name and smiled and waved. But the air was charged with urgency, eyes were distracted-looking. Something had happened up here while she was in the cafeteria drinking Red Zinger and toying with carrot cake. Her steps quickened.

The curtain had been drawn around Hank's bed, and a chill started up her spine.

"It's all right, Dr. McKay's in with him," said Ruth Lilley, the tough little blond nurse who monitored entrance to the ICU. (Fitted top and pants, white leather sneakers. The other day, the new Margo had compulsively noted all the variations on the basic nursing uniform, reminding herself of long car trips when she'd urged her glassy-eyed children to scan passing cars for license plates from different states. On a trip to the White Mountains one December, Skip had seen a blue Honda with Hawaiian plates. He'd let out such an excited yell that Hank had almost driven off route 91.)

"I told him you'd be here on the hour like clockwork," Nurse Lilley said.

"Oh good," Margo said brightly. She noticed the empty bed between the desk and Hank's cubicle, and the chill settled in. "Where's Mr. Lombardy?" she asked. "Getting X rays?"

Nurse Lilley's mouth tightened. She punched letters on her computer keyboard, then hit the enter key.

"We lost him."

Margo put her hand to her breast. Less than an hour ago, parchment-skinned Mr. Lombardy had wiggled his ancient toes at her and she'd blown him a kiss. She raised her fingertips to her lips, then brought them away and looked at them. The kiss was still there and Mr. Lombardy was gone. In the south end of

Hartford generations were weeping.

"No. Poor Mr. Lombardy. Poor everyone." Margo swayed a little. She pictured Mr. Lombardy levitating in spasm, a single cry of pain and disappointment coming from his dry lips. "Oh God. Did Hank see it?"

"It was over in a minute. It happens, Mrs. Corman. He'll be okay."

But he didn't look okay. Around the blotchiness that didn't go away because the fever wouldn't go away, Hank's skin was the putty color of Nurse Lilley's computer console.

"Darling!" She ducked behind the plastic tubing of his glucose drip to kiss his forehead. She could taste the salt of his sweat, and she took a tissue from the box on his bedside stand and tenderly blotted the moisture. She looked across the bed at their doctor and friend. "I don't need a license for this, do I, Gar?"

"You can even do it to me," Gar said. His high, freckled brow was gleaming, but his interest was in the monitor next to Hank's bed. The chill in her back rose up to her shoulders. The men were sweating, and she might never be warm again.

"Everyone wants a Jewish mother." She reached across Hank's restless legs and handed Gar the box of tissues.

"You heard the news?" Hank said. The ventilator tubes he'd had down his throat had made his voice raspier than ever. His words had echoing lapses in between, as if he were calling from Australia.

"Ms. Lilley told me. What a shame, darling. That sweet old man." She walked around the bed so she could hold his hand on the side that didn't have the IV. Gar made space for her. He was wearing a tattersall shirt under his hospital coat, though different from the fabric of the curtains — red, black, and blue, with a uniform thinness of line.

"He knew," Hank rasped. His gray eyes darted in the direction of his neighbor's empty bed, then fixed on Margo, letting her see the terror he'd witnessed. "Only a second, but longer than his life."

Margo squeezed his hand. "It's not going to happen to you. I absolutely refuse. No matter how badly you want to get out of taking me to Paris, a date's a date and I'm holding you to it."

Hank tried to grin. Outrageous red cheeks, steel-wool gray hair wild from the sweat, his neck too thin but with pillows propped behind him he had an extra chin. He looked like a worn-out clown. And beautiful. She saw him in a dark suit that showed off his shoulders, sitting opposite her in a three-star restaurant, beaming as she discussed nuances of wild mushrooms with the captain.

"The rabbi came," he said. "The one person I wanted to see less than my Aunt Becky."

Gar's pager beeped. He went out to use Ms. Lilley's phone. Margo's skin was tightening everywhere.

"So what did the boy wonder have to say?" Margo asked. She wasn't wild about young Rabbi Mitchell Klein, fresh from Oregon.

"He told me golf jokes. I don't think he's ever been on a golf course, but that didn't stop him. Did you hear the one about Jesus and Moses on the fourteenth hole at Rumblestream? Moses hit his ball into the wa-ter—" Hank started to cough, his face screwing up in pain.

Margo fished ice chips out of a bowl, wrapped them in a washcloth, and held it to Hank's lips. "It could have been worse. The rebbe could have brought his guitar," she said.

"And then Mr. Lombardy," Hank said. He looked toward the empty bed again.

"Paris," Margo said. She lightly kissed one of Hank's

naked toes. She should have kissed Mr. Lombardy's toes. Had anyone kissed his toes in eighty years? She'd seen only one visitor with him, a thin grandson in a cracked leather jacket. Hank's nail was yellow, brittle. "What you really need is a toenail transplant. I bet there's a little place on the Left Bank where they do that." She winked. They hadn't made love in two years.

"I don't want Klein"—Hank put his hand to his throat, but he shook his head when she offered the ice chips again—"to do my eulogy. Promise me you'll ask Skip. Even if"—coughing—"he cries all the way through."

Margo sank down next to the bed. "Don't give up, darling. Please, Hank. I love you so."

"Promise me, Margo."

"I promise," she said through her tears.

His eyes closed, and for one roaring black moment she thought he'd gone. But the jagged line that was his heartbeat still pulsed along the monitor screen.

She kissed his cheek, drew back the curtain, and started toward Ms. Lilley's desk.

Gar stood there with his arms folded across his chest. "That was Mickie on the phone. They've bumped him up to category one. Pittsburgh to Maine, he's first on the list for his size. But, Margo"—he shook his head, he opened his arms—"we're running out of time."

Chapter 7

Andrea stared out the kitchen window. The wind had swept the sky clean, and the snow on the hills gleamed hard and waxy against the infinite blue. One of the Ballard boys was skating on the pond, playing hockey against an imaginary opponent. For as long back as she could remember, the Ballards had shoveled off the Spragues' pond in exchange for the privilege of skating, and in a different mood she would have made hot chocolate and brought a thermos down to the pond. But the beauty of the day and the boy were mere technical facts she was registering. She felt heavy and dull and tight all over, as if she were starting a flu, and she couldn't imagine ever feeling differently. The skates she'd bought for John were still in a giftwrapped box hidden under a blanket in the closet beneath the stairs. He didn't know about the skates. Dr. Porter said he would never know.

For three days he had lain in a coma in New Milford Hospital. In an hour a committee of four physicians would run a final battery of tests to confirm what none of them doubted: John Malcolm Pearce was brain-dead, his chance of recovery zero.

If she turned around very slowly, holding her breath, thinking the right thoughts, she would fall through a hole in time and find him sitting at the table stirring sugar into his coffee. Oh sweetie, that was a close call, wasn't it. But now we know. And are safe forever. Let's make love and then cook something yumptious.

She turned around very slowly, holding her breath. Sukie Farraday-Wells and Mark Feingold were sitting at the table, drinking tea. Sukie had flown back from London to New York and Mark had driven her to Kent.

"Oh," she said.

Sukie looked at her tenderly. She had scads of cara-mel-color hair and a creamy, cheeky face though she was only British by marriage. "Think of it this way," she said. "Today is the bottom of the pit. You will probably never again in your life have a day as awful as this one."

"I'd like to go to the hospital now," Andrea said. She'd been virtually living there, sleeping in an arm-chair next to John's bed, coming back to the house on Sprague Road for an hour or so each day to bathe and change her clothes and deal with the incessant tele-phone.

"What about your mother?" Mark said. He was me-dium height and medium weight, fit but not rugged-looking, a cityside jogger with slick dark brown hair he had trimmed every week.

Andrea looked at the clock. Kitty Alexander had come up from New York to Connecticut the day of the accident and was staying at the Inn at Lake Wara-maug. She'd invited Andrea, Sukie, and Mark to join her for lunch at one. The thought of seeing her mother brought Andrea to a new pitch of anxiety. "You're more like me than you want to admit," Kitty had often said, and Kitty was a woman who had lost her husbands.

"I don't want to see my mother," Andrea said. "You go have lunch with her." She didn't care that she sounded childish. "I want to get back to John."

"Mark can take you to the hospital, and I'll have lunch with your mother," Sukie said, pushing up the sleeves of her knee-length white sweater. "After a weekend with that block of granite who claims she gave birth to my husband, Kitty's positively fun."

Mark looked relieved. Kitty Alexander had made it clear that she only put up with his presence because he was John's great friend. "I'm ready," he said to Andrea. "Are you?"

"I have to do my eyes. Spritz on the vanilla." Sukie and Mark exchanged a look, and she said: "He's not dead. He's not going to die. We made a deal. When we decided to get married. That I wouldn't have to be a widow."

"Andrea," Mark groaned. "If only."

"You've got to believe," she said. "There are a lot of deathmongers in the world. We have to stand up to them." The words lightened the weight on her shoulders, cut a pathway through the throbbing in her temples.

"Nobody wants John to be dead," Sukie said. "Believe me, there's nothing on earth those people at the hospital would rather see than John Malcolm Pearce sitting up."

She wasn't sure Sukie was right. She'd had a sickening feeling for the last two days that Phil Porter had written off John, that everyone had. She walked upstairs through air that felt as thick as tapioca and went to her dresser. Fingers taut against trembling, she drew green lines along her swollen eyelids, smudging the lines to a soft blur, debating between azure and moss for the shadow layer, thinking as loudly as she could to drown out all other thoughts. But the mirror was full of John—the times he'd come up behind her and kissed her hair or put mischievous hands on her body, watching with tender amusement as she reinvented her eyes and cheeks. He'd never said, as most men seemed to feel they had to, that she didn't need makeup. He liked her changing faces.

She went downstairs and told Mark she was ready to go to New Milford Hospital.

Phil Porter met them as they got off the elevator on the second floor. His air of resignation, the slump in the military shoulders, confirmed her worst fears before he said the words.

"We did an EEG an hour ago, Andrea, and there's been no change. There's still a complete absence of electrical activity in the brain."

"You've stopped hoping," she said dully, as they walked down the echoing hall to the room where John lay in suspended animation.

"Never. Believe me, a part of me keeps on praying for a miracle no matter what the scientific data are. But hopes are one thing and expectations"—he blinked in that tense way of his—"are another, and we have to know the difference because it's courting emotional disaster to bank on the miracles." She didn't say anything, and he said: "If the miracle doesn't happen, I hope you'll make a miracle of your own and agree to let John be an organ donor. It would be a fitting destiny for the man who wrote that great book. And of course it would mean the difference between death and life for another human being."

Mark's arm went around her to steady her. Everyone meant to be kind, but he had lost all hope too—she could feel it—and she told the faithless men she wanted to be alone with John.

He lay motionless beneath a tightly drawn sheet, white bandaged head square in the middle of his thin pillow, eyes closed, looking as he had looked since he'd emerged from surgery—John who never repeated his jokes, never echoed himself in his work. She dropped her coat and her shoulderbag onto the floor. She went over to the bed and put a fingertip and then her lips against his cheek, and she blew softly against his neck and into his ear, the better to remind him of chaos and other good things.

"Hello, my sweetie. I'm here. Did you sleep well?" The words hung in the air, glassy telephone chatter. She swallowed hard and plunged ahead. "I know you can't say anything, but if you just squeeze my hand"— she pulled a chair up to the bed and took his right hand in both of hers—"or nod, or do anything, I'll figure out what you mean and I'll tell the doctors. Okay?" His hand lay limp and pale in hers and his face remained immobile, and she felt panic rising in her chest. "Now listen, guy. There's no time to fool around. The doctors have done a bunch of tests and they think your brain is dead. You've got to show them that you're still at home. One, two, three now, with all your might, make something move. Or grunt or hiss or anything. Please, sweetie. I love you so much. I wore a ton of eye paint today—doesn't that make you want to smile? Tomorrow's our anniversary, one glorious week, and, oh God, we could have so much to celebrate. It's possible—only just possible, but I'm really hoping—that I'm pregnant, and we need our daddy—"

He lay there still as snow, and she began to massage his hand with frantic motions, kiss it hungrily, and then she was biting it, and harder, so hard that he yelled and she was out-of-her-mind ecstatic, but when Phil and Mark came running in and gathered her up they told her the yells were her own.

"I'm taking you home," Mark said.

She wouldn't go until the four physicians had come to make their determination, though shouldn't it be twelve men good and true, this being a capital case, she said bitterly. She sat unmoving on the chair as the doctors pulled open John's eyelids and noted the staring pupils, but when they took the reflex hammer to his knees, her own legs jerked wildly and she started yelling again, and this time Mark took her home.

She hid in her bed, waiting for the sound of the Jeep. It didn't come and didn't come and she went downstairs because anything was better than the silence.

Mark was telling Sukie about the lunch at Veau d'Or when John had asked him and Andrea to witness his organ donor card. "Then he ordered kidneys in mustard sauce—do you believe it?" Mark was laughing and crying at the same time.

Andrea toyed with the cup of tea Sukie put in front of her. The three of them kept gravitating to the round kitchen table, seemed to have a bottomless need for hot drinks.

"I don't want to do it," she said. "Have his heart and liver and kidneys taken out. His corneas. I want to keep him on the respirator until they figure out how to fix him. His royalties can pay for it."

Sukie bit her lip.

"Andrea, you can't," Mark said.

"I certainly can. You read John's book. The hospital won't go against my wishes no matter how many cards he signed."

"But you made a promise."

"So did John, dammit. He promised to stay with me forever and twenty minutes. I only got the twenty minutes."

She ran retching to the small green powder room off the front hall. She stood over the toilet waiting for the upheaval, craving it, anything to get rid of the hot stone that had lodged in her gut, but her mother's voice still owned her ear and she had to rise above no matter how she longed to cave in. The nausea receded and she edged over to the sink, avoiding the mirror, and splashed her face with cold water until numbness came. She blotted cheeks, nose, chin with a fingertip towel, a small breach of protocol, the smallest, not remotely satisfying, why had she even noticed, oh sweetheart come back and get me off this narrow spiral, only love is large enough.

"I'm sorry," she said, walking back into the kitchen. "I'm not very good at this."

Sukie got up and hugged her. "Don't ever get good at it."

Mark sat with his arms folded across his chest, his face set. "I love him too. Not the way you do, but mine counts. He was going to be the baby's godfather, and now suddenly it doesn't matter as much that the baby is coming. Nothing matters as much. I'd give anything in the world to have him alive. Paraplegic, cockeyed, I wouldn't care. He could make it work somehow. But he can't do anything with death."

"As long as his heart is beating—"

"Let it beat in someone else's chest," Mark said. "Not attached to his wired-up body in some hospital vegetable garden. I was there when he wrote the transplant book. He knew what brain death meant. He hated the thought of beds and money and machines and nursing care tied up in maintaining corpses. He didn't want to die, but he hoped if he did something could be salvaged. He wasn't kidding with that card."

"Once I cut his toenails for him," Andrea said. "It felt like butchery. I'm talking about toenails. Dead protein. And you want me to cut out his heart." She put her head down on the table. "The defense rests." She heaved a sigh. She looked sideways at Sukie. "What do you think I should do."

"Are you sure you want advice?"

She smiled wanly. "This once."

"If they do say he's brain dead, and they know what they're doing, I suppose it's wrong to keep him going. You'd be like those wives whose husbands are MIA in Vietnam, a widow but not a widow. You need to be able to mourn, my poor love."

"And I should give away his bits and pieces?"

"He did seem taken with the idea, God knows," Sukie said. "I suppose you'd feel better for it."

"I don't want to feel better," Andrea said.

"You're not supposed to want it. That's what I'm here for."

"They're very big on transplantation at New Milford Hospital. Phil Porter told me all about it yesterday. I mean, no procurement team a-harvesting with ice chests. Too much risk that way, Phil says. They'd send John to Yale-New Haven or Downtown Medical in Hartford. In an ambulance. Still hooked to the respirator. Then they'd take out his life and give it to someone else. But what if it's someone who's not good enough?" She looked from one to the other, and Sukie groaned.

"No one will be good enough to our minds," Mark said. "But they pick and choose pretty carefully. It will be someone who really, really wants to live, and that's the payoff right there. You have to, Andrea," he said. His eyes were shining. "It was part of your vow."

Andrea and John had taken Cooper Purdys, the judge who would marry them, to lunch at Twenty-One. They'd drank a bottle of the heady champagne they'd chosen for the wedding. She'd gotten hiccups and John had kissed them away and she'd felt seven-

60

teen years old, forever. "You can say 'until death do us part,'" Coop had told them, "but I think 'so long as we both shall live' is a little more upbeat. You know, lime with sugar and a drop of bitters is a great cure for hiccups. It's a good thing you two are getting married."

She had lied to John—little lies, ones he'd forgiven in advance, had just about asked for—but she'd never broken a promise to him. She couldn't start now.

"I'll do it," she said. Mark reached out to her, and she nodded; then the light seemed to change in the kitchen—it got too bright and white and blurry, like a snapshot gone wrong. She balled her hands into tight little fists and pressed them into her cheeks. "Somebody open a window," she cried, rising from her chair. "I can't breathe!"

Chapter 8

Margo couldn't stop thinking about the other woman. Somewhere in the Northeast, in a cheerful house tight against the winter, electrical cords not for fraying and they locked away the shotguns, a woman with shadowy hair stood by a window, weeping. Margo saw her and didn't see her. You never knew much about your donor. Earlier that day Mickie Ross had told the Cormans that the man whose heart Hank was getting had died in an accident. Had been in his early thirties and in great health and there was a wife who had signed the okay. Were there little kids crying for the daddy who would no more walk through the door and swing them up? A couple that young might have postponed their babies. Agony either way, but Margo found herself hoping they hadn't postponed.

Two hours and eleven minutes ago she had kissed a sedated Hank and he had said, "I'll see you in Paris, kid." Now he lay in the operating room, in limbo between two hearts. The procedure would take six or seven hours if no complications arose. Dr. George Fox, who'd done all the transplants at Downtown, was chief surgeon. Dr. Garvin McKay attending.

Months ago, Margo had packed a canvas tote bag against this stretch of intolerable waiting, keeping it ready in her closet the way she'd kept her hospital bag in the last months of her pregnancies, and two mystery novels and a crossword puzzle book lay open on the nubby mixed reds of the living room sofa. But the words blurred or the phone rang or she thought the molasses cookies she was baking for Skip—his train from New York was due in half an hour, and Sue McKay and Debbie had gone down to the station to meet him—were burning. Mostly she looked at the clock and wondered when Gar would call with the bulletins he'd promised from the operating room. And she thought about the other woman.

She could write to her. Should she? Sam Mancuso and his wife had written to the mother of the eighteen-year-old biker whose heart now beat an uncertain tattoo in Sam's chest. Young Bobby Cline hadn't written to his donor's survivors. He didn't want to think of his heart as having had a past and that past now buried in the graveyard. A matter of personal choice, Mickie always said. Whatever helped you to feel good.

A letter, yes—going to her desk for writing paper—but what should she say? What were the words to offer comfort for the loss that had been her gain?

My friend (she began tentatively, blue ink on white paper with a blue deckle edge),

My dear friend,

We will never know each other's names but as I write these words I feel a warmth for you I could feel for no other stranger. This morning my husband was dying and now he is going to live and it is your extraordinary gift that has saved him. How do I thank you, you who have risen above your own grief to perform a miracle for a man you never met? How do I console you for your tragic loss of a young husband? You are my heroine yet you are somehow my child. I would give anything on earth to heal your broken heart.

Two hours ago the transplantation surgery began. Perhaps it is too soon for me to talk of miracles. Yet even if H. dies on the operating table, may God forbid, he will die having tasted hope after years of living in fear. If I had nothing else to thank you for I would be eternally grateful for that.

I have lived on the verge of widowhood for four years and I know how hollow other people's words can be. Friends thought so wrongly that they were being kind when they told me it would be a blessing if my dear H. died. Sometimes they would even raise their eyebrows and clear their throats and mention the name of this or that "eligible" widower as though any husband were as good as any other! I hope with all my being that my words do not hurt and offend you as those well-meant words hurt me. I know that my husband's new life does not make up for your husband's death. Yet I pray that you can take some small measure of comfort from the knowledge that a beloved human being is only alive at the moment because of your greatness.

On behalf of H. and our children and myself please know that whatever we can do for you we are ready to do, whenever you might need us.

With sympathy and affection,

M.

Telephone. Gar. Words tumbling eagerly out. "It's going beautifully. Textbook surgery."

"Is it?" She could feel her face splitting in joy, tears thrilling at the back of her throat. "Beautifully?" She clutched the receiver: "Tell me. Tell me."

"The heart is in. It's beating. Margo"—he was almost shouting—"you can't imagine. It's a sensation. George Fox held that heart in his hands the way we all held our babies, and now it's Hank's heart, doing what every heart does. The rest of the procedure is house-keeping. Mopping up. That's it." His voice bounced and shimmered. He sounded on the edge of tears.

She flung herself on the couch and let her own tears pour out as the news came home. Darling love, you're still here with me? Praised art Thou, oh Lord our God, king of the universe, sustainer of life, granter of miracles. Dear God, make me worthy, though I know there is no being worthy, it is Your infinite goodness and mercy that has given us this moment. And may all who mourn be comforted.

Chapter 9

Sukie answered the telephone, as she'd been doing all day long, but this time she handed it to Andrea.

"It's Dr. Porter," Sukie said softly. She kissed Andrea on the forehead and hurried out of the room.

"Hello, Phil. You're keeping your promise."

"Yes, I am."

She waited for him to say more but he didn't; he was feeding her pain by the spoonful, giving her time to swallow. Decent, and the decency was wasted because her pain was already past measure.

"So the deed is done," she said for him. She looked blankly at the farthest wall, a burgundy blur of history books. "When?"

"About two hours ago. Just after six, said the doctor who called me."

She nodded her head and said, "Oh." Her eyes wanted to find a clock, but she was in her grandfather's library — the timeless room, Papa Sam had always called it, he wouldn't have a clock — and she wasn't wearing a watch. She tried to recall everything she'd done in the last two hours, separating the minutes like so many grains of rice. She'd made a cup of peppermint tea and drunk half of it (which meant she'd put water in the kettle and the kettle on the stove, which meant she'd turned on the kitchen faucet, which meant she'd walked to the kitchen sink from somewhere else). She'd talked with her mother about the virtues of unlined gloves. How had they gotten onto gloves? She'd touched the picture on the jacket of one of John's books. Homely acts that should have felt foreign as Mars because John's heart had been taken out — John was dead.

If she'd loved him more — but she couldn't have loved him more, such a more did not exist, she had no way of knowing this and knew it anyway. She hadn't felt strange because the pain left no room for lesser feelings.

"Tell me all about it," she said to Phil.

"Textbook surgery so far, they say. Everything we could hope for. You did a fine thing, Andrea, and I can't tell you how sorry I am it had to come to this. Is there anything I can do for you?"

"No one can do anything for me now," she said. It was a line from a John O'Hara novel, she wasn't sure which one; her John would have known, and he would have known what she meant. "Unless," she said, spoiling the moment — but it didn't matter because no one else had known it was a moment, "you want to tell me the name of the person who got John's heart."

"I can only tell you again that you're better off without it."

"Some doctors feel differently."

"Yes, and you're probably one of the people who could handle the information, but we've got a policy at the hospital and I happen to subscribe to it. If you can, think of the heart as a gift you gave to humanity and not to just one person."

She saw a United Nations poster, different-colored folk holding hands around the globe, right-minded but vague.

"Humanity isn't enough, Phil. It's not the way John and I think. I want to know about the man who was almost dead and now he's going to be able to romp with his kids. Does he have kids? Will you at least tell me

67

that? Does he need anything? New"—her voice caught—"size-twelve skates?"

"You've given him enough. Find your satisfaction in that. Trust me, Andrea."

For a bitter moment she wanted to say that she'd trusted him to operate on John and look at what had happened, but she knew she would hate herself if the words came out and she bit them back.

"If you will give me the name of the, ah, funeral home handling the arrangements," Phil said, "I can spare you a difficult telephone call."

And that was too much. She held the receiver away from her, looked at it for a moment, and hung up. When Sukie came in, she was leaning back in the maroon leather armchair, staring into the air.

"I hung up on Phil Porter," she said.

Sukie didn't say anything.

"He was trying to help, and I hung up. Because he said 'arrangements' and that's mush talk and John says mush talk is the real profanity. We're going to bring up the children to think of brunch as a four-letter word." She began to cry but tearlessly, making rhythmic little whimpering noises, aching to weep a river but the dam was made of iron.

"I'm sure he'll understand, my love." Sukie knelt down in front of her friend. "Do you have a smidgen of an appetite? Your next-door neighbor with the funny hair brought over a divine-looking chicken pot pie."

Andrea leaned forward and touched Sukie on the shoulder.

"You're being incredibly kind. John thinks I'm kind and I hope he never stops thinking that but I'm an amateur next to you. You would have worried about Phil's feelings and I just paid attention to my own."

"Oh love, I'm sure he has to deal with worse all the time. You really are a good person, and I think what I'll

68

miss most about John is that he was going to make you finally appreciate yourself. Now," she said briskly, "can you bear to tell me the news?"

"The good news is—" The tearless sobs began again, then turned into hiccups, and hiccups reminded her of kissing John, and she saw an image from her childhood dreads, the houselights going up and the audience gathering coats because the play was over.

"The heart is in?" Sukie probed gently.

Andrea squeezed her eyes to make the theater of death go away. " 'Textbook surgery,' he said. Whatever that means. Would you call him back and apologize for me? Grand'Anna never hung up on anyone, not even wrong-number callers at midnight, and I'm not going to let her down now." She took a big breath and gave Sukie a long, slow smile. "Do you know how much my grandparents would have loved John, how glad they would have been for me? Please tell Phil that Colonial Funeral Home will collect the body. I will have it placed in the First Congregational Churchyard, in the Whittlesey-Sprague plot. Just you and Mark and Mother. Mark can have a big service in New York if he needs to."

Later that evening the honeymoon house filled up with people. Kitty Alexander directed the flow, austerely beautiful in a gray wool cowl neck dress and handmade gray suede pumps, blond hair scraped back from immaculate bones, as correct a mother of the widow as she'd been a mother of the bride. Here was the governor's brother from Litchfield, and here was Judy Powell from the bookstore, looking as though she'd been crying all day as she planned the memorial window. Here was this *New Yorker* cartoonist, that retired TV anchor who looked lost without a sheaf of papers. Comfort Hodges came alone in a camel hair coat and took nervous pulls at her scotch.

And, oh God, wasn't this the sort of party she and

John had talked about, a reception for all the people who hadn't been asked to the wedding? And in a way every wedding was a rehearsal for a funeral because if you were marrying for life you were choosing your chief mourner.

"Andrea, you have our deepest sympathy."

I won't let you not be here, my John, I absolutely refuse, I can't face your death without you to see me through it.

"He was such a wonderful man, Andrea."

My love, my shining star, my all and everything; how can a room full of people feel empty, the whole world empty now?

"Our sincere condolences, Andrea."

Making me hear these dusty phrases without you to wink at me. You promised you'd never cheat on me and this is the worst kind of cheating. But I forgive you everything if only you come back.

"He was so alive, Andrea, I can't believe he's dead."

But they do believe it. They insist on it. When in fact you cannot cannot cannot be dead. I will show them the cup in the bathroom, your toothbrush next to mine, and they will see: You cannot be dead.

Her mother told her she was looking unraveled and ought to go upstairs for a rest. Sukie went with her, helped her undress, lay a steaming cloth across her forehead, darkened the room.

"Why do they come?" Andrea said. "They talk about him but in a way that doesn't let me think about him. Canned condolence cards. One size fits all. And I end up talking the same way."

"I suppose that's what the ritual's about," Sukie said.

Andrea huddled under two quilts. "Why?"

"They want to pull him out of you. Because if you keep something dead inside you, how can you live? It's not good form any more for widows to die."

70

"But they're saying he never was. If he so much isn't, then he couldn't ever have been." She moaned, and Sukie leaned over her. "There's no air in here."

"I'll open the window, love."

A knock sounded at the door. Comfort Hodges pushed it open and took a step into the darkened room.

"I'm sorry," Sukie said. "Andrea's having a lie-down."

"I need to see her," Comfort said.

"Later." Sukie hulked her shoulders, ready to bounce.

Andrea watched from her bed. Backlighted from the sconces in the hallway, Comfort, who wasn't thin, looked curiously flattened, like a paper doll. Andrea remembered a book of paper dolls she'd played with as a child, maybe in this very room. Girls and boys from colonial days, with hair parted in the middle and those wide, flat shoes — hadn't one of them been named Comfort?

"I wanted to tell you," Comfort was saying, "Gary was in the store the whole time."

Andrea blinked. "What?"

"I was there, but you don't have to take my word for it. A dozen people saw him. I can give you names. Oh, maybe he went to the basement to get something, but he wasn't gone five minutes. The reason he got to the bridge so quickly is because he monitors the police band."

"The weather band, the rock band, the hair band." Andrea sat up. Her voice was incredulous. "Comfort, are you giving Gary an alibi?"

"I'm not saying he wouldn't have done it if he'd had the chance," Comfort said, "but if people could be arrested for thoughts, we'd all be in jail."

"You can't —" Sukie began, voice high with outrage, but Andrea put out a hand to stop her.

"Comfort. Please. Tell me. We haven't been great pals, but I never thought you disliked me. Did you

71

come here tonight knowing you'd say these things?"

"I came because Gary asked me to. He had to be at the store."

"You could have watched the store and he could have come."

Comfort stood there, picking at her skirt. "I think he was afraid your mother wouldn't let him in the house. Because she knows."

"Knows what?" Andrea shook her head in disbelief. "There's nothing to know. We had a fling when we were kids about a hundred years ago, and now we're friends. Don't you have friends who happen to be men?"

"I love my husband and my children and that's it."

"Comfort, you silly, you lucky," she said with a groan. "Gary loves you and the children and that's it for him. So go home and kiss his elbows and tell him you wouldn't trade them for diamonds. Because I will spend the next fifty years pining for one more glimpse of John's elbows."

Comfort started to cry. "I'm sorry. I know you're sad. I know I shouldn't be here. But I have to tell you, the day of your wedding I think I was as happy as you were. Because I finally felt safe. And when the accident happened, I got so scared again."

"Well, I'm scared too. You can't imagine how scared I am. But I can tell you this. I'm not the enemy. I'm about as dangerous to you as a sack of potatoes." Andrea suddenly felt her eyelids dragging downward, her words spacing out. "Now let me get some sleep. And for God's sake, Comfort, don't tell Gary what you said here tonight, not for anything. This conversation never happened."

Comfort turned and ran down the stairs, and in the stupefied silence that followed her performance, Andrea and Sukie heard the front door open and slam.

"Andrea—"

"No, I'm okay." She leaned back into her pillows. "At least I can't accuse her of mouthing platitudes, can I? Poor Comfort."

"You really feel bad for her, don't you? I could have knocked her block off."

"But she's just like me. I have no right to be sore. There was a time when she thought if she only could have Gary and some babies and a house, she would never stop being grateful . . . and look at her. And me. Can you imagine? John really did love me the way I'd always wanted, and I didn't accept it, I didn't trust it, I sat on his lap and dared him to be bored. I sent him" — she buried her face — "out into the snow."

"I won't let you feel guilty," Sukie said fiercely.

"If I could have another chance. Such a simple thing. I'll be so so so so good."

"You are good." Sukie picked up a new box of tissues from the bedside table, punched out the perforated oval, blew her nose. "Maybe you think you didn't know what you had, but you did know, it came off you in waves, and you made John feel over the moon."

"Do you really think so?"

"Positively I think so. Now how about that sleep?"

"I have to wait for Phil to call."

"He said six hours altogether for the procedure. I'll wake you, I promise."

"Okay. I'll try."

Sukie made tucking motions, kissed a cheek.

"You're some kind of friend," Andrea told her. "Do you need anything? Towels?"

"I'm fine."

"Are you? I mean, ultimately fine? We haven't talked about you for ages." She was almost asleep, but she had to get these words out. "It was Andrea the bride and now it's Andrea the widow, and what about you? Is George still your perfect husband?"

"He's very sweet. It's different from what you had—we spend a lot of time apart even when we're both in London, but I need that."

"You're having affairs." Andrea felt hurt for Sukie and hurt for herself.

Sukie didn't answer, and then she said, "Sometimes that's all right, you know."

"I never slept with married men, not in my wildest days. But maybe what I've had with Gary is worse. I did want him to go on adoring me, and I wanted John to see it. To balance the two ex-wives. And I didn't think of how it must be hurting Comfort."

"Dammit, I said no guilt. No one said you had to be perfect. You're a loving woman, and life shouldn't have turned on you, and I just wish you could cry"—she was crying herself—"and let some of the pain out instead of turning it inward. Now close your eyes. I'll wake you when Phil calls."

Andrea obeyed. Then with darkness came a stabbing pain in her chest, a sensation of remembering what had somehow for an instant been forgotten, and she sat up with her eyes wide open, and she was running down the road after the Jeep, yelling into the snow that he mustn't go, somebody please stop him, oh please dear God don't let him kill us both.

The
Red
Course

When a player's ball is in motion, a loose impediment on his line of play shall not be removed.

—THE RULES OF GOLF

Chapter 10

At two o'clock in the morning, Hank opened his eyes in his glass-walled isolette and asked for a corned beef sandwich. Margo burst into tears.

"If I'd said pastrami, I could see it, but corned beef?" His voice had a post-anesthesia scratchiness; his head lay heavy on the pillow; yet there was a wellness about him she hadn't seen in four years — a different aura she would have said if she believed in auras, and maybe she should consider believing because something was definitely there.

"I think even stringbeans could make me cry today. Happy tears. The happiest." She fumbled for a tissue under her paper gown. "I'm so glad to see you. You look gorgeous."

"I'd say the same, but you'd yank out my catheter."

She smiled behind her surgical mask "Turn your head a little, darling, and you'll see two more masked beauties." Debbie and Skip were on the other side of the glass wall, waving like little kids.

Hank managed to turn his head, to raise the hand that didn't have the glucose drip attached. "College boy made it. Ask him if he wants to go skiing with me tomorrow."

"You can ask him yourself. I better go out and

let them have their turn. I'll be back in a few hours." She got up but she lingered.

"On rye," he said. "A touch of mustard."

"Nothing doing. Chicken on wholewheat pita. We've got to take care of that heart."

"Maybe it's an Irish heart. It runs on corned beef."

She kissed him lightly on the cheek. "As soon as they tell me you can have solids, I'll make you some oatcakes."

He closed his eyes and she knew he was tired but she couldn't bear to leave him. There was so much to say and do.

"They really gave me a new heart?" he said.

Gingerly, mindful of the surgical dressing, she put her ear to his chest and drank in the music of the slow and steady beats. "That is definitely a new heart. A great heart. The nicest sound I've heard since Debbie's first cry."

She floated along the corridors of the SCICU, letting the children have their moment unobserved. Gar McKay caught up with her.

"Happy?"

"You know it." They hugged, and she said, "I can't begin to tell you how much we owe you."

"You don't have to tell me. My secretary will tell you." She made a face at his crassness, and he managed to look chagrined and said: "If anyone ever tells you doctors run from emotion, it's absolutely true. This has been one of the great nights of my life, and yesterday, before we got the news about the heart, when I thought we were going to lose him, I was so low I could hardly move, and that's more feeling than I'm allowed in a year. But I'm not the one you owe. You owe yourself. You've kept that guy going for four years, and don't you forget it. If Jews had saints—"

"Oh sure. What else is new?"

His pale face took on sudden color. "Actually, I've got to ask you a question. Aren't—" He cleared his throat.

Good heaven, was he going to throw her a question about sex? At two o'clock in the morning in the SCICU? She had to squelch the desire to giggle. Though why not giggle when everything was strange and wonderful?

"Aren't Jews"—he looked uncomfortable, as though she might think ill of him for using the word twice—"supposed to keep all their body parts together? We've had trouble on occasion when we've wanted to do an autopsy on an Orthodox Jew, and I seem to remember reading about a Jew whose leg had been amputated and his rabbi said he had to save it to be buried with him. So I was wondering about Hank's heart. Now I know you're Reformed—"

"Reform." Margo smiled. "It's not exactly like being a sinner. But you know something, Gar? I've got no idea. It's wild, isn't it? All this time, all the things I've thought about, and I never wondered what would happen to Hank's old heart. I suppose it goes to pathology, right? And then—" She shrugged. "I had my appendix out, and I never wondered. But a heart's different, isn't it? That's the heart that beat in his mother's uterus, that fell in love with me!"

"So—"

"So I don't know. But I'm very glad you asked. I'll consult Rabbi Klein first thing in the morning, if he isn't off practicing his guitar. I don't know why

79

I mind the guitar so much — he's really quite talented — but I do. It's that hipper-than-thou business. Like his wearing bluejeans all over town. I wear jeans when I eat at Scoler's, and so does Hank, and there's no reason why Mitchell Klein shouldn't, but he's so obviously proud to be a rabbi who wears jeans that it gives me a pain!" She let out a long breath. "I'm blathering. Because I'm so excited about Hank, and I want it to be a month from now and him home, and oh everything. Please ask pathology to hold on to that heart!"

She went back to the isolette. Hank was holding Skip's hand.

"You know what the kid says?" Hank's eyes were bright. He looked another notch stronger. "He's going to make a musical about my life. Called —"

" 'Transplantation Is the Only Way You'll Ever Get a Heart into an Insurance Agent,' " Skip supplied.

"A line he stole from me, though he claims I stole it from him in the first place, and he's only going to cut me in for ten percent."

Debbie was standing at the foot of the bed, looking the way Margo felt — dazed, ready to drop. Margo put an arm around her and said if they didn't leave that minute she would fall asleep at the wheel.

"Don't go," Hank protested. "I've waited too long for this moment." He looked from face to face, drinking them in. "Debbie, when did you get this gorgeous? Now I know why the Moslems want their women veiled — because the eyes are twice as exciting when the mouth is covered. Don't tell me I'm being sexist, darling. I'm so in love with all of you."

"We're in love with you, Daddy," Debbie said, and

Hank fell asleep with a contented little smile on his lips, and Margo got the children out and home.

Exhausted as she was, Margo tossed for what remained of the night. So much excitement! She remembered staying awake the night Skip was born, though she'd labored from noon to midnight, because she was unwilling to let go of the exquisite realization that her son was finally here. And her son was here again and that was part of the excitement, and in the morning the *Courant* would carry a story about Hank's surgery, and tomorrow she and Debbie and Skip had a meeting with Mickie Ross to discuss life after the transplant, and—imagine Gar of all people bringing it up—what about that old heart?

Seven-thirty in the morning was much too early to call Rabbi Klein but not too early to call Hank's Great Aunt Becky, who was always up at dawn and had often called before breakfast.

"Becky, I wanted you to know the good news. Hank has his new heart and he's doing beautifully."

"He should live and be well. So when can I see him?"

"A couple of days, darling. The kids and I had just a few seconds with him after he came out of the recovery room, and you're next on the list." Becky was Hank's mother's sister, the only surviving member of that generation on either side of the family. "Beckelah, tell me, the doctors were wondering, does Jewish law say anything about the disposal of Hank's old heart?"

The old woman let out a spiraling moan. "Don't they teach you anything"—a full-fledged shriek—"at that church you call a temple? What did you think, you should throw away his heart like so much garbage?" Impossible, but her voice was rising. "Forty-nine years it kept him alive—is that its reward?"

"Becky, don't yell at me, please, I'm not arguing with you, I want to do the right thing." Wondering what masochistic impulse had led her to make this phone call.

"Margo, Margo, it has to be buried—that is the law. Because when the Messiah comes, and we are all resurrected, should Hank be without the heart he brought into this life? I just thank God"—Becky's voice was a clogged whisper now—"that Miriam isn't alive to see her baby boy's heart flushed down the toilet."

"Oh, Becky, how can you? It isn't that way." She thought of anti-abortionists with their pictures of mournful fetuses in bottles. Cruel, lying pictures. But her forehead was beaded with sweat. If not a toilet, then what? She visualized Hank's heart lying in red bag waste. She felt ill.

She called Rabbi Klein at home. He was groggy-sounding but sweet, brushing aside Margo's apologies for disturbing him and telling her he was thrilled a heart had come in for Hank.

"Rabbi—"

"Please. Mitch. Or Mitchell, if you prefer."

"Mitchell, you never said anything to us about it, but one of the doctors asked. According to Jewish law, what are we supposed to do with Hank's old heart?"

"I suppose what the doctor was thinking of, Margo, is that the Orthodox and some Conservatives believe in burying any part of the body that is removed before death."

"Saving it to be buried with the body when the person dies? Or—surely not!—it gets its own funeral?"

"The custom is that if the final resting place is known, if there is a family plot, the body part would be buried there in anticipation of eventual reunion. Or"—the rabbi cleared his throat—"it might be laid to rest on top of someone else's coffin if another funeral were being held on the right day. Without any ceremony, I might add."

She nodded, though no one else was there in her bedroom to see her. "Is it just because I haven't had coffee yet, Rabbi? You sound as though you approve. But Hank's Great Aunt Becky, who's Orthodox, told me these parts are buried because of a belief in resurrection. And we—you—Reform—"

"With all due respect to your Great Aunt Becky, the Talmud tells us but a single bone is needed for resurrection. An Orthodox rabbi would have told you that the thinking behind the custom of burying body parts is to show respect for a God-given aspect of ourselves. In Judaism, and I'm talking Orthodox, Conservative, Reform, across the boards, there is no division of flesh and spirit into noble and base. The flesh is the covering of the soul and, like the soul, it is holy."

"We should bury the heart, then? Why didn't you tell us before?" She knew she shouldn't be upset when Hank had a gorgeous new heart beating inside his chest. She was upset anyway. What if (foolish, primitive fear, but it was there) they'd risked all they'd gained by angering God?

He said if she hadn't called, the heart would have gone to a laboratory, and that too showed reverence because out of the study there would come knowledge that might save or prolong Hank's life and other lives. "And if you want my opinion, that heart should still go to the lab and do its good work, and what happens to it after that is secondary."

"But Rabbi, what you told me about burial showing reverence sounds so right. It sounds as though you believe it's right."

"Margo," Mitchell Klein said, "I have a feeling you think of me as being excessively lightweight. You persist in addressing me as Rabbi in hope perhaps that I'll become more rabbinical. But I am not without my complexities. My father's brother, whom I adore though he thinks I'm an apostate, is an eminent Orthodox rabbi in Brooklyn and a leader of a hebrukadisheh, a burial society, with several thousand members. I happen to share some of his beliefs even though I have dedicated my life to fighting others. If you will forgive me now, I smell bacon cooking—it is time for me to go to breakfast. You are a good woman, and I know whatever you decide to do with Hank's old heart, your decision will find favor in the eyes of the Lord."

Would it, though? She thanked the rabbi for his kind words, but in a way his cheerful certainty was harder to take than Becky's yelling. The problem wasn't just Hank's old heart. It was her heart, as the world perceived it. Brave, a good woman, a saint. That was how people saw her, and maybe that was how she wanted people to see her, but it wasn't the whole story. A memory that had been flickering in the back of her mind came into full, terrible, focus. Hank lying feverish in his bed, Gar phoning for an ambulance, and there she was praying for someone to die so Hank could have his heart. Of such prayers saints were not made.

If she shared her thoughts with Hank, he would laugh and tell her she was guilty only of feeling guilty. A wife was supposed to be excessive in her desire to see her husband's existence continue.

Get with it, Margo! Don't maunder! Maybe tonight you'll sleep and everything will look different.

She put on a bright red apron. She reached for the buckwheat flour.

Chapter 11

Mornings were the hardest. Today, the fourth day since the accident, Andrea lay in her bed with her eyes closed, pretending consciousness hadn't come and reality wasn't. She twisted after the vapors of a dream, but her dreams had never stuck and this morning was no different. John. John. She pulled a pillow over her head, to no use. His name was there, echoing, shouting her into the dark places of the world, and his body wasn't there, and this was how life would be until she died.

She had liked waking up first, waking up next to him, his shoulders, his arms, the way he sensed her in his sleep and would gather her in when she shifted. So warm when he slept, a chesty sunbathed seal lying on the rock of her bed. No electric blanket, no hooded down coat, had cozied her chilly bones the way he had. He had changed to meet her needs — his very metabolism had changed. And he'd treasured the coolness of her skin, had called her his mountain brook, his body and soul's refreshment. Oh John, we were a whole, and I am a fragment again.

Last night, when the crowd had gone, she had moved out of the master bedroom, the honeymoon suite, into the single-bedded room of her childhood summers, the better to flee John's not-thereness. Now she threw the useless pillow aside and drank in the familiar details — the dusty roses stenciled on the walls and the window shades, a pair of Audubon robins in pale wooden frames. Anything (fade marks on one of the shades, an Audubon print hanging skewed, and she had never liked robins, the way they swarmed across early spring like rodents) was better than the mocking echo of his name.

She got out of bed, put on his plaid robe. I will never wash it, she thought, but she knew she would wash it, knew life would go on. "How can you?" she shouted at the planet, the robe, herself. "How dare you go on?" She ripped at the robe, hating it, hating him — the emotion surging out of some cave in her soul to the forefront of her being, and there was no way of snatching it back — for bringing her halfway up the mountain and abandoning her. Oh God take me back in time and let me never have known him because I cannot bear this pain and the end of the pain will hurt even more.

Sukie had heard her moving about and was at the door in polka dot sweats, pink on purple for the oversize shirt, purple on pink for the pants.

"Andrea love? Are you all right?"

Andrea managed a nod. "Super." She turned aside to hide the pocket she'd succeeded in ripping.

"Listen, you" — Sukie made Andrea meet her eyes — "you don't have to be super — will you get that through your head? Even your mother told me she thinks you're holding too much in."

"My mother who sent me upstairs last night because I was looking unraveled? Why, I was spoiling the party."

"She was thinking of you, not of the other

87

people."

"Maybe."

"When we're all ourselves again," Sukie said, nodding decisively, "I'm going to put you and your mother together. But I didn't call this meeting to sell you on her virtues. I have some nice news. I just talked to Phil Porter. Mr. X had a very good night. Everyone's thrilled with his progress."

Andrea caught her breath. The anger and the strangeness fell away. His heart was still beating. Nothing else mattered. Her own heart was beating so hard, she felt it in her left shoulder. She took Sukie by the arm, started toward the stairs at a clip. "Tell me more."

"Not much else to tell. Mark called. He'll be back early afternoon. His wife was sick during the night—he wants to take her to the doctor. He's so different when he talks about the baby. Sweet."

"No," Andrea said impatiently. "About the heart." They were in the kitchen, and she saw *The New York Times* lying folded on the kitchen table, and a shutter opened in her mind, a motor raced. "Did we make the paper?"

Sukie nodded. She crumpled a note she'd left propped against the sugar bowl in case Andrea had come down earlier—*Off and running, back in a minute.*

"What's his name?" Andrea reached eagerly for the paper. "Which hospital?"

"Oh no, love. Not that. I thought you meant the obit. Page one, and then it jumps to the usual place. Quite grand, really. As it ought to be. They used the picture from the last dustjacket. Can you bear to see it?"

"Sukie, I just realized. Phil said Downtown Medical in Hartford or Yale—New Haven most likely. So

88

if we get the *Hartford Courant* and the *New Haven Register,* I bet we'll find the story."

"I suppose." Sukie pushed back her mass of hair. "Are you sure you want to know? Phil said—"

"You can't imagine how sure."

Sukie sighed. "Are the keys in the car?"

Andrea listened to the Lamborghini take the turns down the hill, the plowed and sanded hill, safe as a nursery. Somewhere, somehow, John was on that road, alive, heading home to her. She went out to the window and looked out, peering everywhere, searching for the road that had to be, willing herself to find it, feeling her body ache toward that otherness (though her eyes couldn't read it in the snow)—and, oh, was this what her father had felt when he'd leaned out of one world into the next? A chill from the window panes pushed her back across the room. She was standing there still, holding on to the big blue hutch, when Sukie came back with the *Courant* and the *Register.*

"Tell me," she said, thawing, not quite sure where she'd been.

"I didn't peek." Sukie unwound her eight-foot chartreuse scarf and put the papers on the table. "Do you want to look or shall I?"

"You."

Sukie scanned the front page of the *Courant,* turned to page two. She stopped, nodded, folded the paper, handed it to Andrea.

INSURANCE MAN, 49,
GETS DONOR HEART

Andrea read the story three times. There was a coating on her brain that didn't want to let it in.

89

"Wallace Stevens was an insurance man—do you remember that from school? An actuary. Actually an actuary. Not my favorite poet, but a real poet." Her ears were ringing. She put the paper down. "So now I know."

Sukie took her hand. "Yes, and he sounds what we were hoping for. A wife and two children."

"Why did they make such a to-do about its being a secret? When anyone could have put it together."

"I suppose so that if you didn't want to know you wouldn't have to know. Most of the time it's different, isn't it? They have those retrieval teams, and a heart could go anywhere. So people might have a harder time putting it together."

"John liked Wallace Stevens. He said he was heroic in a quiet way."

"Of course we could be wrong," Sukie said. "The heart might have gone to New Haven." She took up the *Register*. "Both papers have front-page stories about John."

"No, it was Hartford," Andrea said. "I'm sure."

"*People* phoned while you were asleep," Sukie said. "I mean *People* the magazine, though there were also lots of people people. And *Us*. And someone from PEN. And your mother. She'd like to have calling hours at the Colonial instead of here. She said—"

"I know. It's too—did she say it right out or just hint—too Jewish to have people call at home. But it's the way I want it. Tell her"—she looked back at the *Courant*—"Henry Corman would want it that way."

"I know some people named Corman in England who aren't Jewish," Sukie said.

"Oh England," Andrea said, and both of them giggled, and Sukie's giggles (though not hers) ended in tears.

"I don't care what he is," she said, and Sukie said she knew that, and then Andrea said, "But I do care. I want to know all his details. What he believes in, and what he looks like, and what he has for breakfast — everything."

"I think this is what Phil was worried about. That if you knew a little bit about the donor you'd want to know more."

"Well, yes. Naturally. The time John went to Guyana — just for five days and we'd only been together a month — I read everything I could find on Guyana. I studied maps because I had to be able to picture where he was. Now he's in a foreign country called Henry Corman, and I have to get to know it."

Sukie put her hands on Andrea's shoulders, got her full attention. "There's a difference this time, my love. He's not coming home."

The breath caught in Andrea's throat. "You didn't have to say that. I know."

"You know in your head but not in your heart. You don't feel it yet."

"Oh God, how can you say that? I don't feel anything else."

Sukie shook her head. "I don't think you feel anything, period."

"How do you know what I feel? Even you?"

"Your obsession with this Henry Corman —"

"You pushed me to be a donor, dammit."

"Yes, because I thought you would dislike yourself if you went against John's wishes, and because I could see you going numb, not accepting the terrible truth. I thought maybe if you knew his heart had been cut out of his body" — she impatiently shoved her sweatshirt sleeves above her elbows—"it would sink in that he was gone. Andrea, believe me, I've seen what it does to people to deny—my mother-in-law thinks the British Empire is still in full flower, and look at your mother, unable to believe the men she married weren't rich—and it's a terrible business. Deny truth, and you deny life. Deny death, and you deny life. No, don't swallow it. Cry!"

"Will crying get me to John? Can I swim to him on this famous river of tears everyone keeps prescribing? You mourn him your way; I'll mourn him mine." She stared dry-eyed out the window, east toward Hartford, and now the panes didn't chill her.

Chapter 12

The phone rang and rang as Margo and the children tried to eat their buckwheat pancakes. The Cormans could have requested anonymity, and as she said goodbye to a breathless Sally Letterman—"I couldn't be more excited, Margo, if that heart were beating in my own chest; I just pray he doesn't reject it"—she reconsidered the wisdom of their decision to have Hank's name in the paper. But she'd wanted everyone to know she was proud and full of hope, like someone announcing a birth. Besides, didn't she and Hank owe something to the other men and women waiting for hearts? So many people were just not aware. Let them phone her during breakfast and disrupt everyone's digestion, she didn't care, she would have them standing in line to bequeath their organs.

And what to do about Hank's old heart? And should she finish that letter and give it to Mickie or Gar to send on to the other woman? And did the rabbi really eat bacon—and why shouldn't he, except that the fat and the nitrites would kill him? And Skip so tall and grown-up looking and Debbie looking fragile, as though the transplant had ended a series of fears only to sponsor another.

"Come here, you." Margo pulled Debbie onto her

lap in the open area next to the kitchen that doubled as dinette and den. She'd made it cozy with a window seat and book and small TV yet had kept the flow of space. "I need a cuddle."

"Cuddle, cuddle. You smell nice. Do you mind if I wear jeans?"

"Of course not, doll. What can I mind today? Anyway, all your father is going to see is the sterile gown and cap. Which from my point of view is just as well. Tomorrow I'm going shopping, and I've got an appointment with John for a cut. A little overdue, wouldn't you say? Now it's my turn for a makeover."

"Is Daddy going to live for a long, long time?" Debbie leaned against her mother's shoulder. "Will he go running with me?"

"That's exactly why we're going to see Mickie. So she can answer our questions and tell us everything we need to know to help Daddy protect his new heart and live a nearly normal life."

"I wish it weren't just nearly normal."

"Sweetie pie, do you know how lucky we are to have Daddy at all? Oh, God—" She thought of the other woman.

"What, Mom?"

"Nothing, darling. I'm just very, very grateful. You be grateful too."

Skip came into the kitchen, waved at them, and opened the refrigerator, though they'd just finished breakfast. He'd grown another inch, gotten to six feet four, was always hungry. When Hank got home from the hospital, he would have the same kind of nonstop appetite because of the prednisone, one of the drugs that was going to keep his body from rejecting the new heart. Some of the wives at clinic had talked about hearing the refrigerator door open

94

and close a dozen times in a night. In her mind, Margo was already scraping celery, scrubbing carrots, shredding cucumbers, inventing low-calorie, no-fat nibbles out of egg whites and air.

"Have an apple," she said to Skip. "There's a bag of golden delicious from the Avon Cider Mill. No, not in the fruit drawer, honey, on the bottom shelf back on the left."

Skip emerged from the refrigerator holding a spotty apple and looking tragic. "Other kids sneak off behind the house to smoke a little dope or drink their parents' vodka. Me, I'm going to hole up in the garage someday with a couple of Big Macs and a gallon of chocolate ice cream."

"The apples are very sweet," Margo said calmly. "Not gorgeous, but full of character, and if you say that sounds like me, I'll paddle you. Skip"—her voice got anxious—"you don't really eat a lot of junk, do you? Please, honey, find some way of rebelling against me without killing yourself."

"How about a girl named Mary Margaret Sheehan?" He took a bite of apple. "Flaming red hair and a wee little mushroom of a nose."

Margo studied him. He didn't look a lot like Hank: he was taller and narrower, and though his hair was the blue-black Hank's had been, it was gently wavy instead of steel wool. But he had his father's way of cracking a joke (or maybe not) with gray eyes slightly narrowed and mouth expectantly ajar.

"You can't scare me," she said. "Though I'd prefer Japanese to Irish—they know the importance of vegetables and fish, and when they fry it they do it lightly."

"When they fry they do it lightly, and they kiss each other nightly," Skip sang. He'd been writing ballads, love songs, intricately rhymed comic riffs, since he was a freshman at Loomis Chaffee. He picked up the *Courant* and looked at the front page. "Hey, the guy who wrote 'Recovery Room' got totaled. That's everyone's favorite TV show in the dorm."

"He wrote a poem your father loves," Margo said. "He turned Dante's nine circles of Hell into nine holes of golf. He was, what, thirty-two? And talented. It's sad."

"How old is this 'girl' you've been dating?" Debbie asked Skip. "Or do you mean 'woman'?"

"Shh, not in front of Mother. She doesn't want to think her little boy is dating women." Skip tugged at Debbie's hair. "If you were a real feminist, you wouldn't be caught up in all this symbology. Deep down underneath, though, you realize that you are inferior to your brother, and you therefore extrapolate—"

"When I get into Harvard, we'll see how inferior I am. I bet you can't set 'extrapolate' to music, rhyme-brain." Debbie jumped down off Margo's lap and ran toward her bedroom.

"Thank you, Skip," Margo said.

"Since when can't Debbie take a little teasing?"

"Since when it's (a) about her politics and (b) the day after her father got a new heart."

Skip opened a cupboard. "She should feel like an ace. Able to handle anything. Do you realize when I got on that train I thought I was coming home for my father's funeral? I was in such a panic I couldn't pack my own suitcase."

He took down a box of righteous honey graham crackers, shook his head, started to put the box back on the shell, then dipped into it.

"Well, Debbie's still in a panic," Margo said.

"She's had to live with the day-to-day reality of the worst of Daddy's illness, and she's going to have to live with a whole new reality of strange medicines and rejection episodes and thihking if she invites a friend over and that friend is coming down with the flu, her father could be in deep trouble."

"Hey, Mom, are you trying to tell me something? Like that it's not fair for me to be off in New York while Debbie's slogging it out with all this reality?"

"Not for a minute. You've had your full share of reality. I think Daddy's illness was harder on you than on Debbie the first couple of years, if you want my opinion, but now maybe it's the other way around, and I want you to be good to her."

"I'll try. I will."

"I know you will." She smiled up at him. "You want to tell me more about this Mary Margaret Sheehan who packed your suitcase for you?"

"Actually, it was Sara Simon who helped me pack my suitcase. Mary Margaret Sheehan's cute, but she can't carry a tune."

"Don't expect me to faint in relief. I'm not hung up on your dating Jewish girls. Women. Whatever. I love being Jewish, and I hope you and Debbie do too, but I'd rather see you both involved with good Christians than bad Jews."

"I don't know if Sara's a good Jew," Skip said, "but she's a good vegetarian."

Margo put her hand over her heart. "Now you're talking my language. So when are you bringing her home? But you know what, doll? We've got to get moving or we'll be late for Mickie."

He went off to get his shoes, looking — what? — disappointed? relieved? that she'd cut off the chat about Sara. Had the rabbi been teasing about the bacon? She'd show Gar the letter to the donor's wife and ask if she should send it. She could have the heart held on ice until Hank was strong enough to decide, but somehow it was her decision. Maybe she should go all the way and become a vegetarian too. And Hank was alive! Alive! She called to the children to hurry.

Chapter 13

She put on a purple sweater and skirt she'd found in a SoHo shop, the skirt the mid-calf length that made her feel most in control, and a pair of black leather boots.

"If I stay home with that phone, I'll go crazy," she said to Sukie. "I'm going to Hartford. See some paintings at the Atheneum, maybe walk around a little."

Sukie nodded. "Do you want me to drive you?"

"I called a taxi. An extravagance, but I'm not ready to drive and you deserve time off, my nanny."

Sukie didn't say anything, and Andrea kissed her on the cheek and thought that letting her go alone was Sukie's greatest kindness yet.

"You want the museum?" the taxi driver said. He was in his late fifties, with a battered nose, a tired brown cap, a humorless voice that made her want to win him to her side.

"Yes, please," Andrea said, and tried for the hourlong ride to think of paintings she had liked at the Atheneum. The one that kept coming to her mind's eye was a sorrowfully beautiful Mondrian, its surface cracked and crazed because the artist had been too poor to buy good paints, and maybe it was

99

dead by now, and that would be too much to bear.

"If you don't mind," she said, as the driver turned off route 44 onto the north end of Main Street, "I'd like to go to the Downtown Medical Center instead."

"I didn't think the museum." He sounded satisfied the way people do when they've won a bet with themselves, and she realized she'd never meant to go to the Atheneum though she'd really thought she did.

The hospital was a part of the newness in Hartford, a twelve-story thrust of bright glass set about with young trees, probably lovely in spring. The driver pulled into a semicircular driveway.

"Half an hour?" he said.

"That sounds about right," she said. She was trembling a little, but she knew that the driver — Ed Spaet, said the name on his hack license — would have refused to bring her here if she shouldn't have come.

She paused inside the revolving door, getting her bearings. Cafeteria and gift shop this side, elevators straight ahead, the all-important visitors' desk to the right. Her head was buzzing. Air too warm even for her.

If her mother were here, the chairman of the board would greet them and smooth the way. She was angry about that, and angry that her mother wasn't there, and angry that she was dissipating energy being angry at her mother. What was it Sukie had said? "When we're all ourselves again, I'm going to put you and your mother together." When John was himself again?

She walked over to the visitors' desk. She stood up tall in the Burberry John had bought for her in London, twin to his, trying to project a rightness.

"I'm here to see Henry Corman."

Gray lady with a bun and a smock had no need to consult her monitor. Nicely but definitely: "Mr. Corman's in the ICU. Immediate family only."

"I know. Of course. And I'm not going to claim to be his mother"—smiling, suddenly knowing just what to do—"but I think he would want—" She delicately let the sentence go unfinished.

The face behind the desk tightened. "Other visitors only at the discretion of Dr. McKay. Yes?" she said to a couple breathing down Andrea's neck.

Andrea didn't move. She had lost everything; who could frighten her now? "Oh, I'm just what the doctor ordered. If you'll page him for me."

"Dr. McKay. Dr. Garvin McKay. Please dial reception."

He was tall and thin with receding red hair and he bothered to tell the gray lady—Peg o' My Heart, he called her—that he'd come instead of phoning because he'd been right there in the cafeteria drinking the unspeakable coffee. "What's up?" he finally asked.

"I am," Andrea said. "I'm Andrea Pearce, and I want to see Henry Corman."

"Are you a reporter?"

She laughed a little. "Not today. I'm Andrea Pearce. Mrs. John Malcolm Pearce."

"Oh Jesus." He took her arm and led her away from the desk. "What are you doing here?"

"I want to see—"

"Yes, yes. Who the hell told you?"

"Nobody told me. I put page one and page two together. Just a glimpse. Please."

"Look"—he held up a police officer's hand to reroute her—"I didn't mean to snap—"

She shrugged. What was snapping after what

101

she'd been through?

"—but we've got a delicate situation here. Don't misunderstand me, Mrs. Pearce, you're a heroine, and God knows you deserve anyone's sympathy, but I've got to say no. Please. Be a heroine all over again and turn around and go home."

"Why?"

"Can you think of it as one more gift to the Corman family? The right to privacy at a very trying time? And for your own sake too. Believe me."

"Privacy. I bet all over the country people are adding up page one and page two and getting John Malcolm Pearce's heart in Henry Corman's body. You'll have the TV crews here any minute. A glimpse. I love him so much. Give me a thread."

"Oh boy." He sighed and shook his head and compressed his lips, and then he took her arm again and led her toward the elevators. The middle car was open and waiting. He pushed the button for four, which wouldn't light up. The elevator took them right up anyway.

He held on to her as they walked down a busy corridor and past a desk presided over by a small nurse who gave him a hot-eyed look. "Hank is in an isolette," Dr. McKay said. "No one goes in without cap, gown, booties, mask. The drugs that are going to keep him from rejecting the heart depress the hell out of his immune system. Cold germs could kill him. You'll get a look through the window."

Something caught at the back of her throat. "The way you do with babies."

"There he is, Mrs. Pearce," the doctor said more gently.

She stood with her nose to the transparent wall, her breaths coming fast and shallow. There. He.

102

Was. Lying face up, white sheet and blanket nearly to his chin, a man with steel wool hair and a clown's rosy cheeks, but the nose was serious and fine and the mouth—just open, cornering a smile—was the mouth of a what? A what? She was seeing without seeing. Help.

"Is he all right?" The monitors were gibberish to her. Open your eyes. Just for a moment. Please.

"He's doing beautifully."

"Is he?" She felt numb, incapable even of being frightened about being numb, which in itself was frightening and yet wasn't. Save me, John. Help. "And he's—decent? We've kept a good life going?"

"He's a fine man," the doctor said. "My friend as well as my patient. With two good kids and an exemplary wife. Your husband's heart couldn't have found a better home." His hand tightened on her elbow. "It's time. I hope you saw what you wanted to see."

She scrunched against the window. "Hungry," she said.

"What?"

"His smile. Like a salmon going after a fly. Look."

"Well, I wouldn't doubt it. He hasn't eaten in a couple of days. When he came out of the anesthesia, he started talking about corned beef."

"No," she said impatiently, staying at the window, knowing him better every minute. "It isn't food hunger. It isn't sexual hunger, either."

"Mrs. Pearce. Before someone in his family shows up. Let's go."

Oh God, a family, such a simple thing. You didn't have to be good or bright or beautiful or rich to be in a family; you didn't even have to want to be in a family to get there; for billions of people all

103

over the world it just happened, mothers and fathers and sisters and brothers and husbands and wives and children. But not for her. She felt empty, hollower than John's chest with the heart pulled out of it, a bleak and airless cave, cold as the moon. Somehow she was walking and talking, thanking the doctor for his kindness, dealing with doors, trying to hold on to the image of that hungry smile, but without her John to warm her to life, she wasn't really there.

As she got into the cab, the driver said, "Thirty-four minutes. Not bad."

"How long would you have waited?"

"I was wondering that myself."

"Did you get coffee? Stretch your legs?"

"What this trip is costing you, you don't have to worry about me. I think maybe someone should worry about you."

"I'm fine, Mr. Spaet. I'm super."

She huddled into the backseat, arms wrapped around herself, aching, exhausted. She didn't know what she'd come to Hartford to find, but she knew she hadn't found it.

"I thought 84 back to vary the scenery, if that's okay with you," Ed Spaet said.

She said it was okay with her, and she looked out the window, searching for something that would matter to her one way or the other. She saw the capitol building, gold dome on dripped sand; Papa Sam had taken her there to see the portrait of her great grandfather the governor. Oh God, so many deaths. Grandfather, father, husband, all her men, as if she'd been born in one of those countries ever at war. And Comfort Hodges was jealous of her.

She opened the window a crack to let in the winter air. She leaned back and fell into a thick sleep

104

and stayed asleep until the wooden planks of Bull's Bridge caught at the wheels of the cab and changed their rhyme and rhythm. Ahead was the stretch of road where John had crashed. She made herself look down toward the Housatonic. Come and get me, she dared the river. Anything is better than this.

The driver turned up Sprague Road. The house rose in front of them, a red clapboard sprawl with white trim, cozy attic windows peeping out from under the roof, an open porch off the kitchen and a woodshed behind. The safe house of everyone's childhood fantasies, John had said the first time he'd seen it.

She gave the driver two fifty-dollar bills she'd taken from John's sock drawer. She went inside.

Chapter 14

Margo and the children had read and reread the cardiac transplant patients' twenty-page handbook—the medical team at Downtown made sure that all prospective patients and their families knew what they were in for—but it had a new heft now that it was going to be the bible of Hank's daily life. From the early morning orange juice laced with cyclosporine to the midnight dose of persantine, Hank's existence would be a series of prescriptions, and not just for drugs. Do your exercises, take your temperature, floss after every meal and rinse with fluoride, wear a surgical mask in crowds, avoid demolition sites (old bacteria might be let loose), and of course pay strict attention to your diet.

"What if Daddy just doesn't want to take all this stuff?" a pale Debbie asked, nervous fingers zigging and zagging across the medication chart. She and Margo and Skip were gathered in mismatched chairs around Mickie Ross's chaotic desk. "Or is that"—catching a look from Skip—"a dumb question?"

"It's a very smart question," Mickie said. "Nearly all my patients gripe at some time or other. The cyclosporine makes their juice taste bitter, and the prednisone makes them ravenous and puffy, and they hate coming around to clinic every week and getting needles stuck in their necks for their biopsies. Or you know what else happens?" She picked a minuscule bit of fuzz off the two-toned red sweater she was wearing under her lab coat. "They get arrogant. We want them to think of their new hearts as ordinary, healthy hearts, and sometimes we get too successful. Then they start thinking they don't have to follow their regimen because no way are they going to reject. But, honey, believe me, I know how to straighten them out when that happens. I just ask them to swap their heart with one of those guys"—her right hand swept broadly through space—"hanging by a thread out there. Oh, don't look so terrified. No one's accepted yet."

Margo put her hand on Debbie's knee. "Mickie is a famous kidder."

"Who's kidding?" Mickie said. "You think Hank's going to wake up every morning thanking God for sparing his life? Some mornings. Maybe most mornings. But you better be prepared for the days when he wakes up groaning, 'Why me?' "

"Why me?" Skip sang. "That could be the second-act opener."

"You are the most incredibly insensitive—" Debbie began.

"Hey, I'm sorry," Skip said. "In my own cloddish way I'm trying to cope with things, too."

"It's going to be okay," Margo said. "We're all going to be better than we've been in years."

"Why do you keep saying things like that?" Debbie began to cry, a small girl's hiccuping sobs. "What if Daddy rejects or gets an infection or—"

"If he rejects, we'll up his dosage of prednisone,

107

and if he gets an infection, we'll lower his imuran," Mickie said. "And we'll deal with the other 'what ifs' when they happen. You've met Bobby Cline, right?"

Debbie blew her nose.

"Well, Bobby Cline, who got his heart exactly eight months tomorrow, has just decided to go back to school fulltime. Yes, that's the same Bobby Cline who had to be tutored for three years because he was too weak to walk the corridors at school. Furthermore, he just got permission from Dr. Fox and Dr. McKay to take his girlfriend to Florida for a week. Where he will swim, dance, ride a bike, maybe play a little tennis. Okay?"

Debbie's face got red, and her breath came fast, and when she opened her mouth she all but screamed. "You're just like my mother, always looking on the bright side of things, and I can't stand it any more!"

"Phew." Skip collapsed back in his chair.

"Debbie," Margo said. "Debbie."

Debbie whirled on her. "Yell at me or hit me or anything, but stop being so understanding! How many of your patients"—she turned back to Mickie—"are still alive?"

"We've done ten transplants in two years, and eight are still alive. One died in a car accident, the other of rejection. Judging from the statistics coming out of Stamford and Pittsburgh and Columbia-Presbyterian in New York, five of the remaining eight will still be alive five years after their surgery, thanks mostly to cyclosporine. A couple of transplants are twenty years old and going strong, so there's nothing wrong with big hopes. One thing I can tell you absolutely." Mickie folded her arms across her chest. "All the patients who got hearts at

108

Downtown would be dead if they hadn't been transplanted. Including your father."

Debbie nodded and didn't say anything and then said quietly, "I want to see Daddy again and then go home."

"That sounds like a good agenda," Mickie said. "I think we've covered what we need to here. Remember, I'm always at the end of a phone if you want me. Any of you."

"No tears in front of Daddy," Margo said. "And I've got to find Gar before we go."

"I won't," Debbie said.

Margo opened her bag and put a blue envelope on Mickie's desk. "I wrote a letter to the wife of the donor. Maybe it's too soon, but I had to do it. So please, whenever she's ready for it. Do you feel a little better?" she said to Debbie. "Why don't you go splash some cold water on your face?"

"Oh, by the way," Skip said to Mickie, as he got up, "you forgot to tell us the name of the donor."

"Very funny."

"Ghoul," Debbie said.

"No," Mickie said, "its perfectly natural to be curious, but the fact is you know everything you need to know. He was young, healthy, athletic, about your father's size — an ideal donor."

"Was he nice?" Skip said.

"Maybe he was and maybe he wasn't. It doesn't matter. Nice comes from somewhere else than the heart. Nice your father still has wherever he kept it before. In abundant quantity, I might add."

Debbie went into Mickie's washroom, and Skip said, "I guess I want to know it wasn't a mass murderer."

"Oh, Skip," Margo said. She started gathering

109

coat, scarf, gloves. "At least you waited until your sister was out of hearing."

"There's been talk about death row transplants," Mickie said to Skip, "but nobody's done anything about it, I'm happy to say. As far as I know, the donor never even got a parking ticket."

"You mean," Skip said triumphantly, "you wouldn't want to use a murderer's heart?"

"That's right," Mickie said. "First of all because your average murderer has lived on a diet of pork and beans and smack, and second because I have to worry about my patients' psyches as well as their bodies. I know, and you know even though you're baiting me, that good and evil do not reside in the atria and ventricles. But take someone just emerging from a long illness—he's got a lot on his mind and I don't need him worrying that he's about to turn into a killer. Anyway, I don't believe in capital punishment. I wouldn't want to be a part of anything that made it more palatable."

"Zap," Skip said, with a finger across his throat, for a moment looking so much like his father that Margo had to hide a smile. "But I'd still like to know whose heart it is."

"It's Hank Corman's heart," Mickie said. "His healthy young heart. Be satisfied with that."

"He's asleep," Nurse Lilley said, when the Cormans got to the surgical cardiac intensive care unit. A TV monitor on her desk gave her a close-up view of the bed in the isolette. Displays stacked alongside it relayed Hank's vital signs.

Skip stared at the picture of his motionless father. "I bet this is where Andy Warhol got the idea for those eight-hour videotapes of people doing nothing. Maybe we could nominate Dad for an Emmy."

"Yeah, he's a great napper," Ms. Lilley said.

"I wish he'd wake up," Debbie said.

"He had a big night," the nurse said. "He's still sleeping it off. By dinner time he'll be bouncing."

"I'm going to go down and see him anyway," Debbie said.

"I'll come with you," Skip said.

"Is Dr. McKay around?" Margo said to Ms. Lilley.

"Around but not awake. He had a big night too. And some morning surprises." She snorted. "Can it hold? I'll have him call you when he gets up."

"If you could give him a message from me." Margo looked over her shoulder to make sure the kids were out of earshot. She'd have to share her decision with them, but she wasn't in any hurry. "Tell him I want to bury the heart and I'll call him this afternoon when I've got the details."

When Margo drove into the garage, she could hear the telephone ringing. It started ringing again as she and Debbie and Skip walked into the house.

"In Hartford, nearly everyone reads the *Courant*," Skip said.

Margo answered the phone. "Hello?"

"Mrs. Corman?"

"That's right." She could hear a keyboard clicking in the background.

"This is Gretchen Davis at *The New York Post*. Congratulations on your husband's surgery."

"Thank you."

"He's doing very well, I understand from the hospital."

"He's doing beautifully, thank God." Margo wondered if she should feel strange talking to a reporter but she didn't.

"You've seen him since the surgery?"

"Three times." Margo shrugged off her coat. "*New York Post*," she mouthed to Debbie and Skip. "But he was only awake once," she said into the telephone. "I hope we'll have a real visit later in the day."

"Mrs. Corman, I'm sure everyone feels special when there's been a transplant in the family, but is it extra special knowing that the donor heart comes from the man who wrote the book?"

Margo's shoulders got cold and her eyebrows got hot. She sat down.

Chapter 15

Sukie didn't ask where she'd gone in Hartford, and Andrea didn't tell her. She had nothing really to tell; that was the awful part.

She changed her purple clothes for jeans and toasted an English muffin and ate half of it. She and John had eaten English muffins for breakfast the first time she'd stayed at his apartment. He liked his lightly done, with a touch of butter and lots of marmalade. She liked hers charred, with raspberry preserves. "We'll need separate but equal toasters if we keep this up," he'd said. Silliness that had filled her with joy.

Kitty Alexander came over from Lake Waramaug. "Someone has to pick out a coffin," she said, in her let's-face-facts voice. Then she began to weep. Sukie scurried off for tissues. Andrea stared. She had watched Kitty bury two husbands and her parents and had never before seen her cry.

"Are you all right, Mother?"

Kitty's impeccable blond head inclined fractionally. "I'm very, very sad for you, Andrea." She plucked a tissue from the box Sukie had brought and she dabbed at her eyes. If it had been Andrea, she would have cried a river of mascara, but Kitty had her eyelashes dyed once a month and was flawless even in tears. "And I'm sad that you can't seem to"—she looked away from Andrea, then back again—"let go. Is it my fault? You once told me I found emotions intolerably intrusive. Is that what you think?"

"Invasive," she said softly. "I said you found them intolerably invasive. I was eighteen. Has it been eating at you all this time?"

Sukie stood up. "Ladies, I'm going to head for the Colonial and do the deed. Any instructions, Andrea?"

" 'A rough plain hearse then,' " she murmured, shaking her head for wonder and sorrow. Ah God, that they had once been smug enough—newly in love and time on their side—to have read the William Carlos Williams lines to each other, and there had been no prescient shudder. It was other people who died.

And now she was on her feet, grabbing at Sukie, telling her not to go, a mistake had been made.

Sukie hugged her, but Kitty said sharply that maybe it would help if Andrea were the one to choose the coffin.

"Help? Help?" Her voice bubbled with trembly laughter; then she was shouting the word, shouting for her life, "Help!" as loud as she could; then she was sinking back into her chair, covering her face with her hands, the word a soft breath against her skin, "Help. Help. Help."

When she looked up, she saw that Sukie was crying the tears she couldn't shed herself. "My designated weeper," she said. "Plain pine. Gold filigree. I don't care." A table lamp seemed to be blinking. "Don't make me go."

"Of course not," Sukie said, and Kitty nodded her

114

assent though no one had asked, and Sukie left with a little wave of her hand.

Andrea and Kitty looked at each other.

"So," Kitty said.

"So, Mother."

"You seem very angry at me," Kitty said.

"I'm angry at life."

"I'm not going to tell you you shouldn't be. You've been dealt the most wretchedly unfair blow imaginable. But you have to get past your anger, I think the phrase is. Well, maybe tomorrow. I suppose that's part of what funerals are for."

"Can you really say that to me? I was there. When Daddy was cremated. And at Brady's funeral. And Grand'Anna and Papa Sam's. You were dry-eyed."

"Do you want to know the great joke?" Kitty threw her head back in a brief trill of laughter. "I was holding myself in for your sake. You were such a weepy little girl, Andrea. Tears from morning to night. Everything touched you. It seemed to me if I didn't toughen you up life would dissolve you. So I put on a mask to show you a different way."

Andrea wanted to believe her, but something was in the way — maybe the truth, or maybe the lie, and did it matter which? She couldn't muster the words of thanks, forgiveness, love that Kitty wanted. She couldn't give her the simple warmth she'd given Ed Spaet, the cab driver. Someday, John had said, she would accept herself, realize how special she was, and when that day came she would accept her mother too and give her some credit. But had Kitty ever truly accepted her?

Enough questions. The important thing right now was not to add to the sum of pain in the world.

"Don't let's fight, Mother," she said.

115

"It's the last thing I want. I want to help you. Sukie's a wonderful friend—"

"And Mark."

"And Mark, I suppose, though I think you know I'm not wild about him. But I can't help thinking you need me too."

"I do," she said. "But not as an editor. This is my story. You mustn't tell me when to cry and when not to. And Mark really is my friend. We disagreed yesterday, but we made up, and I'd appreciate it if you stopped frosting him."

"I think 'frosting' is a bit much. I suppose he sees me as some kind of superWASP, and I know a lot of Jews have these enemy camp feelings—"

"Mother, stop. I've got an awful headache. I'm going to lie down now. Come back this evening, will you? I suppose we'll have another crowd."

She took four aspirin with a glass of milk and dozed until Mark showed up.

"I'm starved," he said, not taking off his coat. "Are you allowed to be seen in a restaurant?"

"I'm a Whittlesey and a Sprague. I can do anything I want in Kent. I just had breakfast, but I need something sweet. Let's go to the Villager. Tuna melts, fried potato skins, rhubarb crunch."

"Are you serious?"

"Absolutely. It's my primal food."

"Then we're off. Where's M'lady Farraday-Wells?"

Andrea felt the air go out of her. "She went to the Colonial. I couldn't do it, Mark. Choose a coffin. Are you going to get mad at me?"

"I cared about the heart. Because he did. The gift-wrapping doesn't matter." He sighed heavily.

"Are you okay?" she said.

"Sure, sure."

"I'll call Sukie and ask her to meet us. Actually, if

you could call."

In Mark's mushroom-colored BMW she started to fasten her seatbelt and then released it.

"Put it on," Mark said. He fastened his.

"No."

"Andrea, what is this? Fasten that belt or we're not going. No rhubarb crunch."

"Are you sure John wore his? The day he crashed?"

Incredulous: "John? Of course he did."

"The worst storm of the year, and he went out. Do you think he was running away from me?"

"For God's sake." He put his right arm on the back of his seat as he turned toward her, and she had a memory of her father making the same move, or maybe it was the New York City country gentleman clothes—a cashmere polo coat, discreet plaid scarf, pigskin driving gloves, cuffed gray flannels over pale suede boots—that reminded her of Frank Olinger in Kent.

"He took intellectual risks," Mark said, "emotional risks—"

"You mean marrying me."

"Andrea. Come on. I mean, he didn't do crazy things with his body. He wasn't a coward; he just had a very strong sense of self-preservation. There's the man who, as far as I know, never once snorted coke. He didn't want to die that day. He didn't want to leave you. He was wearing his seatbelt."

"Do you really think so?"

"I know so." He hunched his shoulders, rubbed his hands. "Listen, it's effing cold in this car and I want to have lunch. Are you going to buckle up, or should we go back inside the house?"

"I'll buckle up. Please don't—"

He started down the hill. "Please don't what?"

117

"Tell him. About my doubts. I know he loved me."

"He was so nuts about you, it was scary," Mark said. "I saw him with a lot of women. You were it."

"I thought I'd hear from Linda," Andrea said. "When we met at parties she called me her wife-in-law. John said we'd be friends someday."

"She's in Italy; no one's quite sure where."

"She reads the papers, doesn't she? I can't see Linda going twenty minutes without a paper. The accident must have made the *International Trib.*"

"I'm sure she likes you, but she didn't much like the idea of John marrying you. She probably picked up some cute little postcard vendor when she got off the plane and she's been screwing her brains out ever since. Christ." A yellow truck was parked on the road. A crew was working on the wooden guard rail the Jeep had broken through.

"Don't stop," Andrea said. "Don't even slow down."

"Okay. Okay." His hands tensed on the wheel. "Take it easy."

"Tell me more about Linda. Not liking our marriage." She looked straight ahead, waiting for the other bridge—the covered bridge, Bull's Bridge. People came from miles away to see it. How good of John not to take it with him.

"It isn't anything against you," Mark said. "She just liked having an ex-husband around."

"John hadn't exactly been 'around' for a while," Andrea said.

"No, but getting married is getting married. She would have liked to do it first."

They slowed down for Bull's Bridge: one lane.

"Isn't this a splendid bridge?" Andrea said. "George Washington crossed here."

118

"Ole devil George. At least he didn't call it New Jersey."

"Mark, did Sukie give you the message? It's okay with me if you have something for John at Frank E. Campbell's."

"That's very kind of you, Andrea. I want it for him and I need it for myself. I'm having trouble believing he's gone."

"Oh, don't believe it. I'm never going to. I know it but I don't believe it. The Villager is up ahead on the right. Park anywhere."

She had always loved the look of winter in Kent. The town wasn't postcard-perfect, like Washington or Litchfield or Cornwall Bridge, but on a day like today—blue sky, a few puffy clouds, cold enough to keep the drifts left by the blizzard from turning to mush—the town looked real and eternal and right. Yes, they'd done that hokey renovation of the old railroad station up near the town green, but otherwise the single-story buildings lining Main Street were what they were, an architectural jumble of shops honestly serving the needs of daily life. Here were Mrs. Goode's yeasty breads; here were Judy Powell's carefully chosen books; here Hodges' Market and the garden center. No fresh pasta, she said to Mark, as if fresh pasta were on their minds, but New York didn't have clean snow.

Her favorite table was waiting at the Villager, back in a corner under a painting of covered wagons. If she sat against the wall she could see the counter, the grill, the front door with its yellow half valence curtain on the window, and she could smell cheese sandwiches toasting and melting without getting the flavor in her hair.

She concentrated on details, pretending they were still important. She waved at Patti the waitress. She

119

took her usual seat. She handed Mark a menu sheathed in clear plastic. "My treat. Sky's the limit. Specials on the blackboard."

He turned to look "Macaroni and sausage casserole. Shepherd's pie. You weren't kidding about this place. It's the most goyishe joint I've ever been in. You're sure I'm allowed in here?"

"Just don't let my mother catch you. I'm going to have a vanilla milkshake. There's Sukie."

Sukie dropped her shearling cape over a chair at the next table. "All set, love. Tomorrow morning at eleven."

Andrea closed her eyes. "Thank you, Sukie."

The milkshake was wonderful, just the right amount of syrup, but she thought about John with his lips on her neck, her ear, murmuring of vanilla, and she couldn't take another sip, risk getting to the bottom, everything sweet and good sucked up and swallowed, the love that was meant to change the world nothing but a stickiness in a glass.

Chapter 16

"What we would like," Gar McKay said, "is to turn this situation to our advantage."

"Margo, it's a God-given chance to raise public consciousness about the donor program," Mickie said. "I know that's something you're very eager to do."

Margo nodded. She felt a little dazed, a little out of it, as if her life were happening in one room and she were in another. Skip and Debbie, sitting on either side of her on the nubby red living room sofa, weren't much help. Skip was humming melody lines, the way he did when he was turning the moment into musical comedy, and Debbie was hovering between tears and clenched fists, lost to reason.

And what was reasonable, what was right? Gar and Mickie, doctor and nurse, sitting on the edge of heather armchairs, coffee untasted on the small round table between them, seemed sure they knew. Some clever reporters had figured out the truth, and now the thing to do was stage-manage the story.

"I can see a picture of Hank sitting up in the isolette, reading John Malcolm Pearce's book on kidney transplants," Mickie said. "That's front-page stuff."

Debbie groaned her disgust. "Otherwise known as exploitation."

"Otherwise known as a thousand people who've

121

been meaning to sign organ donor cards getting around to doing it," Mickie said.

"That's a very good point, honey," Margo said to Debbie.

"Mom, you're hopelessly naïve."

"She's right," Gar said. "Mickie, we better come clean. What we're really interested in is the kickback we get every time we do a transplant." He took a sip from his coffee cup.

"It must be icy," Margo said, rising. "Let me get you some hot."

"It's fine, Margo. Considering what I'm used to drinking at the hospital, it's ambrosia."

"How a doctor can drink that poison—" Margo said.

"We can't all be decaffeinated saints like you, Mom," Debbie said.

"Debbie!" Margo said. "What's gotten into you today?"

'It's just that you're all leaving out Daddy." Her mouth quivered but she didn't cry. "Why can't Daddy decide what to do? It's his heart."

"Frankly," Gar said, "whatever decision is made is going to affect the three of you more than it does Hank. By the time he's out of the hospital, his transplant will be old news. If his heart gets buried with John Malcolm Pearce's body—"

"What?" Skip shouted.

"I hadn't gone into that with the children," Margo said to Gar. She drew Skip and Debbie close to her. "According to traditional Jewish law, any part of the body that's removed before death is buried. To show respect. I'd thought"—she swallowed—"to have Daddy's old heart buried in the cemetery where he and I will someday rest."

Debbie began to howl. "You can't do this to me.

Daddy's alive and we're going to bury him anyway."

"Darling. Darling. We're not going to bury him."

"I'm with Debbie," Skip said. "That's the most macabre thing I ever heard of. Are Jews really supposed to do that? Mary Margaret Sheehan, you're looking better every minute."

"You think it's less macabre to toss his heart into a garbage pail?" Aunt Becky's words and intonation—how could you, Margo? "Oh kids, I'm sorry. That was ugly. I apologize. But I've been thinking about that old heart all morning. I even talked to Rabbi Klein, who was actually terrific, and it feels right to me. Burial for an old friend. The way"—a sudden flash of inspiration—"you buried the flag that got ripped at camp, do you remember, Deb? You wrote me a long letter about it, I still have it somewhere. You thought that was beautiful." She looked at Gar. "But with John Malcolm Pearce's body?"

"It just came to me," he said. "It seems to me it would be rather poetic."

"Good copy, you mean," Skip said.

"Yes, good copy, Skip. I'm not trying to hide my interest here. I want to publicize transplantation. You've met Sam Mancuso. Great guy, right? With four little kids. Well, Sam was admitted to Intensive Care about an hour ago—"

"Oh no," Margo said.

"—and I think he's going to reject the heart he has before we can get another one for him. Because people die in accidents and they go to their graves with the hearts and the livers and the kidneys that could save lives, and you know what?" He slapped the arm of his chair. "I just can't stand the waste. I think future civilizations are going to look back on us and judge those buried organs the way we judge the ancient pharaohs who filled their tombs with food and gold. Hey, who

123

were they kidding? Didn't they know you can't take it with you? But we're worse than the pharaohs because what we're burying every day is someone else's only hope. Don't think badly of your mother for wanting to bury a useless heart. Think badly of the people who bury hearts that could beat again."

"Bravo," Mickie said softly. "Bravo."

Margo sagged. "Poor Sam. I've got to call Elaine."

"But all the stuff Mickie told me earlier about keeping donors and recipients apart," Skip said.

"Yeah," Debbie said.

"It's still the best basic rule," Gar said. "But every once in a while there's more good to be gotten from breaking the rule."

"Did you leak the story to that *Post* reporter?" Debbie asked.

"Debbie! That's incredibly rude," Margo said. "I want you to apologize to Gar."

"Come on, Deb," Gar said. "Give me a little credit. If I'd leaked it, at least I would have called *The New York Times*. But I can't say I'm appalled that the story got out. Aside from John Malcolm Pearce's fame, there's the solidity of this family. I don't think I have to worry about you all coming apart in the glare of publicity."

"If we do Johnny Carson," Skip said, "maybe I can perform some of my stuff."

"You give me your heart, and I'll give you mine," Debbie sang.

"Hey, that's not bad," Skip said. "To think, my ideal collaborator has been right here under my nose all these years."

"On the other hand—" Gar said with a little groan, but he was smiling. He leaned back in his chair. "I'll take you up on the hot coffee, Margo."

She gathered cups. "About the old heart," she said.

"Do you think Mrs. Pearce might let it be buried with her husband? It does seem poetic. Less spooky than what I was thinking of."

"A lot less spooky," Debbie said.

"But is it right to ask her to do that? When she's already done so much for us?"

"I have a feeling it would be just right," Gar said, and Mickie nodded. "You've given her something too, Margo. You've helped her to cheat death that little bit."

"Have I? Oh, I hope so. I wrote her a letter. Mickie has it."

"No, I have it." He tapped the breast pocket of his sport coat. "I'm going to see her later this afternoon. To discuss the whole publicity business. I'll give it to her and ask her about Hank's heart."

"Are there kids?" Margo held her breath.

"They were on their honeymoon."

"Sad!" Debbie said. She took her mother's hand.

"I'd like to go to the funeral," Margo said. "Whether or not Hank's old heart gets buried there."

"I'll go with you," Debbie said.

Margo hugged her. "Would you, darling? How lovely of you."

"Well, not to be upstaged by my little sister," Skip said. "I guess it wasn't a waste to bring my dark suit home."

"I take back everything I was thinking about you brats," Mickie said.

Gar looked at his watch.

"I'll get your coffee," Margo said.

Chapter 17

Late in the afternoon she answered a *rap-tap* at the door and saw Phil and Gar standing there together, faces twinned in intensity. The air jammed in her throat.

"Is he all right? Tell me quickly. He isn't rejecting, is he?"

"He's doing beautifully," Gar said. Phil nodded for emphasis. "Wow, you guys gave me a scare. Come on in. It's the tag-team doctors," she announced almost merrily to the small group in the living room. She introduced Gar to her mother and Sukie and Mark, and she offered Papa Sam's rainwater Madeira all around. Phil, who was on call, said no thanks.

"Well, you predicted it," Gar said. He sat down uncertainly in a Shaker chair built for someone with shorter legs. "The press caught on. Mrs. Corman got a call from *The New York Post.*"

"Mrs. Corman?" Kitty said.

Andrea told her what she'd guessed that morning and where she'd gone. Mark put his head in his hands. Sukie, the careless nanny, looked down.

"Oh Andrea," Kitty said. "You're always so hard on yourself." It was the same voice, virtually the same words, Kitty had used years ago when Andrea had brought bags of carefully folded sweaters and skirts, not all of them unwanted, to a shelter for homeless women. Kitty sent checks.

"I'm not," Andrea said. "This was an act of self-indulgence." She'd thought of the visit to the shelter that way too. "Ask Dr. McKay. He was upset with me for coming."

Gar tendered a conciliatory smile. "I'm sorry I gave you a hard time, Mrs. Pearce. You caught me off-guard. Once I stopped to think about it, and talked with Phil and some of my colleagues at Downtown, I realized that no way could we could keep this story secret, and maybe that's a good thing. You'd be amazed at how few people understand that we are all potential donors and recipients. This is the kind of publicity, with your consent of course, that can do a tremendous amount to raise the public consciousness. I didn't get a chance to tell you earlier, but I admired your husband's book on transplantation. I must have bought a dozen copies for various doubting Thomases in the profession when we were trying to get our program going at Downtown."

"Dr. McKay," Kitty said, "hasn't my daughter given you enough?"

"I haven't given anything," Andrea said. "It's John who's done the giving. I just said okay."

"There, dear, I wasn't going to say it but you did. This whole transplantation business was always John's pet, not yours. I admire you for carrying out his wishes, and now it's time for you to seal that chapter and get on with your life."

Andrea looked down, too embarrassed for her mother to meet her eyes. Kitty wanted her to put away her John-ish things to clear the decks for her next marriage. Don't you realize this is it? So long as we both shall live.

"We often find," Gar McKay was saying, "that the act of giving helps the bereaved to heal. I like to think we've given Andrea something too."

"And now she has a chance to give more, to help save hundreds, maybe thousands, of lives," Phil said to Kitty. "Is that really something you want to protect her from?"

"Yes, if it means she has to sacrifice herself. She has a history of that. They'll put her picture in every supermarket tabloid. Is that what you want for her? She's had reporters on the phone all day as it is. Imagine how they'll hound her if she lets them."

"I'm a reporter, Mother."

"But you're you. You're different. You're not really a reporter." She sighed and looked at Sukie, grown-up to grown-up. "How did I raise such an innocent? You tell her, Sukie. What she needs is a month somewhere warm. Or maybe London with you would be more distracting."

"Lovely," Sukie said. "But I don't think you'll convince her."

"I brought you a letter from Mrs. Corman," Gar said to Andrea. "She wrote it while her husband was in surgery, before she knew who you were, and she asked me to hold onto it until I thought you could handle it. Under the circumstances—"

Andrea smiled. Mush talk. "Under the circumstances" was high on John's hit list. Because, as you would see if you gave it a moment's thought, there were always circumstances. Bread and circumstances.

She took the blue envelope. A chill got hold of her, and she huddled into her sweater. She wanted to bury the letter in a heap of mail, the way she now and then did with a bill for something long gone or not successful.

Gar gave her an encouraging nod. "It's a nice letter. She's a remarkable woman. One of the warmest people I've ever known. A real Jewish mother." Mark cleared his throat and rolled his eyes—John would have been on the floor with laughter—and Gar had the grace to blush. "She'd do anything for you, Andrea. For us. She wants everyone to be as lucky as she thinks she and Hank are."

Andrea got a finger under the flap and opened the envelope, but she couldn't read the letter. Smoke rose up off the paper, obscuring the words. She faked it, nodding the way a reasonable person might do, counting beats, turning the page over at the right moment. She managed to make out the signature—"your devoted friend, M."

"Margo," Gar said.

Margo sounded too young. Oh, let's say M for Mama.

She read the letter twice. The chills subsided.

"I want to meet her," she said. "So she knows she doesn't have to worry about me."

"Actually," Gar said, "she'd like to come tomorrow. To the funeral. To pay her respects to you, and because it's a Jewish custom"—he smiled deferentially at Mark, who winked—"to bury any part of a living person that's surgically removed, and she thought that if possibly you were willing to have Hank's heart buried with John—"

Andrea got up and walked to a window. So many windows, and how they beckoned, like paintings and doorways, but only John had opened for her, offered the longed-for invitation: Come in, I've been waiting, I have secrets to share, and I've got a fire going. She looked out at the crusted snow waiting

129

to receive his body. A heart, Hank's heart, even that broken heart, might help to melt it.

"Yes," she said softly. "I'd like that. Thank you for offering."

Kitty leaned forward in alarm. "Andrea, what are you doing?"

She pulled out the phrase — an awful phrase, one she'd sworn never to use but she knew she was right to use it — which brooked no argument.

"John would want it that way," she said.

Kitty bit her lip to whiteness, but she didn't say anything; no one said anything.

Andrea put an arm around her mother. "I know this is hard for you. Thank you for being here."

"Once tomorrow is over" — Kitty clutched the hand that clasped her shoulder — "we'll all have an easier time."

Andrea didn't believe her, but she wasn't about to tear the fragile peace between them. She offered more Madeira and put Handel in the air, as if these acts, any acts, made a difference.

Chapter 18

Margo woke all at once in a dark room, jolted out of sleep by a pain below her navel, not nausea but a frightening tightness, as though something she'd ingested had congealed and fused her moving parts. Duck. In the old days, before she'd known that dietary fat could kill, she'd often feasted on Long Island duck with its crisp and buttery skin, never mind that a 4:00 A.M. jolt inevitably followed. She hadn't eaten duck last night. She'd eaten a lightly dressed linguini salad and not much of that. The pain came from fear, plain and simple.

She tried to know the fear, the better to beat it. She was afraid she was going to fall apart at John Malcolm Pearce's interment (but she would never fall apart with Debbie and Skip looking on). She was afraid she would make an ass of herself in front of the press (but if the publicity wooed just one organ donor, that would more than make up for any flubs and blushes). She was afraid she would somehow be wrongly Jewish in the Yankee bastion called Kent (but Sue McKay was coming at eight to advise her on wardrobe and Congregational ways, and this was anyway an unacceptable fear). She was afraid that God would think she was taking too much for granted and He would let Hank die.

The last fear was the real one and would not be butted away. She looked at the telephone on the table that separated her bed from Hank's, and she saw its powder blue plastic skin quivering, getting ready to ring with bad news. If it rang she would scream. She lay there looking and looking at it, cheek glued to her pillow, fingers tensing at the satin edge of her blue electric blanket, feeling the fear grow inside her, until she almost wanted the dreaded call to come and free her from the agony of waiting.

The obscenity of that almost-wanting saved her. She sat up, pulled the telephone onto the bed, dialed Downtown, and got put through to Susan Jackson, the weeknight nurse in charge of the surgical cardiac intensive care unit. "It's Margo Corman," she said, "and I thought I'd call the one person in greater Hartford who was sure to be awake. How's my boyfriend doing?"

"Mrs. Corman, how funny, I just went for a nice little walk with him, all the way from his bed to the window."

"You did?" Tears, so quick these days, sprang to Margo's eyes. "And he was steady on his feet?"

"He just missed being Fred Astaire. You better bring your dancing shoes the next time you visit."

"I won't be in until the afternoon. It's going to feel like an eternity. He's okay, though? I was hoping he'd sleep through the night."

"It's something about transplantation—they rarely sleep through the night. Even months and months later. And I guess it's extra exciting for Mr. Corman, getting a famous heart. He was telling me I had to read this poem John Malcolm Pearce wrote about golf, though what I know about golf you could fit on the head of a pin."

"I'll get you a copy," Margo said. "I don't play golf

and I thought it was terrific. And funny. It's about someone playing nine holes, and each hole is one of Dante's nine circles of Hell."

"Oh yeah? 'Midway in life's journey . . .' I remember Mr. Dante. I read the Inferno when I was in nursing school—don't ask me how I had time—because some wiseguy doctor told me it would give me a good idea of what hospital life was like. Golf, huh? Sounds kind of cute. I'd like to read it."

"I'll try to remember this afternoon. How's Sam Mancuso doing?"

"Holding on," the nurse said, but her voice flattened out.

"Give them both my love."

She pulled on a blue terry robe and padded out to the kitchen to make peppermint tea. While the water was coming to a boil, she went to the bookshelf in the den next to the kitchen and looked for *Pin High.* Hank had read it and loved it when it had appeared in *Sports Illustrated,* and when it had come out as a thin paperback, after John Malcolm Pearce had won the Pulitzer for the kidney transplant book, she'd bought it for him.

She felt a strange thrill go through her as she opened the book and read the printed dedication. "To Linda, a Class A player at the game of life." Oh John. You were sweet, I think. I will read all your books. I will take good care of your heart.

But (as she sipped her tea) who was Linda? His widow was Andrea; was Linda his sister? And why did the question nag, why did I care who Linda was? Because Andrea cared, she decided. Andrea needed the solace of knowing her John had never loved anyone else.

"No, I need it," she said aloud, surprising herself, as she rinsed out the cup. A primitive need, one that flew in the face of all she knew (she'd never confess it to Gar or Mickie or her son): She wanted Hank to have another one-woman heart.

Oh, but think of Andrea, devastated, clutching at the air, weeping, telling God that she'd pay any price to have John back, he could cheat on her, play poker, drink too much, just as long as he came home to her.

Dear God, let Hank flirt with the nurses, I don't care, it's enough that he's alive.

She was glad when Sue McKay showed up and put an end to these thoughts.

Sue, blond and rangy, plowed efficiently through Margo's closetful of dark petites. She pulled out a navy suit, checked the hem on the skirt, made approving noises, then noticed the missing button on the jacket. "Margo," she said, "are you sure you're Jewish?"

Intolerable from anyone else, but this was part of the game that she and Sue liked to play. "I know. I better brush up on my princessing." She was standing in front of her mirror, dressed in an ivory slip, drawing a thin brown line under her lower lashes. She dropped her pencil, poked at her hair. "I actually had an appointment with John this morning, and I had to cancel it." Shivering, wrapping her arms around her chest: "To keep a date with another John."

"He was married twice before, did you know that?" Sue said, inspecting a gray tweed suit with deep lapels.

"I knew he dedicated a book to a Linda. The golf poem." She felt a little relieved. At least he married his loves.

"Linda Ammiccare," Sue said. "I listened to an interview on NPR on my way over here. She was wife number two. And his number one editor. Even after the divorce. I couldn't do that, could you? Why don't you wear this suit? And you've got that gray cashmere turtleneck, if it's clean. It'll photograph well."

"The turtleneck just came back from French. It's in the laundry room closet. I guess the warmth will feel good in the graveyard. The service is really only five minutes?"

Sue nodded. "We Congregationalists are very merciful. 'Ashes to ashes,' and then a little prayer and a benediction. That's it. Because there's usually a proper funeral before, though this isn't the first time I've heard of a family opting for just the committal service."

"There are going to be enough firsts," Margo said, shivering again.

She got into her sweater and suit and knee-high black leather boots that would stand up to the graveyard but wouldn't look klutzy indoors. After the burial, she would call at Andrea's house. Oh God, please tell me my acts are good in Thy sight.

Sue McKay was looking at her from all the angles. "You're a perfect Connecticut Yankee."

"Too perfect. I think I'll wear my mink coat so no one will think I'm trying to pass."

"I didn't know you had a mink coat."

"I don't."

"Gar came home late twice last week, and I told him if he had a mistress I thought I should get a new fur coat."

"Doctors always come home late, don't they?"

"This didn't feel like doctors' lateness," Sue said.

"So what did he say?"

"He said did it work the other way? If I got a new fur coat, did he get a mistress?"

"That's a pretty good answer," Margo said.

"Do you think so? Maybe I'm being stupid," Sue said. "Maybe on a day like today I should just be glad my husband's alive."

A limousine from the Colonial Funeral Home came at ten to nine. The driver was pale with dark polished hair—he couldn't have been anything but what he was. He had Hank's old heart in a small wooden box next to him on the front seat. Were heart boxes stock in trade now? Margo and the children sat in the back. Even Skip was hard pressed for talk.

At the graveyard Margo wished she did have a mink because she had never in all her life been so cold. She clutched Debbie on one side and Skip on the other, and still the chill seeped through her gray down coat and her several layers of wool. It was a pretty place, though, right behind the simple white church, with snowcrusted trees all around and powdered hills beyond, enchanting if you kept your eyes from the chasm waiting to receive the coffin and its precious stowaway heart.

The minister looked from Margo and the children to a man and two women standing together but not touching—the younger one had to be Andrea, though she didn't look the way Margo had imagined her—to the small clutch of reporters at one side. His bony nose and elegant ears and closely-shaven cheeks were bright red, but if he felt the cold—surely he felt the cold—he did not let on. He said, without preamble: " 'I heard a voice from heaven saying, Blessed are the dead which die in the Lord; they rest from their labors, and their works do follow them.' "

His manner of speaking was so conversational, so free of clerical bombast—and he didn't open the dark blue leather-covered Book of Free Worship, which he held in his gloved hands — that at first Margo thought he was telling her he had heard a voice. Then she realized the service had begun, the end was here, and her body seemed to collapse in on itself, as though she'd been punctured and the air had escaped. She had been holding the children to her, but now Skip was holding her up.

The minister opened his book.

" 'For as much as it hath pleased almighty God to take out of the world the soul of our brother John departed, we therefore commit his body to the ground; earth to earth, ashes to ashes, dust to dust, remembering that if our earthly house of this tabernacle be dissolved, we have a building of God, a house not made with hands, eternal in the heavens.' "

A stranger but no one could be less a stranger, she would sleep with his heart until it stopped. Merciful God, forgive me.

" 'O Lord, support us all the day long, until the shadows lengthen, and the evening comes, and the busy world is hushed, and the fever of life is over, and our work is done. Then, in Thy great mercy, grant us a safe lodging and a holy rest, and peace at the last; through Jesus Christ our Lord. Amen.' "

As he said the name of his God, the opening words of the kaddish rose up in her and came out: "Yis-gad-dal, v'yis-kad-dash, sh'meh rab-bo."

The minister looked up, and then nodded, almost smiled, and said the words with her. "B'ol-mo di'v-ro kir-u-seh v'yam-lich malchu-seh." In the time of deepest grief, adoration of the Almighty.

Mr. Taft let the world hang silent for a moment; then he said: " 'Death taunted me: Shoot out of bounds! / But the Greenskeeper saved me, and with His help / it was my fortune to play a birdie

137

round.' "

Margo saw that the younger of the women and the man were weeping. The older woman stared straight ahead.

The pale driver placed the box containing Hank's heart on top of the coffin.

" 'Unto God's gracious mercy and protection we commit you. The Lord bless you and keep you; the Lord make His face to shine upon you, and be gracious unto you; the Lord lift up His countenance upon you, and give you peace, both now and forever more. Amen.' "

Margo drew a deep breath, looked at her children for fresh courage, then started over to Andrea to offer as best she could to share the burden of grief. But the weeping young woman who clasped her hands and thanked her for coming was Sukie some-one—Andrea's bridesmaid, she said; Andrea had gone to Hartford to be with Hank.

The
Blue
Course

Except as provided for under the Rules, the player shall not use any artificial device:—

a. Which might assist him in making a stroke or in his play;

b. For the purpose of gauging or measuring distance or conditions which might affect his play; or

c. Which, not being part of the grip is designed to give him artificial aid in gripping the club.

—THE RULES OF GOLF

Chapter 19

She said nothing for the first half of the trip and then she leaned forward and told Ed Spaet: "They're burying my husband. Right now. In Kent. And I'm in your taxi."

The words hung there, part of the awful gray mist that had shrouded her since she'd emerged from a night of fragmented sleep. She thought he hadn't heard her or didn't believe her, and she burst out, "Because I have to be here and not there, do you understand?"

He calmly scratched under his cap. "The way I see it," he said, "if you loved him it makes no difference where you are, and if you didn't love him, it makes no difference either. Maybe it matters to the neighbors, but they don't count right now."

She leaned back against the seat, trembling, tears on the brink but still not falling. "Do you mean it?" Willing to accept his judgment; eager for it, though she'd been telling other people since dawn that they mustn't judge her.

He took them up a curving, wooded road. Avon Mountain, she remembered, and knowing the name made her want to cry out because she needed her mind to be free to steer her through the mist. Her fingers scrabbled over the cracks in the backseat, as if they were a map that might tell her where she really was and how to get anywhere else.

"I heard about you on the radio this morning," Ed Spaet said. "Gil Gross—don't always agree with him but he's never boring. He said how you'd donated your husband's heart and now you were letting the other guy's heart be buried with him. He liked the sound of that and so did I. Told my wife I'd driven you, in fact. Kind of proud of it. Then the dispatcher called and said you'd asked for me."

Even in her dark gray cloud she was touched. "Thank you. My mother and my friends are so upset. About Henry Corman's heart and my not being there today. They think I'm running away. They're sure I'll feel wildly guilty. But I think I would feel guilty being there. Because John and I weren't about funerals. Oh, we weren't babies—we realized we'd have our terrors and horrors—but I'm sure I'm doing the right thing even though I don't know why."

"Maybe you'll know why when you get there," he said. Not words to clear a mist but a tacit blessing, much needed after the tears and frowns at home.

They were at the top of the mountain and she could see the Hartford skyline. John had written about skylines, how moving they were, the mark of humankind daring to thrust toward God. She wanted to share the thought with Ed Spaet, wanted to share John with him. She would have to give him a book. She had one with her but it was for Henry Corman, a signed first edition of *Pin High*.

She reached out and touched it for a talisman. Its smooth cool lines unexpectedly made her shudder, brought her down into a new darkness. Because what were a dead author's books but coffins for his

142

words? And, oh God, now, she could feel it and smell it: the other coffin, lying helpless under a thundering rain of earth, weighting him, sealing him in, extinguishing the light, squeezing out the last breath of air.

"Stop!" she yelled, and Ed Spaet pulled off the road in a squealing hurry, and she bolted from the taxi still yelling, but she couldn't drown out the thunder.

He came around to where she stood and looked at her, making her feel his presence—humorless, shabby, solid, forgiving. He didn't say anything, just waited, and at last the thundering stopped, and she took great gasping breaths of snow air and let him help her back into the taxi.

Churchbells were ringing the hour as they got to the hospital. She left the shelter of the taxi and went through the revolving door feeling that people were looking at her, had somehow expected her. Yes, this was where she had to be. The gray lady at the visitors' desk didn't exactly smile but her stern mouth softened and she handed over an orange plastic pass before Andrea had to ask.

A dark-haired woman who said she was Mickie Ross was waiting for her when she got to the intensive care unit, hands outstretched, offering words of commiseration and thanks. "Dr. McKay isn't here, but he said you were welcome anytime, just like family. Hank's awake and eager to meet you, so let's find you a mask and gown."

"I've brought him a book," Andrea said. "May I give it to him? It's wearing its own paper cover." She was sure they had rehearsed this exchange.

"I know he'd like that very much. Our public relations people would too." Mickie's voice was brisk, unapologetic. "I took the liberty of asking them to send a team up."

"Of course," Andrea said. "I'm here to help the cause." Though she didn't yet know why she was there.

Henry Corman stood for her. No smile but she got the eyes, wide open and very bright.

"Andrea," he said. He seemed to want to say more and didn't.

She clasped his hands. Their warmth thrilled through her. She could hardly believe his wellness. It became a physical fact about her, lifting her shoulders, as though his illness had been the burden she was bearing. "You look—glorious," she said.

"I wouldn't dare look any other way. Not after—" His lips fought to hold the line. His eyes filled with tears. "Hey, I'm sorry," he said, looking at the publicist, a tiny woman whose isolation gown came to her ankles. "This isn't in the script."

"Never mind. You're crying for both of us." She handed him the copy of *Pin High*. "I've brought you a present," she said, aware of the photographer framing them from different angles.

Hank shrugged eloquently. "What can I say? I thank you with all John's heart."

She had been here many times, knew the script as well as he did. "It's your heart, Hank."

He opened the book to the beginning. "I meant to write him a letter. To tell him how much I liked his writing."

"Now he knows," Andrea said. She could hear the publicist's satisfied rhythms as she pinged at her lap computer.

"I hoped he would write a second volume. The back nine."

"He thought about it, but he couldn't get it started. Maybe"—tingles dancing up her cheeks—"you can write it. That could be your present to me."

"If Wallace Stevens wrote poems, why not me?"

"Under the circumstances," she said, and started to laugh.

Mickie Ross took a step forward. "I think it's time for Hank to get some rest."

"I never felt better. I could play eighteen holes right now. Hell, thirty-six. What was John's handicap?"

"He played scratch," Andrea said. "Not the longest hitter in the world, but he was something else with a putter. What's your handicap?"

"It used to be my heart. How's that?" he said to the publicist.

"I love it."

"Mrs. Pearce—" Mickie Ross said. "I want a shot of her listening to the heart," the photographer said.

Hank did funny things with his eyebrows. "Is my heart up to the excitement?"

"Oh, it's used to me," Andrea said. She waved away the proffered stethoscope and put her ear to Hank's pajama'd chest.

Dan-dy, said the heart.

She leaned into the gorgeous music, instantly drunk.

My John. Is it really you? Say the words.

Dan-dy. Dan-dy. Sweet as. Can-dy. I love Dan-dy.

"I have to tell you, Mickie," Hank said, "that a warm ear feels a helluva lot nicer on my chest than a cold stethoscope. Her perfume's nicer too."

She tried to tune in the only real voice, but there was too much static. Then she was standing back

145

and looking into Hank's eyes, those hungry eyes, wildly alive, and she didn't need anything else — she had what she had come for: a map through the mist, an escape from the smothering ice of the grave.

Chapter 20

HEARTFELT
A Transplant Wife's Story
exclusive to *The New York Post*

*by Margo Kovner Corman
with Gretchen Davis*

Life has been a series of ups and downs in the four years since my husband, Hank, suffered a massive coronary at 45.

After our initial thankfulness that he had survived the attack came the crushing realization that his condition could not be helped by bypass surgery and he was doomed to death at an early age.

Hank had the finest medical care possible, and I became an expert in low-fat cookery, but our two children and I saw him deteriorate from a tireless life-of-the-party kind of guy into a bedridden ghost watching the sands of time run out.

You can imagine our ecstasy when he was accepted as a candidate for a heart transplant at Downtown Medical Center in Hartford. Then, just a week ago, came a day of both joy and grief—joy that a heart was available for Hank, who was growing weaker every day, and grief that the donor, unknown to us but oh-so-cherished, had lost the young life he was posthumously giving to my husband.

Only after the successful transplant surgery came the startling telephone call from *The New York Post* informing me that the donor was the writer John Malcolm Pearce.

Again, I felt conflicting emotions in my breast. What an honor for our family to give a home to the heart of this talented author and athlete, long a hero of ours. And yet my sorrow was intensified because so promising a life had been snuffed out. For not only was this a man with many great books yet to write, this was a bridegroom on his honeymoon with the beautiful young woman who had hoped to bear his children.

Andrea Pearce and I communicated through our doctors, and she performed a second act of magnificent generosity. Jewish law requires that all body parts be buried, and she allowed Hank's old heart to be interred with her husband's body. In a snow-covered graveyard in Kent, Connecticut, my children and I bid a tearful farewell to John Malcolm Pearce and to a part of Henry Corman.

This Friday evening, just six days after the transplant surgery, Andrea will come to our house for dinner. If the President and First Lady were due, I could not feel more excited. On the menu are some of our tried-and-true family favorites, festive yet simple. We'll start with hot winter fruit soup, a combination of fresh and nonsulphured dried fruits, garnished with a dollop of nonfat yogurt. Then on to Skinny Skinned Roast Chicken,* baked new potatoes in their jackets, steamed asparagus, whole-wheat challah, and a big tossed salad with sesame dressing.

For dessert, I'm going to rush the calendar and present Andrea with a carob confection I invented for Hank shortly after he became ill, Valentine for a Broken Heart.*

For my children and myself, tonight represents a magnificent opportunity that many organ recipient families never have to express our overwhelming gratitude to the donor. I deliberately say "donor" and not "donor's wife" because I feel that Andrea, as well as John, has given her heart.

I know that we can never repay the Pearces and all the other good people everywhere who have turned the dream of transplantation into reality. But if my story encourages even one person to fill out an organ donor card, perhaps I can pay the interest on our debt.

(To be continued.)

*Clip 'n' save recipe below.

Exclusive: Margo Kovner Corman's Low-Fat Cooking Secrets

Skinny Skinned Roast Chicken

HAVE your butcher SKIN a 4-pound chicken or do the job yourself, loosening the skin with the tip of a sharp knife and pulling off the skin with the help of paper towels. REMOVE the fat from inside the body cavity.

RINSE the chicken and PAT dry. In a bowl big enough to hold the chicken, PLACE 1/2 cup low-fat, no-salt buttermilk, a few scallions, some slices of fresh ginger, and some fresh parsley or coriander. PUT the bird in this bath, TURN several times to coat, COVER the bowl with plastic wrap, and REFRIGERATE overnight. Meanwhile, MAKE about one cup of fine cracker crumbs (I use unsalted whole grain sesame crackers). SCRUB AND RINSE two lemons.

SET oven to 450.

Working over waxed paper, COVER the bird with crumbs. ROLL the lemons to make them juicy and INSERT them into the bird's cavity.

SPRAY a roasting rack with vegetable oil, PUT the bird on breast-side up, PLACE in oven, and REDUCE the temperature to 350.

ROAST for about 1 1/2 hours, turning twice, until chicken is golden brown and the juices run clear.

HOT or cold, no one will miss the skin on this crisp and tasty bird!

Valentine Cake for a Broken Heart

No, it's not quite the same as chocolate! But this easy-to-make, low-sugar, no-fat confection has a sophisticated mocha flavor and a satisfying chewy texture.

SET oven at 300.

COAT a four-cup capacity heart-shape baking tin

with vegetable oil spray.

BEAT 3 extra-large egg whites with 1/4 tsp cream of tartar until peaks form.

BEAT in gradually 1/2 cup sugar sifted with 1/4 cup carob powder.

FOLD in 1 capful pure vanilla extract and 1/2 cup unsweetened carob chips.

BAKE for 1 hour. COOL on rack for 1/2 hour.

INVERT onto plate and SERVE with water-washed de-caffeinated espresso and lemon ice. ENJOY!

P.S. You should feel no more compunction about throwing away the leftover egg yolks than you do about trimming the fat off meat!

Chapter 21

She decided to drive to the Cormans'. Everyone argued with her but in resigned voices as though it were understood that she had passed beyond the reach of reason. She promised she wouldn't crash because the irony would be too tidy—Margo and the children siphoning their blood to save her—and life didn't work that way. She wouldn't crash. She wouldn't get lost. Her only worry was that the Lamborghini, so red and rich, so careless, might embarrass the Cormans' driveway. Mark took the train back to New York to leave her the mushroom-colored BMW. Truly a friend.

She wanted to bring the Cormans a present, the one right present. Not flowers in this week of drowning lilies, not chocolates for a woman who skinned her chickens. Something of John's and not a book. Oh God. His putter.

When she was a child, six or seven, she'd heard about a man being buried with his putter. He was a business associate of her father's, some kind of supplier, and when her father had come back from the funeral, he'd had that red bursting look he sometimes got over little things (at least they seemed little to his young daughter). "An open casket—the barbarity of it," Frank Olinger had fumed to Kitty.

"Face rouged, they plucked his damn eyebrows, and then they would go and lay his putter on his body and arrange his hands on the shaft. How could she do it to him?"

I'll make up for it, Daddy. An anti-death putter.

John's clubs were in the closet underneath the stairs. On Driver and Mashie and Sand Wedge and Blitzen.

Six or seven or eight and she'd asked her father what kind of sandwich he carried in his golf bag. Forever after (he'd loved telling her) he would ask his caddy for his sandwich when he had a ball in the bunker.

John liked the story, but he still said "sand wedge." He didn't want to be Daddy — that would complicate bed and gray his hair — and anyway, he never stole other men's riffs.

Why did you do it then, sweetie? Jump off that bridge not wearing your suspenders?

She crushed sheets of green tissue around the putter. Neat little tears of tape. A yellow bow from the messy drawer in the kitchen.

She put on a long thick yellow sweater to match, a simple mid-calf gray skirt, pale gray leather boots. A reporter's clothes, though tonight she would be the story.

"Let me drive you," Sukie pleaded again. "Or call that taxi driver."

She didn't want to call Ed Spaet for fear he would see that the hope she'd found in Hartford was a slippery kind of hope and she didn't have her hands on it now. "I'll be fine," she said. "I've got to do it sometime."

"But to Hartford?"

"If I don't feel in control I'll come back."

153

She stepped out into a fine sharp winter night, stars above and snow below silvering the infinite dark, and for one lovely moment as she breathed in the purifying dark, possibility lived again. She opened the door to the car, and her mind turned in on itself. If anything might happen, why shouldn't the car explode when she put the key in the ignition? John laughed, leaned back in the passenger seat, teased her with adoring eyes. This is what comes of buying you trenchcoats. Let it blow, let it blow, let it blow.

She turned the key. The car started.

She considered heading up, not down, Sprague Road, heading for the hills and New York State and around to some other bridge, but the car nosed to the left and down. You can do it, Dandy. Show them. The road was clear now, though narrowed by the drifts the plows had made. She took the curves slowly, precisely, holding tight to the steering wheel, braced against the moment when it would try to drag her down to the river. And oh God if she loved him more, but she couldn't love him more, she would be racing for the river.

Silly Dandy. That's not where I am.

Where are you then?

You have to find me. That's the game.

Were you there in Hank's room, or was I just hearing things?

Silence.

She got to the other side of the bridge without having been aware that she was crossing it. To town, through town, opposite the church with its terrible yard hidden behind the blameless white of the building. Shuddering: Is this where you are?

Reverend Taft had come calling. What may I do

to offer comfort? Would you like me to accompany you to the grave?

Please. Please just tell me I don't have to go.

Have to, no. But I think you would find it helpful. Denial won't sustain you.

Are you here my John my love my God do you know how much I miss you?

Silence.

She drove on, following Ed Spaet's route as far as Bishop's Corner in West Hartford. Then left to Mohawk and four blocks down. We call this part of town the Reservation, Margo had said. If you get to Navajo Drive you've gone too far.

Pocahontas. Houses a pleasant jumble, one of everything. Mustard colonial, two-tone Tudor, a thrust of aluminum angles. Tenderly swollen white lawns bordered by crisp shoveled walks and driveways.

Number fifty-four. Brick and glass in comforting proportions, cozy yet open. A welcoming light in the freestanding lamppost. I'm home, Mama.

She parked in front but didn't get out. Had she worn the right clothes? Was tonight the night? Maybe Kitty knew what was what for once. Don't get involved, they'll eat you up. But Skinny Skinned Roast Chicken was on the menu—she'd read it in *The New York Post*. Gary Hodges had seen to that.

She put the car keys in her bag and got the putter from the backseat. Not her car, she'd better lock it, even on this street where nothing bad ever happened.

Her feet dragged and then she was running because this was his house now, he was eager for her to know it, the sidewalk with its artful curve, the two front steps, the keyhole where someday his

155

key —

"Andrea. Darling. Welcome."

Sassy hair, denim, slender, pixie pretty. Mom but not Mama though the air was full of Skinny Skinned Roast Chicken.

"Oh, you read that," Margo said, flustered and pleased when Andrea named the aroma. She hung the trenchcoat in a closet fragrant with cloves. "What that woman did to my words! You probably think I'm the dreariest sort of health food nut, but I'm not so bad, I promise, the children keep me in line. Come on into the living room and meet them, and how about what Hank likes to call some all-natural fat-free Scotch? Or bourbon, Canadian, vodka, gin, beer, wine, you name it. And no bean sprouts in it, I promise."

"A beer would be very nice. John converted me from wine and I stopped getting headaches." Margo's eyes hooded when the name was named and Andrea rescued her from the obligatory solemnity by thrusting the giftwrapped putter at her. "This is for Hank. From himself."

"Andrea. What a thoughtful thing to do. As if you had to give us anything else. I'll bring it to the hospital first thing tomorrow. He'll be so thrilled." She gently laid the putter on the front hall table and took Andrea by the elbow. "Now a beer for you. There's Dos Equis, Miller Lite, and Guinness Stout. And of course wouldn't you know there's beer without alcohol. I bought it originally for Skip's friends because I simply will not serve them booze until they're twenty-one."

"Guinness. Please. They say it makes milk."

Margo stopped and looked at her, hugged her lightly. "That's very wonderful news. When I heard

156

how young you were, I did so hope there might be a child. Do I dare ask? Did he"—she shook her head at her own audacity—"know?"

Oh but the audacity was lovely. The questions Kitty had never asked because prying was so human.

"No," Andrea said. "I'm still not sure, you see. But I think so."

"Just one very small glass of Guinness, then," Margo said, tenderly stern.

The children rose, smiling but uncertain, to greet her. How frightened the young were of mourners and they were right. Every mourner was a traitor. Can't you see that I'm different?

Mom saved them. (Kitty would have made them face the music if she'd had them there at all.) "Andrea, I want you to meet my Debbie and my Skip. If you ever need a crew to help you move a mountain, these two will head the list of volunteers."

"I think they already moved a mountain for me." She held out her hand to the girl and then the boy. "Standing in for me the other day. Thank you."

"How can you thank us?" Debbie said. "We'd do anything for you. We were sad at the cemetery, but we were glad to be there." Her face got hot-looking, and she turned to her mother. "Was that an incredibly dumb thing to say?"

"I think it was a fine thing to say. Don't you, Andrea?"

To be swaddled like that! "Of course it was fine because it was true. The things we've been through together, we have to talk true. How's my friend Hank tonight?"

"Antsy," Debbie said, and Skip nodded. "Ready to come home."

157

"Well, it's only a matter of days now, isn't it?"

"Three or four," Skip said. "That's some heart."

"Make yourself comfortable, Andrea," Margo said. "I'll get the drinks." She left her children with the stranger. Swaddling but not suffocating.

Andrea sat down in a big red chair opposite the sofa. Was this the Daddy chair, or did he sprawl on the sofa? "I like the colors here," she said.

"Mickie Ross says red is the color of life," Debbie said.

"Not that it's such an original idea," Skip said. "I studied tantric yoga, and red is very big in Eastern symbology."

"My mother's house is blue," Andrea said. "I was married in her living room and I had so many yellow flowers in there that the walls looked green."

"People with blue bedrooms have trouble," Skip said.

"Oh Skip," Debbie said.

"Well, it's true. I did a paper on the psychology of color, and that's a fact. Blue is associated with poison in people's minds. Someone did experiments with mashed potatoes, tinting them all different colors, and nobody would eat the blue ones. It's probably some defensive mechanism built into the species."

"Well, what about seeing red?" Debbie said triumphantly. "Sometimes in this room I see red."

"I guess we all see red in our mother's living room," Andrea said. "But I'd rather see red than be blue. Who plays that serious-looking piano?"

"I do," Skip said.

"And Daddy does. At least he used to."

Andrea smiled. She'd wished throughout her childhood that she had an older brother, and if

158

she'd had one they probably would have tussled endlessly.

"I bet he'll want to play again when he gets home," she said.

Skip nodded knowingly. "I can hear him now. 'You Gotta Have Heart.' Et cetera."

"You should talk," Debbie said. "He's writing a musical called 'Transplantation Is the Only Way to Get a Heart into an Insurance Agent.' "

Andrea obliged with a laugh, then said to Debbie, "And what are you writing? Something, I bet."

"Political tracts," Skip said. "Behold the feminist conscience of Pocahontas Drive."

"Ever hear of Leonora Whittlesey? She was my great-great-great aunt. I'm writing a novel about her."

Debbie looked as though she might pass out with excitement. "You're kidding me! She was fantastic! Do you remember my telling you about her, Skip? She dressed up in men's clothes so she could go into the political clubhouses and saloons."

"Which, if you've read any Shakespeare, is hardly a startling idea," he said.

"She wasn't trying to be original," Andrea said. "She didn't have the energy left for that kind of thinking. She was just trying to control her own life."

The children didn't say anything, but she was sure she knew what was on their minds: What would Leonora think of a woman who hadn't even been able to run a honeymoon?

"Please," she said, getting up, "if you could tell me where to wash."

They told her, competing for the privilege of giving her directions, and she fled down the hall. The

159

guest bathroom was green and yellow, a fresh yellow rose in a plastic cup in the cerámic toothbrush holder that was devoid of toothbrushes—waiting for hers, yellow this month? She ran cold water over her wrists, a trick Grand'Anna had taught her for freshening if you weren't sure of the water or didn't want to spoil your makeup.

"Hello," she said into the mirror, hoping she wasn't there.

She wandered into the guest room. More yellow—the stripes on the wall, the spread on the four-poster double bed. She touched the spread. It was soft and clean-feeling. Warm.

"If you ever need a place to stay in West Hartford, this room is yours," Margo said softly from the doorway.

Andrea looked up. "You're very kind."

"Would you like a house tour? Or that Guinness first? The drinks are in the living room."

"I want to see the house. Please."

"Houses are irresistible, aren't they? I always peek at parties. This is Debbie's room." Geometric patterns, bold colors, a sleeping loft with a desk built in underneath. "She went on a rampage last year. No more pink, no more frills, and every last doll and stuffed animal went, though I managed to tuck a couple of things away for her children. Hank's illness has been hard on her. She had to grow up too fast in some ways, and in some ways she stayed a little girl longer than she should have. And guess whose room"—wallpapered in *Playbills* and posters from Broadway musicals—"this is."

"I can't imagine," Andrea said.

"And this is the master bedroom."

She stood rooted in the doorway, inhaling the fragrance of Margo's powder and perfume, a soft fruity smell and pleasant but still it was choking her, and how would he breathe in this room?

"We've got masses of forsythia at the window, marvelous in spring."

Did they ever sleep with the window shades up, those massive draperies open, so dawn would come and get them and they could breakfast with the birds? Because life was too precious, said John, to waste on sleep. Wake up, my sweetheart, wake up!

"The twin beds were a concession to Hank's illness, and I can't wait to see them go. They make me feel ancient. I love that double dresser, though; it belonged to my parents. Of course, nothing here has the character of those lovely old pieces in your house in Kent."

"You were in my house?" She wished people would stop surprising her this way.

Margo gave her a worried look. "The day of the funeral," she said hesitantly. "You have to tell me, Andrea, because I do so want to take good care of you, what you want to talk about and what you don't want to talk about."

"But it doesn't matter," Andrea said. "Nothing matters except this bedroom. Is there enough air in here for him?"

"Well, yes. Of course."

"The mattress is firm enough?" She walked to the far bed, surely his, and she sat on it, bounced a little, as if she were in a bed store. "May I lie down on it?"

"If you want to stretch out, you might be more comfortable in the guest room."

"I want to be here." Andrea peeled off her boots and swung her legs up on the bed. Her parents had

161

had separate beds, separate bedrooms in fact, though they'd shared a dressing room with a lovely big square tub where she wasn't allowed to bathe because her mother said she splashed.

"Then this is where you must be." Margo gently covered her with a large loose-knit throw, but Andrea saw distress around her mouth.

"I'm sorry," she started to say and couldn't. Tears were streaming down her face, filling her throat. She grabbed his pillow and wailed into it, sobs swelling up from deep in her chest, shoulders heaving as the waves came and came.

"Yes, oh yes," Margo said, sinking down beside her. "Let it all out, darling."

"I'm crying, Mom," she said in amazement, and then a fresh storm of sobs drowned out all words.

She went on weeping as the chicken cooled and the other children got hungry and nibbled on crackers — weeping for all the men whose bed this was, her father and her husband and Hank the hungry-eyed, keeper of the heart of hearts.

Chapter 22

"Oh, boy somebody's getting lots of presents today," Ruth Lilley, R.N., said, as Margo appeared at the SCICU with two round red tins tied with silver ribbon. "Let me guess. Eggless, sugarless, fatless, flourless chocolate chip cookies?"

Margo laughed. "If I could do that, I'd be a millionaire. Another batch of oatcakes, but you're right about the eggless and sugarless. The secret is frozen apple juice concentrate."

"Ask himself to save me one, will you?"

"No, because this tin is for you."

"Mrs. Corman, you're kidding. You didn't have to do that."

"And you don't have to do everything you do, but thank God you do."

Ruth Lilley's telephone rang. "You're one lovely lady," she said, reaching for the handset. Margo put a red tin on her desk, gave it a little pat, and headed on down toward Hank's isolette.

He was sitting on the chair next to the window, wearing a new blue silk robe his office staff had given him, unwrapping a long, narrow box, when Margo tapped on the window. He glanced up and blew her a kiss, then went back to his task, fingers scrabbling impatiently at the shiny silver paper.

Like a child at Hannukah, Margo thought. So many gifts this week. There were heart-patterned mugs and T-shirts from friends and from strangers, books with heart in the title, golf balls galore, a dozen dispensers of mint- and cinnamon-flavored dental floss from Bobby Cline, and, most exciting, the putter monogrammed JMP. The world loved Hank Corman, wished him well.

Nobody loved him more than she! So why, as she pulled elasticized paper booties over her brown suede flats, did she recognize the undeniable prickings of wifely irritation on the back of her neck? Shame and fear instantly followed recognition. Dear God, I don't mean it. You know I'm just overtired, I will never stop being grateful! But that perfunctory kiss in the air. The haste to get back to unwrapping his package after he'd acknowledged her existence.

"Hey, will you look at this? What a great present!" Hank held up a roll of green plastic grass as she entered the isolette. "And an electric cup."

"I bet it's from the Davidsons. It's their kind of style, isn't it? Is there a card?" She put the tin of oatcakes and her shoulderbag on the table next to his chair.

"Here it is," Hank said. " 'So the putter has something to do. Love, A'."

"Andrea."

"No," he drawled. He gave her a cool, puzzled look not in his everyday vocabulary of expressions. She couldn't quite get a fix on it. "And here I was thinking it was Archibald Abernathy."

"Well, I'm sorry if I was being obvious. I spent most of the morning listening to Dick Jaffe tell me why we can't afford to sell professional liability insurance any more, and Dick doesn't do much for my subtlety quotient."

"Roll out the green for me, would you, honey?" As if she'd said nothing. He took the putter from its parking place at the foot of his bed and caressed the snub-nosed brass head.

Margo stretched the nine-foot grass carpet alongside the bed. "Don't you want to know what I told Dick?"

He put his hand over his heart. "Please. No business talk until I build up my strength. What do you think, I want malpractice on my mind? If Dr. Fox did anything wrong, I'm not going to be around to enjoy the fruits of the settlement. Where are those Titleists the Hollanders sent?"

"First of all," Margo said, "you're not actually putting until you get the medical okay. Second, we're not plugging in that cup until I check with Ruth Lilley. It would be nice to see that ball come bouncing back at you, darling, but not if you're going to short out Sam Mancuso's respirator."

She expected a laugh, but he gave her that puzzled look again, as though — she fumbled for a minute and then she had it — he'd dialed a wrong number and couldn't quite bend his mind around the reality at the other end. The medicines, she told herself. Gar and Mickie had warned them. Many strangenesses in the beginning.

"I'm riding an exercise bike and you're telling me I can't putt?" Hank said. "Gar said to hold off on swinging a driver, but putt?"

"I admit it sounds foolish, but we're not experts. We don't know what action creates what kind of stress, so let's get a knowledgeable opinion, okay?"

Hank pulled himself out of the chair with a kind of theatrical stiffness that reminded her of Lyndon Johnson on TV after his gallbladder surgery. Well, the man had a right, didn't he? He had a wound from his throat nearly to his navel! She asked him if he were feeling his stitches.

"It's the damned gas," he said. "It's like knives inside."

"Have you been taking all your Maalox?"

"Sure, sure. I don't want to hurt your feelings, kid, but I think maybe those oatcakes were too much too soon."

Margo looked out the window. Down on the street a man was taking off his coat, flinging it over his shoulder, as though he'd decided he'd had it with winter, he was launching a personal springtime, never mind the calendar or weather. Oh I know how you feel. And Paris seemed further away than it had before Hank's surgery. Because before the surgery she'd thought: If only that heart would come in, dayenu, sufficient. And, God forgive her, sometimes it wasn't enough.

A rap on the door. Gar McKay. He took in the length of plastic grass, the cup. He watched Hank ready his grip on the putter. "If you start one-putting the green," he said to Hank, "medical science is going to be very interested."

Margo shuddered. "Don't say things like that, Gar." Should she give Gar the red tin of oatcakes? If Hank hadn't liked the other batch, he wouldn't like this one. She'd thought the recipe a success and had used it again.

"I can talk like that to you," Gar said, "because I know you know I'm not even slightly serious."

"Dr. Margo here tells me I'm not allowed to putt," Hank said. "Putt!"

"Hank, honey, that's a little unfair. I simply said we should get the okay." And it would be unfair to put

166

Gar in the middle by giving him the oatcakes with Hank right there.

Gar looked from one Corman to the other. His eyes were anxious, and Margo's stomach tightened. Sam Mancuso? But he would have told them.

Hank persisted. "Is Gar high enough authority?"

"Excuse me," Margo said, "you two chat. I'm going to say hello to Sam."

She picked up the red tin and whisked out of the isolette and down the hall toward Sam's bed, then made a different turn and went to Mickie's office.

Mickie was on the phone, but as soon as she saw Margo, she told the person at the other end she had to go. She folded her hands expectantly. "To what do I owe?"

"I have a tin of oatcakes looking for a taker."

"Look no further."

"Oh good." Margo gave Mickie the tin. She perched on the arm of the stuffed green chair she'd sat in the day Debbie had carried on. "Do you have a minute? I was wondering—you're sure he'll be ready to go home in two days?"

"You're kidding me. He was ready the day after the surgery."

"You know what I mean," Margo said. "Is he really well enough?"

"What, you're worried about a little gas? He's beautiful."

Margo looked out Mickie's window. Windows were magnets these days. "Kind of, I don't know, moody, though. But I guess you warned me."

"Ahah."

"No, it's nothing." Margo started to get up. "I'd be edgy if I were living in that plastic cage."

"Sure, but would you let anyone see it?" Mickie shook her head. "You'd be telling Hank everything

167

was fine, terrific, and he was a doll for coming to see you every day, bringing you such wonderful presents. You know your problem? You're a Pollyanna. Maybe they told you different when you were little, but lightning won't strike if you complain. We won't give Hank back his old heart."

Margo nodded, forced a smile. "You're right."

"No, what you really want to say is, 'Stuff it.' Margo, you've been the model transplant wife until now, but you know what? It's not because you're so goddam cheerful all the time, if you'll pardon my French. It's because you're wildly in love with that scrawny smart-ass clown who hasn't been able to get it up in what, a year and a half? Two years?"

Margo didn't answer.

"You really do have a right to be very, very, very pissed off at people you love. Even when they've come this close to dying. You have a right to hate them sometimes. In fact, you have a kind of obligation to hate them sometimes because they hate you sometimes and you don't want them to feel like they're some lower order. Or do you? Now don't you dare thank me for my helpful little speech!"

"I wasn't planning to!" Margo said, and she wasn't smiling.

"I apologize for being rough. I know you've been through the mill. What I was really trying to do is tell you that you are so genuinely good a person, you can be bad once in a while and still be good. And if you're feeling anxiety about having him back home again, that's okay too. Par for the course."

"Are you sure that's your message? Or are you trying to tell me you just can't stand my style? Or maybe"—daring—"you have to be the queen bee around here, and I've got too many friends on the floor? Enjoy the oatcakes."

168

She was still smarting when she left Mickie's office, but she stopped at the first pay phone she saw and called her haircutter, John, to remake her thrice-postponed appointment. That editor from *Redbook* was coming. And she just wanted to do it, dammit.

She went to see Sam Mancuso. He was sprawled face up, a medium-size, medium-color man in his early thirties who always made Margo think of boiled new potatoes, asleep but restless, his pale legs making little frog-kick motions, echoing memories of Skip as an endlessly physical two-year-old, swimming in his dreams. Elaine, his wife, stood by the bed staring off into space, dark circles under her violet eyes but stunning, her face as angled and detailed as poor Sam's was potato-vague.

"It wasn't supposed to be like this," Elaine said. "He hasn't had a single good moment with that heart. He looks a hundred, doesn't he? You know what he said yesterday? If it weren't for the kids, he'd curl up like an old dog and let go of life."

"I'm sorry it's been so terrible for both of you," Margo said.

"What if he gets another heart and it's the same thing all over again?"

Margo shook her head. "I'm sure the doctors have learned from what's happened. If they didn't think he could do better with a different heart, they wouldn't be looking for one."

"Don't be so sure. They have to try to make themselves look good. Maybe it's not the heart. Maybe it's the way they put it in or the drug dosages. Look at that guy. A hundred thirty-two pounds. How is he supposed to tolerate all that poison? You could fit two of him in Hank."

"They know that, Elaine. Don't be angry and please don't give up."

She went back to Hank's room. He was lying in bed.

"I'm sorry if I was bossy," she said.

"Hey, kid, who can blame you? You've had to be in charge more than you should have been and it just stuck, I guess."

"How did you make out on the green?"

"You ever see a cardiologist eat his heart out? At the end of twelve holes Gar and I were even. You were right about the electric cup, though. They won't let me plug it in. And I'm not supposed to bend to hole out."

Margo raised her eyebrows. "May I suggest you be careful to whom you repeat that phrase?"

"You're a wicked broad, you know that? Thank God."

"I can't wait for Paris."

"Good, because I'm not going to let you wait for Paris. I may not even let you wait for the Plaza."

"Well, you better let me wait for somewhere because people who live in glass houses shouldn't do much at all." She kissed him on the forehead. "You want to nap?"

"It's not what I want to do, but"—eyelids closing—"I have the feeling I ain't got much choice."

She kissed his lips. Dry lips, but her mouth sizzled and she came back for more.

"Love you," she said.

He snored.

Chapter 23

But in its own way dirty snow was beautiful. Like ink-stained fingertips, and cracked leather bags, and a Lamborghini that bore the dust of the Grand Corniche. History. Character. Snow that had lived, that knew what there was to know.

Her father had liked dirty snow, or was she making that up? Probably she was. Weather hadn't impressed him for better or for worse. He'd never exulted in the yielding of April, the crunch of October. He'd never changed his plans because of a storm. He'd thought of nature, the whole of it, from birth to death and the crabgrass in between, as a problem for engineers to solve. What little nontechnical reading he'd done had been in science fiction, and Andrea clearly remembered him rasping at a dinner guest who'd invoked capital-N Nostalgia for the fifties: "Nostalgia? I'm nostalgic for the twenty-first century. That's when they knew how to live." His suicide had been widely blamed on Kitty's marriage to Brady Alexander, but Andrea sometimes believed that he'd chosen death by his own machinery to ward off the insult of death by natural causes.

She was walking east along West Twelfth Street, toward Hudson Street. Pamela Wallett was going to cut her hair—because she was going to be on the radio in a couple of hours, wasn't that funny?

She'd come back to New York so she could publicize the cause. So Mark could have his car. So Sukie could go back to London. So she could meet with John's lawyer:

"He left everything to you, Andrea. You won't have to worry about money."

"My father went bankrupt twice. I'll always worry."

She turned up Hudson and stopped in front of Peanut Butter and Jane, the fantastical shop for children's things, darling tiny French denim jumpsuits in the window, perfect for the baby of the woman who didn't have to worry about money. Fingertips on her belly. Are you here, my love?

Across the street to Pamela's.

Pamela hugged her. "Andrea, I'm so sorry."

"He adored my hair. Laser-crisp, he called it. It was one of the first things." She sat in Pamela's chair, in front of the triptych mirror. "I guess I told you that a hundred times."

"Never mind. You can tell me a hundred more." Pamela — short-haired, sassy and sweet, something woodsy in her New York Now face — took up her crisping scissors, assumed her wide-legged dancer's stance. "As usual?"

There was a sudden tightness in her throat as she looked at the two of them reflected. "Yes, but I can't bear the mirrors. Will you turn me around?"

It was a small shop, very pink, reflections in reflections in reflections. Pamela faced her toward the door.

"The Jews cover the mirrors after a death," Andrea said, "so the angel of death can't come in." But that wasn't it. She strained after dream vapors, lost them. "I think mirrors just know too damn much. They remember. Do you have that feeling ever with your

172

scissors? Do they remember cutting John's hair? I mean, really remember?"

Clip. Clip. Clip. "Oh honey. Be careful. Sit very still now. Good."

"Why should I be careful? What do I have to lose?"

"There's always more to lose. Believe me. There are things you don't want to mess with. You be really careful."

Andrea had been sticking to the straight press, avoiding the fringes, but she'd agreed to do the "Steve Coe on the Line" radio show because of a sentimental memory. A few days after she'd met John, he'd gone on the show to promote the paperback edition of the kidney transplant book, and a telephone caller had asked him what his next book would be about, and he'd said, "Andrea. All my books from now on are going to be about Andrea. The next one may have a little acupuncture thrown in." That quote had made Liz Smith's column, and John Malcolm Pearce and Andrea Olinger had officially become an item.

Now she sat wearing headphones at a long wooden table in an acoustic-tiled room. Her host, a tall stringy man known for tolerating, even egging on, cranky callers (but they tested your faith in your givens and they helped sell books, John had said), was eyeing his engineer through a wide glass window, leaning toward the mike.

"WKNO. Hello, you've got Steve Coe on the line."

"Hello?"

"Turn down your radio, you're on the air."

"Oh hi, Steve, my name is Mary, and I want to say something to your guest."

"I'm here. Go ahead."

"Oh hi, Andrea. First I want to say, I'm sorry for your loss."

"Thank you, Mary."

"I've been a widow for two years, and, well, my husband died of meningitis, so I couldn't have his heart transplanted, and to tell you the truth, I didn't know from transplants at the time, but what I really want to say is, I don't think God meant us to do this because it mixes up the races."

"Are you serious? You tell that to someone who was ten minutes from death and then got an organ transplant."

"And that's another thing. I think it's kind of dirty the way you people keep talking about organs."

"Thanks for your opinions, Mary. Gotta take another call here. Hello, you're on the line with Steve Coe and my guest, Andrea Pearce."

"Hello, Steve, my name is Curt, and what I want to know is, can you get AIDS from an organ transplant?"

"All depends on what organ you transplant to where. Hey, sorry about that. Any comment, Andrea?"

"Somebody could get AIDS from a transplant, but nobody will get AIDS from a transplant because it's one of the defects that's screened for."

"Well, I still say that it ought to be a law that no gay can be an organ donor except to another gay because they're going to kill each other off anyway and it's a good thing."

"Oh, now, wait a minute—"

"Keep those cards and letters coming, Curt. Hello, you're on the air."

"Hello?"

"Hello, hello, hello. I bet I can say it more times than you can."

174

"Oh Steve, you're such a tease. My name is Georgia, and I never miss your show, and I have just one question for Andrea. I read where you were visiting at the hospital during your own husband's funeral. If you loved him, why weren't you there when they put him in the ground?"

"Do I have to answer her, Steve? Why isn't anyone nice calling? I'm having trouble breathing. I loved him so so much."

"I'll tell you what love is, missy. When my husband died, he got a proper Christian burial, with all his parts inside him, and I wore mourning for a full year, and I didn't go putting my head against other men's chests because I loved my husband and I love our blessed Lord and I don't aim to burn in Hell the way you will."

"Steve, this isn't fair. I had to be where I was. Doesn't anyone understand? Why do your listeners hate me?"

"For those of you who just tuned in, my guest today is Andrea Olinger Pearce, widow of writer John Malcolm Pearce, who joined the noble ranks of organ donors when she gave her husband's heart to businessman Harvey Corman."

"Henry."

"Sorry about that. Henry Corman. We've got three lines open here at 999-8888 if you've got a question for Andrea Pearce. First, an earth-shaking message."

Half a beat, and the resonant voice of the pitchman came over the loudspeakers. Steve Coe took off his headphones, gestured for Andrea to take off hers.

"Two minutes of public service announcements, a couple of commercials, then we're on for another eight minutes. You live all the way west on Twelfth Street? I know some great restaurants down there.

Love that Gulf Coast. Fantabulous crayfish. Messy as hell, you don't want to wear white, but really sweet and fresh. Hey, they're not even a sponsor. This is an unsolicited testimonial."

Andrea looked at him. "It doesn't bother you? That your listeners seem to think I did something sleazy? Maybe you do too."

"Hey, don't take it personally." He flapped his skinny shoulders. "Maybe Curt just lost his job to a gay and Georgia has acid indigestion."

"What do you think a transplant is, the latest hair-style? My husband gave a stranger his heart. People say it all the time, that someone gave his heart, but my husband," she choked, "really gave his heart!"

"Save it for the next segment. It's okay to be mad—it makes a better show."

She was running out of air. She put her hand to her throat. "Hot in here. I've got to get something to drink."

Steve depressed a button on his microphone. "Francine—"

"No, I'll go out and get it." She edged toward the door, afraid he would try to stop her, those long skinny arms capable of anything. "I know where the Coke machine is. I like putting the coins in. My father used to take me to the Automat."

She made it out into the hallway, looked at the Coke machine, and kept going. Her coat was in the producer's closet, but she was wearing a bulky black and white sweater that came almost to her knees, would keep her from freezing. She got into the elevator, pressed the lobby button, and found herself standing on Broadway between Forty-second and Forty-third. The air was cold, but at least there was enough of it. She stood on the corner just breathing, trying to get rid of Steve Coe and his listeners.

176

Then she sensed that people were looking at her, that Georgia might materialize out of the throng, and she crossed Broadway and started uptown.

She'd told Mark she would meet him and Annette at Sardi's. She drank in the crowds and the blazing marquees and the towering animated ads, squinting a little to turn the scene into a lush blur. Her father had loved Times Square, and for once she wasn't inventing him. Oh Daddy. Why did you leave me? I need you more than ever.

She turned left on Forty-fourth Street, started past *The New York Times* garage, big trucks nosing out. Through the revolving door at Sardi's, waves to people she knew but moving quickly so she wouldn't have to talk, up to the second-floor bar.

She and Mark kissed cheeks and he said she was cold as ice and needed a drink in a hurry: cognac? Her hands flew to her belly, though she tried to cover the motion, and she said nothing these days but Guinness. He shouldered his way through the crush of *Times* reporters and theatergoers and emerged with a foamy goblet. "Well?" he said, as she sipped gratefully. "Did you further the cause?"

"I couldn't handle them, Mark. They hated me, and he egged them on. 'Organ' is a dirty word and how come I wasn't there with John when I was! They couldn't begin to understand. I walked out. I'm glad I told you not to listen."

"I was stupid, dammit. I should have warned you off him. He's an effing tough piece of work. A thuggish audience."

"John used to handle them. Next time I'll have him on with me and won't Georgia sing another tune."

Mark worked them into a corner opposite the bar—two free stools and a ledge for their drinks.

"You need a vacation," he said. "I hate to sound like your mother, but some sun would be nice, wouldn't it?"

"I was thinking more of the Hartford Hilton. I don't dare get too far away."

"From what?" His eyes seemed to snap to attention.

"Oh, you know," she said, though she didn't quite know herself. She glanced vaguely around the bar. Down at the other end a tall dark woman with wild hair was taking off her long strand of pearls and putting them around the neck of a redhead who wouldn't stop laughing. A story, and John would have gotten it. If Hank were there, would he get it? She shivered violently. "Mark, were you ever halfway between believing something but not wanting to and not believing it but wanting to?"

He thought a while and then he said, "No. Here comes Annette."

She was a small woman with scattery dark hair, cute in a voluminous plaid maternity dress she didn't yet need. "Andrea. What a lovely surprise. I thought you were on the radio." She kissed Mark on both cheeks.

"On and off," Andrea said. "How are you feeling?"

"Would you believe fantastic? Probably a typographical error, as this one would say." His arm went around her and she looked up at him. "Did you tell Andrea our great news?"

He couldn't quite meet Andrea's eyes. "We got the amnio results. The kid is okay. You want an orange juice, Mama?"

"Oh, that's lovely," Andrea said. "I'm so glad for you. Is it a boy or a girl—are you telling?"

"A boy." His eyes misted. "I really wanted my first child to have John for a godfather."

"He will," Andrea said. "You'll see."

"She's right," Annette said softly. "It's the way we'll do it. Because it wouldn't seem right to ask anyone else. A symbolic godfather. I'd love that o.j., Mark."

"He's going to be a luck baby," Andrea said. "Out of the ordinary, like his godfather. I feel it. Have you decided on a name?"

"We want to name him John," Annette said. "John Malcolm Feingold." Her face was shining. "I hope that sounds as beautiful to you as it does to us."

Andrea tried to smile — she wanted very much to smile at these nice people — but a wind had whistled in from the north and she couldn't move a muscle.

"Andrea?"

A Canadian wind, I think. They must not know that I married. A man who was born in Toronto.

"Andrea?"

Somebody call the Mounties. I never liked maple walnut ice cream.

"Let's get you over to a table. Have you eaten anything today? Steak, a baked potato, salad — that's an order."

Jews didn't name babies after people who were still alive. Everyone knew that.

She told the captain she wanted Skinny Skinned Roast Chicken.

Chapter 24

She had to get the oatcakes right. The ones Hank hadn't liked had been made according to a recipe she'd gotten from Sue McKay, substituting whole-wheat pastry flour for the white flour, soy margarine for the tablespoon of lard, and apple juice concentrate for the sugar, and of course leaving out the salt. A great favor for your heart, but they didn't do you any good unless you ate them!

As she poked around her kitchen, getting spices out of the cupboards and putting them back, re-thinking the recipe—maybe orange juice concentrate would have a lighter taste and feeling—she heard the voice of a long-ago gynecologist saying, "Just remember, Margo, it doesn't do you any good sitting on a shelf in your bathroom." Imagine remembering him—what was his name? Dr. Miller?—after all these years. Mueller, that was it, Alfred Mueller, the sort of patronizing doctor she would no longer put up with, and wouldn't her daughter be proud of that? She opened the freezer door and took out the frost-bearded plastic container of orange concentrate. Or maybe she should use the dessertspoonful of sugar in Sue's recipe. Would even Pritikin have objected to a dessertspoonful? Yes, he would have! But would Hank eat orange-flavored oatcakes?

She went to the little den off the kitchen, to her shelf of cookbooks. The Irish weren't the only ones who knew their oats. She got down a Scandinavian cookbook, but the one recipe for oatcakes was a nursery sweet, mostly butter and sugar. Oh, the things we do to our children in the name of love!

Was it still on a shelf in the master bathroom? She knew perfectly well it was, but she went to see anyway. Opened the blue plastic case and held the funny old thing up to the light to check for holes. None, but bodies changed and rubber deteriorated. She should be refitted and the thing replaced. Or maybe — Hank might want to make up for lost time — she should get an IUD, though they were out of favor now. The idea made her tingle just behind the ears. She'd ask Joe Berger, who'd delivered Debbie and had been her GYN since. Overdue for a checkup anyway.

She stood in the bedroom, in a long triangle of winter sun splash, looking at the way the cool light climbed up the dust ruffle and onto Hank's bed. She had never been in that bed. He had come into her bed from time to time, to whisper sweet words and fool around a little, but no matter how often she told him she loved those cuddly moments, he seemed convinced that they awoke unbearable longings. Well, maybe for him, which was why he'd stopped the visits and had made her feel that his bed was his alone. But for her those moments had been precious, delicious. She'd always been big on the notion that something was better than nothing. A couple of times after their cuddles, she'd had dreams in which she'd actually climaxed. Without touching herself, which she didn't do because it seemed like a form of cheating.

181

Hank. Dearest. Do you have any idea? She took his pillow out of its sham and peeled the spread off, then pulled back the top sheet and blanket. She had Amanda change his sheets every time she changed Margo's—this week a mauve and jade herringbone with a Navajo feeling—so they would be in phase whenever he got home. She knelt down next to the bed and laid her cheek on the sheet, right in the middle, where his middle would go. Oh, isn't it strange? I can't say the words any more, not even inside my mind with all the doors locked. I say "penis" at the hospital, but that's different—it's to talk about catheters, and anyway it never was our bed word. Cock. There, I thought it. "Cock," a whisper, then again, louder. And, "I love your cock, darling."

In the old days, before his heart attack, he'd gotten turned on when she'd talked a certain way. At first she'd been reluctant when he'd asked her to say those words: it felt awkward, the way it felt now. Wasn't life wild? They'd been making love for almost a quarter of a century, and she'd borne two children and breastfed them, been endlessly earthy with them; and here she was feeling shy about the words for her husband's body and her own. His cock. Touch me, darling. There. My tits. Yes. Like that—yes. The orange juice concentrate! She'd left it sitting on the counter next to the sink—the whole thing was going to defrost.

She pulled the bed together and went to the kitchen. She mixed oatmeal, flour, and baking soda, cut in the soy margarine, and added enough concentrate to make a stiff dough. There were still ice crystals in the remaining concentrate, so she put it back in the freezer, but a minute later she took it out again and tossed it in the garbage. After all she and Hank had been through, was she going to start taking chances to save eighty-nine cents? She rolled out the dough and went to work with her heart-shaped cookie cutter. She'd been using a traditional round cutter. Maybe eye-appeal would make the difference!

She put the oatcakes in the oven.

She called Joe Berger's office to schedule a checkup. The secretary was new and didn't recognize her name—that's how long it had been since her last appointment. Little anxiety pangs danced up and down her arms. Vaginas weren't like cars. They accumulated mileage even when they just sat there and nobody touched the ignition. Two, maybe three years, since she'd had a Pap smear—anything could be going on inside her. The pangs turned to waves of heat, and she thought of hot flashes; she thought of Hank with a thirty-two-year-old heart and a menopausal wife.

Come on, Margo! The only thing hot around here is the oven. If you can't stand the heat . . .

The oatcakes smelled done. Were done. A lovely golden brown and you got a whiff of the orange. Hardly traditional, but who was counting? She loosened them from the foil-covered baking sheet and transferred them to a rack. A name came to her in a flash: Heart-y Oatcakes.

The mail arrived. She had twenty-odd letters on top of the usual bills and magazines. Poor carrier! She invited him in for decaf and Heart-y Oat Cakes; he said thanks, he would take a raincheck. Most of the mail was for Hank, though he also got a lot at the hospital, but a bunch was for her. Skip had sent a tearsheet from the NYU *Courier:* a photo of him and a dozen other kids—was the cute short-haired girl with her hand on his shoulder Sara Simon?—gathered around a television set. "Skip Corman's heart is in his mouth as he watches a harrowing episode of 'The Recovery Room,' written by the man who gave his father a heart. John Malcolm Pearce was killed . . ." There was a note from Barb Epstein, the editor of the Temple Sisterhood cookbook wanting to know if Margo would like to add a recipe for the updated edition. Heart-y Oatcakes! They're crunchy, fruity, satisfying, and as good for you as they're delicious.

She made a pot of chamomile tea, set the kitchen table prettily for one—a woven oval placemat, a French country napkin with bright tiny pansies on a field of deep blue—and arranged the oatcakes on a gilt-edged plate with handles. Skip had always called it the ear plate. I developed this recipe when Hank was in the hospital. It quickly became a family favorite. Orange juice concentrate makes the difference.

She took a bite. But horrible! Soapy-tasting, and as heavy as Aunt Becky's matzo balls. The concentrate was a disaster.

She pushed oatcake after oatcake into the garbage disposal, a strange satisfaction rippling through her body as the cookies crumbled, and then the feeling turned to panic, a nightmare sensation of falling, spiraling through the emptiness of space. She gripped the edge of the sink, swallowing screams. Breathe in, breathe out. Breathe in, breathe out. Breathe in, breathe out.

Because that wasn't a short-haired girl cozying up to Skip in the blurry newspaper clipping, was it? It was a boy. And the single earring told the whole story, didn't it? Shouldn't she have guessed, the way

184

Skip had laid it on so thick about this terrific Sara and this terrific Mary Margaret he couldn't choose between?

She made herself look at the NYU kids again, over by the window, and now she wasn't sure. Even John Pluskowski here in West Hartford was giving buzz cuts to some of the young girls. And skinny like that and wearing a sweatshirt: How were you supposed to tell if someone had breasts? Really, it could be a girl. Absolutely it could. But it could be a boy, and how would she know? Her baby was living his own life now, letting her see what he wanted her to see. But he would want her to know a big truth like that about himself, wouldn't he? Was the clipping a message to her? And hadn't she way down deep inside been wondering for a while? Or had the question been born that minute? She was no more certain about her own state of mind than about Skip's state of body and being.

"Gay," she tried aloud. "My son is gay." She put her head to one side and then the other, trying to hear the real meaning in the words, in her own tone of voice. "Maybe my son is gay," she added, then immediately pounced on herself inwardly for wanting this particular truth not to be true. A person was or wasn't gay, wasn't that the wisdom now? You couldn't properly want it or not want it for yourself or someone you loved. Could you?

She ran to the telephone and dialed Sue's number because she knew if she didn't tell her that minute she would lose the nerve to tell her, and if she didn't tell her she would choke.

"I think Skip's gay," she blurted, describing the photograph, bringing up supporting evidence as if somehow she wanted to convince her friend. "It doesn't bother me—that's not why I'm calling. What I can't stand is that he didn't think he could tell me in plain words."

"No," Sue said, "what you can't stand is that he's gay."

"You're right, you're right, because Hank will go crazy. And Aunt Becky—oh my God."

"Hank nothing," Sue said firmly at the other end. "You can't stand it, period. 'Gay, shmay, who cares,' I can hear you saying, as long as it's about, what's her name, Sally Letterman's brother, but your own baby, that's different."

Margo closed her eyes. "God, it's true," she said. "I hate myself, but it's true. I want"—hot tears tracked down her cheeks—"grandchildren."

"Margo, you're still running away from the truth. You don't want him to be gay, period and end of sentence. You want him to be normal. Straight. Whatever you want to call it. You want him to be like you."

Suddenly Margo was laughing through her tears, great waves of hiccuped giggles coming and coming. "Are you kidding? Like me? I wouldn't wish that on my worst enemy. At least he's getting it from someone."

Sue didn't say anything for a moment; then she said, in a flight attendant's lilt, "Good morning. Welcome to the wonderful world of marriage."

"Oh God," Margo said, still trembling between tears and laughter. "Oh God. What am I going to do?"

"What would you tell me to do?"

Margo didn't hesitate a minute. Advice came so easy as long as it wasn't to herself. "I'd tell you to find a way to get used to the idea. Didn't we always say we would love our children even if they were murderers? So what's the big deal about gay? But"—her voice swung in panic—"what about AIDS?"

"What about it?" Sue said. "Don't you worry about it anyway if he's sleeping with different girls?"

Margo felt as if someone had punched her in the gut. "No. I don't. At least I didn't until this minute. The way I didn't think about going to Joe Berger for a checkup for three years. And what about Debbie? Am I supposed to worry that she's doing drugs? I guess I worried so much about keeping everyone's arteries unclogged that I didn't have room to worry about the rest. But oatcakes don't prevent AIDS, do they?"

"Maybe if you use them as prophylactics," Sue said.

"Very funny. Do you think Debbie takes drugs?"

"No. But I think you better talk to Skip about AIDS. Whether he's gay or straight or whatever."

Margo paced her kitchen rehearsing opening lines to her son, but they sounded so strained—"Darling, I just happened to read an article about parents of gays, and I was almost jealous"—that she kept shaking her head in dismissal. And how on earth would she break the news to Hank? And Debbie? How would she handle it with her friends? Sally Letterman would understand her to death . . . and that would almost be worse than the friends who cooled! Of course she would play it proud, march on Washington or whatever it was that right-minded parents of gays did . . . but why, Skip, why? Is it something I did or didn't do?

She looked at the newspaper photo again, trying to approach Skip's friend with the predisposition to warmth she would feel if it were Sara (and maybe after all it was Sara). A nice smile something intelligent about the eyes . . . clean-looking even in the sweatshirt . . . really likes Skip, you can tell.

God.

She went to the phone, dialed his number in New York listened without breathing while the phone rang, almost died when he actually answered. Said simply, "Hi, darling, I got the picture you sent me."

"Your famous son," Skip said. "Dad okay?"

"Terrific," she said. She realized guiltily that she'd scared him by calling during daytime rates. "How are you? I didn't really expect to find you in. You're not cutting class, are you?"

"This isn't Loomis, Mom. I only have one class today, psych, at two o'clock. The rest of the time I'm supposed to be working on my own."

Margo heard a giggle in the background, and her heart clutched.

"Or not on my own," Skip said. "Want to say hello to Sara Simon?"

"Hi, Mrs. Corman," a perky voice said.

"Well, hello, Sara. This is an unexpected pleasure." Such a pleasure that Margo slumped with relief. "Skip says such nice things about you."

"You too," Sara said. "Hope to meet you for real sometime. Here's Skip."

"The little slut," Margo was saying ecstatically to Sue a few moments later. "She knew I knew she was in bed with him and she didn't even care."

"Did you bring up AIDS?" Sue said.

"Oh sure," Margo said. "But I will. Though, when you think about it, I bet those NYU freshmen know more about it than we do. Sue, I'm drenched

188

with perspiration. I better go take a shower. Do you believe this whole episode? What's the matter with me, that I could look at the picture and be so sure it was a boy? And then the way I felt about it. I'm not proud of myself."

"Maybe," Sue said, "you needed to make something up to keep your mind off your real worry."

"What's to worry about now? Hank's healing so fast, he may make the *Guinness Book of Records*."

"His body is healing," Sue said.

"He's fine," Margo said firmly. "I talked to Mickie about the moods, and she told me I should worry more about my own. I've got to take that shower, Sue. Need anything from the Crown?"

But as she stood under the cascading water soaping herself, she thought about what Joe Berger was going to find—Joe, who was such a sweetie that she was sorrier for him than for herself because he would feel so bad about having to break the news. And then Hank would be the well one, and then the only one. And Andrea would come to console him.

Chapter 25

She knew she had thoughts to think but didn't know how to think them. There were distortions in the way, and knowing what they were didn't free her. Time felt rubbery and too big. The angles in the apartment seemed to have widened. The new bathroom was complete, and the two-level living room was airy and bright even when sleet fell outside, but she couldn't get comfortable there, couldn't just be. She was watching herself watching herself, less the conscious person John loved than a self-conscious mockery.

She tried to work, but she didn't feel worthy of her heroine. Leonora had kept her husband alive into his eighties.

Her telephone rang and rang. Everyone had advice. Her mother thought she should go to a spa and get herself pummeled into condition. Sukie wanted her in London. Mark kept trying to involve her in the details of the memorial service for John. Should he ask Bill Hurt to read a short story of John's?

She kept thinking about going to Hartford, had all the train times written down, but she was afraid of what she would find or wouldn't find—she wasn't sure which.

Steve Coe called, just like that. "Andrea? Got the cravings for Cajun, started thinking about the Gulf Coast. Join me for dinner tonight? Hey, I'll even bring your coat — my producer forgot to send it — all you need to do is change your jeans."

As if she were single, available, ripe. She ran to the bathroom, the brand-new bathroom, vomiting into her hands, onto the floor, into the squared-off oval bowl, another one of Kitty's barriers broken but oh dear God the awful loneliness.

She woke the next morning feeling as though she'd downed a gallon of Guinness. She set small specific goals to get herself through the day. She walked purposefully to Balducci's and bought veal and pistachio nuts to make John's favorite pate. She went to Foul Play and bought a dozen mysteries, all red covers and no death in the titles.

She didn't cook. Didn't read.

The doorbell rang. Pete, the tenderhearted day doorman, with a UPS carton, holding it gingerly, his mouth scrunched to convey commiseration.

"Another one, looks like," he said.

"Oh well," Andrea said.

"Want me to just send it back for you?"

"Better not, Pete, but thanks. I have to write a note and all. At least we're down to a trickle now."

Inside the carton was a white bridal box tied up in yards of silver ribbon. She folded back puffy layers of tissue. She found bold deco plastic placemats and bright solid unmatched napkins, nice though she wouldn't have picked them. "Wishing you and John every joy. Barbara and Jerry Coyne." Thank you, we will do our best. She set the box down with the others in her bedroom and knelt there in a white and silver haze until the telephone released

191

her.

And this call, she realized as it started to happen—realized with a whir of the consciousness John cherished, was the call she had been waiting for without knowing she'd been waiting.

Linda Ammiccare was on the line.

"Andrea, dearest, what can I say? It's just too wretched. I got back to my hotel in Rome yesterday after two weeks of oblivion, and there was the telegram. And here I am. Are you all right?"

"As all right as I need to be."

"Of course you are. All right enough but not really all right—will we ever be? And don't shoot me down for saying 'we.' You were his great love, but he was mine; and if you don't understand that, who will? Now listen."

"I'm here, Linda." That purposefully hush voice, the billowing words. How could John have loved them both?

"On the flight back I read all the stories. This nice guy Henry Corman lying there in his bed with a copy of *Pin High.* And the wife who puts water in her salads—do we like her? She seems too good to be true."

"I like them both. Very much. And the kids. Especially the girl."

"So I'm sitting there on the plane, crying like crazy, looking at the pictures in *People,* and I got an idea. For a book. We get this Henry to write a sequel to *Pin High.* I know you've got to go for it because really it was your idea, I read it right there in *People,* you said it that day at the hospital—he plays golf, Wallace Stevens, he's got a poet's heart."

"I don't know," Andrea said, because hearing the idea from Linda was different from hearing it inside her head. And if he tried and failed what would that say? "I don't think Mark will much like it," she said to buy time, and it was true.

"I'll make him like it. It's you I'm thinking about. You and John. I think wherever he is it would make him smile."

She shivered but wonderful shivers. We'll do it all before we're finished. Yes. And she would be needed. Would get to hang out with the heart.

"And it will show Georgia, won't it?" she said aloud.

"And Missouri too," Linda said. "I'll call Mark and set up a meeting."

Andrea worked on her book for an hour, feeling Leonora Whittlesey's benediction.

Chapter 26

Margo couldn't get used to the idea. Hank, the poet laureate of Pocahontas Road—it was wild! Maybe Andrea and this Linda Ammiccare believed (did they?) that Hank could write because he wore a writer's heart. That didn't make it true. (Did it?)

A heart is a pump. Period and end of sentence. Gar kept saying it, Mickie said it, she had said it herself to the children, to friends. She'd needed a blood transfusion after Debbie had been born, and the plasma of strangers had not changed her, and Hank was no different for having John Malcolm Pearce's heart than he would have been for having any other. That was stone fact.

Critical illness changed a person, though. That was also a truth. How had Gar put it? You walk around all your life knowing you're mortal and now you capital-K know it, and you want to try for the brass ring. But poetry?

He liked *Pin High*. He liked the lyrics of Cole Porter and Larry Hart, something he and Skip had in common. And there his relationship with poetry seemed to end. Oh, he'd read through a volume of Wallace Stevens that Margo had given him years ago because you couldn't be a Hartford insurance man and not have a little feeling for the actuary-poet. He occasionally read some verse in *The New Yorker* if Margo nagged him enough. But he and poetry had never been important to each other, and before his surgery he would have been the first to say so.

Maybe poetry wasn't really the issue. Look at how he was carrying on about golf. He'd held John's putter in his hand when they'd wheeled him out of the hospital, had waved it as if it were his flag, and he toted it around the house with him, stroking imaginary golf balls across invisible greens. Sometimes he just held onto it the way Skip had held onto that precious yellow blanket of his when he was a baby.

Good, Gar and Mickie told her. Hank was identifying with health and strength, daring to dream big dreams again—what could be more tonic? Maybe it was Margo who needed her head straightened out. What did she want, a perpetual invalid gasping for breath, his hand clutched to his heart? Linda Ammiccare's offer of an advance for the sequel to *Pin High* was a ten-thousand-dollar bet that he could be ever so much more.

He had a right to try. No one wanted him to try more than she. She took her stationery and checkbooks and warranties and household records out of the living room desk and dedicated it to Hank's new life as a writer. She bought a high-intensity light (though she thought it looked harsh in that setting) because he said her cloth-shaded hurricane lamp cast too ladylike a light. She went to Huntington's bookstore on Asylum Street and put together a little library: *The Elements of Style*, the Untermeyer anthology of poetry, Rilke's *Letters to a Young Poet*, Plutarch's *Lives of the Poets*, and the John Ciardi translation of Dante's *Inferno*, which John Malcolm Pearce had credited with inspiring *Pin High*. Hank said he was too old to learn to type, much less use a word-processor, and she gathered a variety of pads—pocket-size to legal, lined and unlined, even graph paper (though it reminded her of the curtains in the SCICU)—so he could see which inspired him. A box of virgin number two pencils.

In the week since he'd left the hospital, she'd devised a routine that was supposed to free him to do what poets did. They exercised together and ate a high-protein breakfast with Debbie; she made the bed and tidied the kitchen and checked the low-cal snack supply; then she took Debbie to her bus and went on to the office; and at eleven-thirty (when he would start feeling ravenous) she came home and made them lunch.

"So?" She walked into the house with a big smile on her face. "How did it go?"

Hank tipped back the desk chair. He gestured at the wastebasket. "Damn phone kept ringing. Every time I got halfway into a thought—zap."

"Like Samuel Coleridge."

"Who?"

"Oh, you must have been told the story by some English teacher. Remember 'Kubla Khan'? 'Caverns measureless to man . . .' He dreamed the poem in a trance and was writing it down when some businessman came calling and that was the end of it."

"Opium," Hank said. "I remember. He had opium, and I have cyclosporine. He had a salesman, I have Sue McKay and Sally Letterman and Elaine Mancuso. I think every broad in town called to gossip."

"And I bet Mr. Coleridge didn't say 'broad.' Anyone I'm supposed to call back?"

"I tell you I couldn't get a damned thing done" — he brought the chair down to earth with a bang — "and you're worried about Sally's feelings?"

"Please don't snap at me, Hank. You know how much I care about your work. Maybe we should get an answering machine — what do you think? I'm going to make us a salad. Tuna Temptation sound good?"

"I'm starved. I want pastrami."

"Hank you sound like a child. You know you can't have pastrami."

"Yeah, yeah. I'm sorry, kid. Chalk it up to creative temperament, huh?" He had the grace to wrap the phrase in self-mockery. "Tempestuous Tuna sounds great."

She set the small table in the den off the kitchen. Miniature bran muffins in a wicker basket, a single streaky red and yellow tulip, the big goblets that made seltzer taste important. A red napkin for him, yellow for her, to pick up on the colors of the flower. She set out the salad and called him.

"Well, I did it," she said, as Hank helped himself to chunks of water-packed Albacore, celery curls, alfalfa sprouts, watercress, and spaghetti-like strands of carrot and turnip she created with a special Japanese vegetable cutter. "That co-op in Farmington. I made them realize that they're grossly underinsured at three-point-five million, and they're going for a very nice comprehensive liability package."

Hank pushed a hard round green tailed something across the serving platter with the back of a serving spoon. "What's this? A kidney stone with goiter?"

"A sprouted pea. I steamed them for a minute

197

and they're very sweet, almost like corn. I'm glad I didn't listen to you and Dick Jaffe on the subject of co-ops. They're sprouting up everywhere, and it's a good thing I went to that seminar."

"So we get sprouted co-ops in the salad next? Listen, I had an idea this morning."

Margo looked out the window for a moment. She blinked. "Tell me."

"I was thinking about those writers' colonies they have. You get a studio, and they fix all your meals for you, and you don't have to think about anything but your work."

"Gee, darling, that sounds like a description of life around here. Maybe I should advertise." She took a bite of bran muffin. She'd used currants instead of raisins, and she loved the way they popped in the mouth, releasing sweetness.

Hank reached across the table and patted her hand. "Don't get all sensitive on me, will you? You do everything just right, but I ask you, does this look like a place where poems happen?" His accusing glance fell on the potted herbs along the windowsill, the tea-cozy shaped like a house, a dozen other artifacts of comfort. He had the look she'd seen on first Skip's and then Debbie's face when they'd learned there was such a thing as the middle class and it wasn't where the action was.

She swallowed a sigh. If sighs had calories, she would be a size eighteen. "Look, I'm sure John Malcolm Pearce had plenty of bad mornings. I'm sure Mr. Dante did. You've only been at this a week. But if you think you'd do better in the attic, or should I call it the garret—"

His hand worked his napkin into a wad. "Don't humor me. You know you don't believe I'll ever write anything worth reading. I think you've forgotten I had literary dreams before."

"Oh?"

"Those editorials I wrote for my high school paper — I don't know if I ever told you, but they really set heads spinning. You have any idea where those clips are? I was thinking they might help me unblock."

"Somewhere in the attic. I remember thumbing through your scrapbooks when we were packing for the move. They're safe for posterity," she said, and then wished she hadn't, "along with my pottery."

"Your pottery was very nice, Margo, but I'm not talking hobby here. No question I could have gotten a job in journalism. Of course it made more sense to go into my father's business when we decided to get married."

She felt the color drain from her face. "I'm sorry our marriage came between you and your true vocation."

"Oh now, Margo" — he reached for her hand — "you know that's not what I'm saying. I just want you to remember that there's a little history here. So when I start thinking literary, don't treat me like an imposter."

"That's just not fair! Haven't I done everything possible to help make the work go well? The desk, and the books, and giving you the house to yourself —"

"I've seen you this way with the kids," Hank said. "When you didn't believe in something they were doing. Sure, you let them go ahead and do it, but you were sitting there smiling to yourself waiting for them to come to their senses. I know what you're thinking. Any minute he'll give up this *narishkeit* poetry business and he'll go back to the office. You think I came this close to death"—he signed an inch with his thumb and forefinger, the way Mickie always did—"to worry about whether some co-op is going to go for the lower deductible?"

"All of a sudden selling insurance isn't nice?"

"Look it's great. It's beautiful. But that doesn't mean I have to do it forever and ever. You're the one who was smart enough to go to the co-op seminar—what do you need me at the office for? So you can go back to hanging around the kitchen all day and invent the ultimate bran muffin?"

Tears blurred her eyes. "I cook the way I do because I want you to live."

"I know you do. You're a great cook. I didn't mean—"

"Yes you did." There was a burning pain in her chest, and it wasn't going to go away unless she threw it away. She picked up the basket of bran muffins and hurled it against the wall. "You can wallow in chicken fat for all I care."

She ran to their bedroom and got into bed with her clothes still on. Hank was wearing corduroys and a flannel shirt, proper poet's clothes. She was an office drudge in white silk and gray flannel. Office drudge, kitchen drudge. Fuck me and I'll stop cooking. No!

"No, what, honey?" He was there on her bed, peeling back the quilt she'd pulled over her head, looking so much like her funny old Hank.

She let her eyes get their fill of him and then her arms were reaching out, pulling him toward her, kissing his mouth. Dry lips, cracked lips, and his mouth tasted different, his skin was foreign, the medicine had changed him or maybe John's heart had done the work. She wept.

"Tell me." He held her against his chest, soothed her hair. "I've been a clod, you can say it. Tell me."

"It's just that everyone wants you to change, you want it, and I think you have changed and maybe it's good, but I loved you so much the way you were. Don't I get any credit for wanting the original old unimproved you?"

"Of course you do, kid. You get credit for everything. You're the heroine of this story, you think I don't know it?"

"Then why don't you want"—the words shooting out before she could stop them—"to make love to me?"

He did tricky things with his eyebrows. "Who says I don't want?"

"You've been home a week and you haven't touched me. Oh, a pat on the fanny or something, but that just made it worse. Because you were so obviously not stirred. And I'm coming on all heavy and hurt and demanding, which is just what I promised myself not to do. I know—" She broke off. She took his hand, she placed it on her breast. "Do you remember what this is?"

"That's the elbow, isn't it, Ms. Kovner?"

"No, Henry. No. You'll have to go to the principal's office if you can't do better than that. Six letters. Begins with b."

He scratched his head. "Maybe if I got a good look at it." He unbuttoned her shirt, poked about beneath her and unfastened her bra. He looked from this angle, from that. "Kinda cute, but I can't remember. What you call it. Unless it's a what-you-call-it."

"And you were once so promising, Henry. Six letters, begins and ends with consonants, has a diph-thong in the middle. Rhymes with 'zest.' "

He dragged tender fingertips across the pale flesh. "I've got it! But you were kidding me about how it's spelled. Three letters, begins and ends with t."

"Henry Corman, are you thinking what I think you're thinking?"

"Maybe."

"You're thinking 'tit,' aren't you? Is that what you're thinking? 'Tit'?"

He guided her hand to his corduroy epicenter. She felt a friendly stirring. He looked wonderful to her, his face thinner than it had been but still cheeky and pouchy, the most interesting face she knew.

"I really should send you to the principal," she said, "but I'm going to let you off easy this time. You'll have to clean my erasers, though, and apologize to my breasts for calling them 'tits.' "

"I didn't call them 'tits,' you did."

"I did? I called them 'tits'? I suppose next you're going to tell me I called that a 'cock.' "

"Oh no, Ms. Kovner, I wouldn't dream of saying that."

"Saying what?"

"Saying you said 'cock.' "

"Henry, I did not say 'cock.' " Her hand on his zipper.

"That's what I said, you didn't say it."

"Say what? Say 'cock'? I just can't believe you are sitting there on the edge of my desk accusing me of saying 'cock.' " She folded her hands behind her head, smiled outside the game. "Hi."

"Hi, kid."

"This is more fun than throwing bran muffins."

"Less mess to clean up."

"Did you clean up? You're a love. I never did anything like that before. Maybe I'm changing too."

"No you don't. Not this year. Someone's got to stay the same for the kids."

She tapped the corner of his mouth. "I'm not sure either of them would notice if we became Marxist nudists. There's watermelon for dessert."

"I thought you were dessert. Isn't that my line?"

"Is it?"

"I think you're getting cold feet."

"I don't want to rush you. Just because I've been chewing my nails for two years—"

"It won't be great." He started undoing her skirt. "I can't make up for two years in one afternoon."

"I know that. I'll settle for a cuddle."

"Like hell you will. Move over. Now about your erasers—"

Chapter 27

She looked at a sketch of Leonora Whittlesey in men's clothing, and an idea she'd been chasing came together in a phrase: Leonora Whittlesey had to become a man to be all the women she was.

She got up from her desk to show the words to John, actually rose and took two steps across the angled oak boards of the floor. Her realization of what was what slammed her back into her chair.

"Sweetie," she whimpered. "No."

No, he said back. Absolutely not. Think negative.

She sat there rubbing the base of her spine, breathing rapid shallow breaths, conjuring his face behind closed eyelids (she had his picture on her desk, he was sitting on the grass by the pond in Kent, but its fixity stung her, she preferred the movies in her mind), trying to remember all the naysayings she knew. No, no, a thousand times no. We shall not, we shall not be moved. Hell, no, we won't go.

Help.

Mother.

She started to dial the number of the Park Avenue apartment; pictured the telephone ringing in one of the cold blue rooms; stopped. She called

Connecticut, the office number, and gave her name to the secretary. Had to wait only seconds.

"Andrea, darling?"

"Is it a bad time? I just needed to hear your voice."

"Well, I'm thrilled to hear yours. I did one of those telephone interviews, some radio station in Tennessee—I'm getting to be such a pro I did it right from my desk while I signed the payroll checks—and of course I was thinking of you. Tell me everything. Are you working? Sleeping?"

"Working a little, but I'll go along for an hour and then—wham. It should be a comfort to forget him for a while, but really it isn't because remembering is such a blow. How"—she coiled the phone cord around her finger—"is Hank?"

"Working so hard, you can't imagine. And then it gets ripped up."

"All writers rip. Par for the course, as my father used to say." She'd told him when she was twelve or so that someday she would write a mystery called *Par for the Corpse* and he'd told her he thought someone had already done it but he'd never found a copy for her. Because he hadn't tried to find it?

"Only this time," Margo was saying, "he's taking a lighter approach, comedy really, and I think maybe it's going to work. Why don't you come to Hartford, darling, have a look at what he's doing, just visit with us. I think it would be tonic for both of you. Come tonight, spur of the moment, what do you say?"

"Tonight?" Though she was already mentally packing.

"Why not? I have a great meal planned. Venus on the half shell. We're starting with fishysoisse— yes, you heard that right—and we're going on to grilled shrimp and fresh spinach fettucini with chopped tomatoes and herbs. What train are you taking?"

Andrea laughed her relief, her pleasure. "You mean it?"

"Let's see, I've got the schedule right here, you can take the 2:06 and get to Hartford at 4:46 and you don't even have to change in New Haven. I'll be out in front in a dark blue Chevy, and don't start to argue that you want to take a cab. I don't have to meet the school bus because Debbie's having dinner at her friend Ginger's—they're rehearsing a play—so I've got time on my hands. Of course you'll stay over with us."

She slept all the way to Hartford, warm and cradled.

She didn't have to search for the Chevy because Hank was standing on the sidewalk in front of the station waving at her, grinning behind his surgical mask. They hugged, and she told him he looked as healthy as a bear, and she kissed Margo's cheek through her half-open window and insisted, over Hank's protests, on sitting in the back.

He kept turning around, his mask in his hand, to talk to her, and she drank in the brightness of his face. She'd thought him miraculously changed the second time she'd seen him at the hospital; now she saw a whole new increment of health. The small-boy winter apple cheeks (gone the sad clown de-flated balloons); gray eyes wide open and reflecting diamonds of light (gone the heavy lids, the foggy whites); and the lips that had been cracked and tremulous were plump with smiles. Even his hair had changed, the black as shiny as paint, the gray a dancing silver, the ringlets fat and springy.

Full-blooded. Heart's blood. You did it, miracle

man. Your magnum opus. Nobody ever but you.

"And this is Asylum Avenue," he was narrating vividly, hands making music, "one-way west from four to six, or it would really make you ready for the asylum. There's Elizabeth Park, we call it Lizzie, it can't compare with Central Park, but when June rolls around we'll take you to see the roses and you'll swoon. Let's go over on Prospect, Margo, and show her the big houses and get the sun out of our eyes. That's the Governor's mansion on your right there, Andrea, used to belong to Beatrice Auerbach, who owned G. Fox, it was the Bloomingdale's of Hartford, I guess it still is. Look at the plantation up ahead, the columns, you'd need an army of dusters for that one."

"You can't scare me," Margo said.

"Good, because our place has started feeling small. My feet are hungry for stairs. Dammit, why did I say 'hungry'? What do you say we swing around by Scoler's, pick up a pound of chopped liver to keep us going to dinner? Nobody," he said to Andrea, "chops a liver like Scoler's."

"Open my bag, darling," Margo said, "you'll find a box of cherry fruit bars. Can I tempt you, Andrea? Sweet as candy and they're just pure fruit."

Hank and Andrea passed on the fruit bars.

At home Margo suggested Hank lie down until dinner, but he pooh-poohed her, said he wanted to stretch his legs, drink the air, and then play the piano for Andrea, he'd just dug out his Rodgers and Hart songbook, she seemed like a Rodgers and Hart kind of girl.

"I don't believe his energy," Andrea said. She was helping Margo skin tomatoes while Hank took his walk. "The doctors must be marveling."

"I'm marveling," Margo said. "This isn't just a

207

great recuperation, it's a whole new Hank."

"He wasn't like this before he got ill?"

"Oh, he always had lots of pizzazz, but, well, it's different enough so I asked Gar McKay if he'd mixed some stimulants in with the immunosuppressants!" Margo took a skinned tomato in each hand and deftly squeezed out the seeds. "Do you know what he reminds me of? A three-year-old. I remember Skip at that age — Debbie too but Skip more so — wanting something new every minute: a toy he'd seen on TV, a ride in an airplane, a cookie and it had to be exactly the right cookie, a trip to his grandmother's house, a drink, a story, I want, I want, and he had to have it instantly, and no matter how full each day was he went to sleep wanting more."

Andrea looked out the window. The night they'd arrived in Kent, John had made love to her, gone running, come in tasting of winter and made love to her again, and when she'd fallen asleep he'd gone downstairs and read two of Papa Sam's books on the American Revolution. She'd been excited by his energy, his hunger, but a little frightened too because at that moment she'd needed only him. If she'd known then what she knew now, she wouldn't have squandered her fear.

"Don't be afraid," she said — pushed at the skin of time to tell it to herself but Margo caught it.

Margo gave her a funny little smile. "Who said 'afraid'? I just get exhausted trying to keep up. Would you chop the parsley for me?"

Hank came into the kitchen, stomping snow from his running shoes, grabbed a fistful of carrots, and summoned Andrea to the living room to hear him on piano. His playing was rippling, light, oceanic — Ellis Larkin at two in the morning with smoke and

208

laughter rising. She leaned back into her chair and closed her eyes and thought of the many times when John had asked a piano player to do "Fine and Dandy" for her.

Margo announced dinner.

"You're talented," Andrea told Hank. "The sort of music that makes people never want to go home."

"So don't ever go home."

"Absolutely," Margo said.

"If I don't make it as a poet," Hank said, "maybe I can get myself a gig at some joint in Greenwich Village."

Margo ladled soup into Chinese rice-pattern bowls.

"How's the poem coming?" Andrea said. "May I see it?"

"It's coming, but I'm not ready for the critics."

"Tease." She tasted the soup, a thick but airy puree intense with flavors of earth and sea. "Delicious, Margo."

"No butter, no cream, that's the beauty part. Show her the poem, honey," she said to Hank. And to Andrea, "It's very amusing."

"Maybe later," Hank said.

"This isn't like you!" Margo said.

"Oh, I'm used to it," Andrea said. "John never let me look at his work until he thought it was perfect. Not like me, showing him everything in a hundred different drafts."

"You two writers talk shop. I'm going to run the shrimp under the broiler." Margo picked up her soup bowl and spoon and headed for the kitchen.

Hank made a great business of cutting into a loaf of homemade Anadama bread. "Can I give you a slice?"

"No. Thank you."

He put bread on his plate and broke off a piece but didn't eat it.

"I hear you're writing a novel," he said.

"Getting ready to," she said. "I'm still making notes, doing research."

"Debbie says it sounds great. You made a big hit with her."

Andrea noticed that he wasn't quite looking at her. "Debbie's terrific," she said. "Skip too. There's a lot of creative energy in this household."

"I think Skip had the right idea, heading for New York. You want to create, you have to feel it happening around you. It's not just the Broadway stage; he goes out to buy a newspaper and there's theater all around him. I say 'street life' to my friends, and they tell me about getting mugged. You know what I tell them back? I tell them I was mugged right here in West Hartford. In my own bed behind my own locked doors. I was mugged"—he put his hand over his chest—"by my own heart. I didn't put it together for four years because I was too sick to think straight. All I cared about was making it through one more night. But that's not enough for me now."

"Of course it isn't," she said.

Her quick, warm words brought his head around, and she thought she saw a giddy relief in those hungry eyes, as though he hadn't dared hope that someone—that she—could hear what he was saying.

"Would you—" he began.

The door from the kitchen flapped open. Margo flourished a parsley-strewn platter of shrimp and fettucini. "Voilà," she said. "Protein."

She seemed so far from the real reality that Andrea ached to bursting with the strain of wanting to pull her in. Oh God, did women never get it right?

210

Her mother was a white bread cook and her father had craved wild spiced stews, aphrodisiacal rose water puddings.

"Andrea?"

And she and John had cooked together, no galantine beyond them, but then there was the question of milk.

"Andrea? Are you all right?"

Please please one more chance, I got the message, this time I'll do it right, I'll square it for all of us.

"Andrea?"

"Andrea?"

"Headache," she mumbled.

Margo gave her a knowing look of hormonal sisterhood. "The baby?" she mouthed.

Andrea put a hand to her belly. The pounding behind her eyes came louder, faster. She wasn't pregnant, she was on the verge of getting her period, that was half the headache. Could Margo be the surrogate mother or something?

She fled to the yellow room.

Margo brought her cool compresses, un-aspirin, hot chamomile tea, concern.

"I'm sorry," Andrea kept saying. "Such a nice dinner. Kitty would be appalled. Please don't call a doctor. I'm sorry."

She heard Debbie come in. Doors were locked and the darkness deepened. She drifted into sleep. She woke up not knowing the time, groping toward her headache but the clutter of pain was gone, and she lay there for a while enjoying the emptiness. Then a shower and into the pale peach robe she'd bought for her honeymoon. Her empty stomach signaled. She headed out to the kitchen.

"Good morning," Hank said. He was sitting at the

dinette table eating cereal and reading yesterday's paper.

"What time is it?" she said.

"Three o'clock and change. Want some Familia? It's the kind without sugar. Of course."

"Yes, please," Andrea said.

He got a bowl from a cupboard and milk from the refrigerator. "Low-fat milk, I'm afraid," he said.

"I don't mind," she said.

"I do." He poured cereal out of the box, enough for three people. "Tell me when."

"That's fine. Thank you. I bet you only mind a little. About the milk."

"And the pastrami. That's how part two of *Pin High* begins. With pastrami. I don't know why I was so coy about letting you see the poem — I guess because I really care what you think. Did John like pastrami?"

"I don't know. There wasn't time to find out. I don't know if he liked Familia." She felt stricken.

"I used to think it tasted like horse fodder, but I've gotten attached to it. Margo says oats are the key to immortality."

"One of the keys, maybe."

They finished their cereal and carried their bowls to the sink. He turned on the water, hard.

"If you don't rinse the bowls right away, the stuff never comes off," he said.

"That's why it sticks to your ribs."

He smiled. He picked up a sponge and made a pass at the drainboard.

"I guess I'll try to go back to sleep," he said.

"Me too," she said.

"Walk you home?"

"That would be nice. I don't know the neighborhood."

He turned off the kitchen light. "You'd think that my bouncing up and down this way would make Margo crazy, but she sleeps right through it. I bet she could sleep through a hurricane. Debbie too."

Andrea didn't say anything.

They got to the door of the guest room.

They looked at each other in the dimness.

"Dandy," he said.

The breath caught in her throat.

"I want to call you Dandy," he said. "Because that's what you are. Did anyone ever think of that before?" He touched her cheek.

Her skin blazed beneath his finger. The way it always did.

"No one but you," she said.

His arms went around her and he held her and dropped kisses into her hair and let her soak his shoulder with her tears of gorgeous relief.

The
Yellow
Course

If a player play when his partner should have played, his side shall lose the hole.

—THE RULES OF GOLF

Chapter 28

"Another waffle, Andrea?"

"No thanks, Margo. They're delicious, but I'm not used to eating a big breakfast."

"I'll have more, Mom," Debbie said. "Is there any maple syrup? I hate that fruit gunk."

"It's twice the food value of maple syrup. And I happen to think it's delicious. Next time I'll buy the blueberry instead of the black cherry."

"I'm with Debbie," Hank said. "Bring back maple syrup." He held up his plate as Margo served Debbie. "Great waffles, though."

Margo shook her head. "I have to hold you to two, honey. Your weight was up nearly a pound this morning."

"The damn Maalox is binding me. Something is. All I need is a good—"

"Please, Daddy. I'm eating," Debbie said.

Margo looked at the kitchen clock. "Ten minutes to blast off," she said to Debbie.

"Not for Daddy."

"Very funny," Hank said, but he laughed. They all did.

"If Skip were here, he'd set this moment to music," Margo said.

"Rhyming h-e-a-r-t and f-a-r-t," Debbie said.

217

Margo groaned. She got up and carried fruit syrup-stained plates to the sink. "Leave enough time to brush your teeth," she said to Debbie. "Especially after that remark."

"Margo, let me take care of the clean-up," Andrea said. "It's the least I can do."

"If you're going to get the 9:23, you've got less time than you think. The cab company will insist on picking you up at quarter of, even though it's only fifteen minutes to the station."

"Maybe I'll get a later train. What do I have to rush back to? And I want to read Hank's poem before I go."

Debbie coughed. Her parents looked at her and she coughed again.

"Mom, I don't feel well," she said. "I think maybe I better stay home."

"What's this?" Margo put the back of her hand to Debbie's forehead. "A math test today? You don't have any fever. You're fine."

"Really, I woke up feeling scratchy—"

"And wolfed down three waffles," Margo said. "Your color's perfect. Run and do your teeth. We've got to go."

She thought she understood the cough. As she and Debbie drove down Albany Avenue, she said: "I'm sorry you weren't home for dinner last night. I know how much you like Andrea. I'm sure she'll be back again soon."

Debbie stared out the window. "I guess so."

"What's the matter, honey?"

"I don't think I'm going to have a family when I grow up," Debbie said. "Too many illusions. It all looks so cozy and solid—and poof."

"Oh, you're always cynical after dinner at Ginger's house." Ginger's mother looked to be on the verge of her third divorce, and her father had vanished to Australia. "Nobody ever notices the families who stay together. I'm not saying it's always easy, but it's worth the struggle."

"You struggle and struggle, and then someone like Andrea comes along—"

Margo slowed for a light. "And what? Saves a life."

"Mom, I don't mean to make you nervous, but I think maybe she's like the man in that Chinese story. She saved Daddy's life, so now she owns it."

"That's not the way the story goes. The Chinese believe—at least we're told they do—that if they save a life, they're responsible for it. Anyway, what are you talking about? I thought you adored her."

"I do, at least I did, but I thought it was pretty strange, us leaving the house and there they are, Daddy in his pajamas and Andrea in a negligee."

"Now wait a minute. Let's not start turning our life into a soap opera. Daddy was wearing a robe over his pajamas. And I would hardly call what Andrea was wearing a 'negligee.'"

"Whatever you want to call it, you don't have one that nice."

Margo had been meaning to replace her blue-and-white-checked no-iron housecoat, but she didn't have much use for robes because they were awkward if you were cooking and she was nearly always cooking. "No, I suppose I don't. Poor Andrea. She probably bought that robe for her trousseau."

"Well, I hate to sound Barbie-ish, but maybe you should go on a shopping splurge. And get a facial or something. You've got a couple of hairs on your chin." Debbie started to cry.

"Honey?"

"I feel so bad, saying that, but it seemed only

219

sisterly." Debbie cried harder. "It's really painful sometimes."

"What is?" She turned onto Sigourney Road and parked. No sign of the bus or the other families who used that stop. Either they'd missed the bus or—no, they were early.

"Everything. And please don't make a Pollyanna speech. I'm scared. I think Andrea wants Daddy for herself."

"Don't be ridiculous, Debbie."

"Either you think I'm a baby who can't face the facts or you're the most incredibly naïve woman in America. I'm not being ridiculous. I don't want to hurt your feelings, but she's very attractive, and she's got money—"

"And your father and I have a great relationship. Honey, if he wanted a younger, richer, more beautiful woman, greater Hartford is full of them. I don't know if these fears come out of your feminism or what, but there happen to be some men in the world who have solid values, and your father is one of them."

"I wish you still slept in a double bed."

"Let's keep the conversation in line, Deb. Though I can't resist telling you, when you were two or three, there was a long stretch when you came into our bed every night and got between us. Believe me, you would have been a lot happier if we'd had twin beds. Better yet, separate bedrooms! Here come the Palmers. And there's the bus. Honey?"

Debbie gathered books. "Uh huh?"

"I think it took a lot of guts to say what you said, and I admire you for it, even though I don't think there's a shred of a reason for you to worry."

"Mom, I do think you're beautiful. It's just—"

"I don't do much with it, I know, I know. But if I

220

spent more time trying to be glamorous, you'd lecture me on my priorities, admit it. Give me a big hug. Tell me I haven't been too much of a Pollyanna. I've been trying not to be one lately, you know. The other day—I probably shouldn't tell you this—I threw a basket of bran muffins against the wall."

"You did? You're kidding. What happened?"

"They crumbled—what do you think happened?"

"I love you, Mom. Maybe you should cover up the gray in your hair. You really have a very youthful spirit."

"Get one thing straight, kiddo. I am not yet old enough to be youthful. And I can't believe how much you sound like Sally Letterman. I've got my much-postponed appointment with John for a cut this afternoon. Don't be surprised if you come home and find me a bleached blonde."

"You wouldn't!"

"You're right. Now go. I love you too. I never loved you more than I do this minute."

Margo sat unmoving until the school bus had disappeared from sight. Then she headed down Asylum Street toward her office, thinking hard about what to make for dinner.

Chapter 29

Andrea stared out the kitchen window. The wind had swept the sky clean, and the snow on the rooftops gleamed hard and waxy against the infinite blue. A mud-and-snow-color bird pecked away at a feeder hanging from a bare-branched tree. John would have given it a name, invented its love life, had her laughing or in tears.

If she turned around very slowly, holding her breath, thinking the right thoughts, she would fall through a hole in time and find him sitting at the table stirring sugar into his coffee. Oh sweetie, that was a close call, wasn't it? But now we know. And are safe forever. Let's make love and then cook something yumptious.

She turned around very slowly, holding her breath.

And there dear God dear God.

Surfaces. Couldn't fool her. When she wanted so very much not to be fooled. And the smile was everything new was old again. Radiating a warmth that called to her chilly bones.

He put his hands on either side of her face. His lips bowed to hers, gentlemanly, shy: May I please have this kiss? Then swooped and tore her open to the ankles.

She smoked. She flamed. He drew back to look at her, to show his wonderment.

"Then again, he said, fingertips trembling on her lips, "maybe I died and went to heaven." He pulled her against him, folded his arms around her.

She sank into the feeling of completeness. She pressed her lips to the part of his chest left exposed by the V of his robe. She caught a single curly hair in her teeth and wove it into her web. Never. Ever. Leave me again.

"You didn't die," she said. "I kept telling Phil Porter. Everyone. No matter what the tests showed."

"I don't want to think about tests. Just about you. You smell so good. Like a vanilla milkshake."

"Drink me," she said.

He held her away from him so she could see his lips coming home. He hummed into her mouth and she vibrated everywhere.

"I want—"

"Me too."

"You're so—"

"I know."

The kitchen was wrong and he felt it too and they floated to the guest room but somehow the yellow didn't work, too much sun when they needed stars and a moon. They sat on the edge of the unmade bed barely touching.

"You ran away from me last night," he said. Softly, not really chiding, wanting to understand.

"I felt confused. Do you blame me?"

He shook his head. "Maybe I would have run if you hadn't. Twenty-two years and I never touched another woman."

"You think I don't know that? And I like her too. Maybe even"—she picked up one of his hands, played with the knuckles—"love her. If I didn't I couldn't have stood it, the two of you together."

Sympathy made an oval of his mouth. "What you've

lost. It's so unfair."

"I don't want to think about that part. I don't have to now." She raised his hand to her lips and covered it with kisses. "Last night I saw you as hers. A married man. But I woke up knowing that skin is only skin. It's time for the heart to come home."

"What are you saying, Andrea?"

"Nothing you haven't thought of yourself. Nothing you haven't felt. Look at me. Am I just another woman? Or your once and forever Dandy?"

He looked, he touched, he kissed — kissed her kissing him kissing kisses, nothing in the world but this sacred hunger.

"We have a right," he said. "I feel it."

"Yes," she said to the taste of him. "Yes."

"But how can we make it work?" He groaned the question against her lips.

"Take the train to New York with me." She felt him yearning and then resisting, and she said: "I don't mean forever. I know I have to share you. But life isn't either/or, remember? Not for you and me. So think both/and. The way you always have."

He did a long slow take on her face, and she saw wonder in his eyes and excitement and a little bit of fear but only a little. "Nobody ever went from being so close to dead to feeling so alive. By God, you're what the doctor ordered."

She threw back her head in joyous laughter. "That's what I told them at the hospital the first time I went to see you. When they thought I had no right to be there."

"Damn the hospital anyway. They made me swear in blood that I'll stay within fifty miles."

"Then we'll go to Kent. That's close enough. Take up where we left off."

"I've got clinic tomorrow morning," he said.

"I'll bring you back. I'll be a part of it." She sat up, wrapping her arms around her knees. "I want to know your new details. Everything. What do they do at clinic?"

"Blood chemistry, weight, the weekly pain"—he put his hand to his jugular—"in the neck."

"What's that?"

"Nothing much. They just send little forceps down through a vein and cut off a piece of the graft, that's all. That's how they know if I'm rejecting. Hey, how did we get from Rodgers and Hart to here?" He began singing "Nobody's Heart Belongs to Me," then stopped and looked chagrined—at least gave her a look that said he knew he should feel chagrined and sorry that he didn't.

The same look as the day he'd brought out his organ donor's card and then ordered kidneys in mustard sauce. And the day in France when he'd said he knew he didn't deserve to be so happy, no one could earn such happiness, it was God or luck or something too big to name; and damned if he were going to insult the Giver by feeling guilty.

"Oh, your eyes," he said now. "I can't believe how hot they are."

"Ask me if I feel like running."

"Do you feel like running?"

"Try me."

He put his hands on her shoulders, then slid them around to meet behind her back. Tumbling weightless to the yellow blankets that had covered but not warmed her last night. Noses playful as pups but mouths absolutely meant it. Peach silk breasts ecstatic as he pressed her into the hardness of his chest.

"Dandy."

"Sweetheart," she said.

"Say my name," he said.

"You know and you know that I know."

"I want you to love me for myself."

"Oh, tell me what a self is. Leonora Whittlesey had to become a man to be all the woman she was. You're John but I think you're more Hank than you ever were before."

His hands fell away. Air slid between them.

"My turn to run," he said. "You're beautiful and I want you but I can't." He pounded the mattress with his fists. "It's this house, dammit. It's small and it's making me think small."

She held onto the saving words. "You're absolutely right. This house just isn't us. And I won't push for Kent again, not after what happened last time. You go to clinic tomorrow and show them how well you are. I'll work on getting you to New York."

"The truth is, I promised Margo New York. A weekend at the Plaza. As soon as they'll let me go."

"It's a big city. Room for everyone. When did we ever"—confidence surged through her and she propped herself up on an elbow—"let logistics get in our way?"

"Do you know what you're asking me to do?"

"Sure I do. Because, I told you, I know who you are. That's no ordinary heart beating in your chest, mister."

"You are a very heady girl."

"Well, yes. You always made it clear. That nothing less would do."

They lay there in silence for a while, and then she said, "What time is it?"

"Believe it or not, it's only eight-twenty."

"I can still make the nine-twenty-three. Call me a taxi, will you, while I shower and dress?"

She was stripping the bed when the doorbell rang. She stuffed the sheets into the pillowcase the way

Grand'Anna had taught her, picked up her overnight bag, and went out to the living room.

"Why is the taxi early the one time I want it to be late?" Hank said. "I was hoping you could read the poem."

"Now you decide."

"Maybe it's just as well. You might not like me if you didn't like it. Zap." He drew a finger across his throat. Then he beamed at her, started dancing around her, like the photographer back in the hospital wanting to see the picture from every angle. "Why do I find it so interesting to watch you button your coat? I want to see you do everything. Open your mail. Brush your teeth. Until I know you by heart."

The words were so nearly an echo, they staggered her. "That's all the poetry I can handle," she said.

She looked back as the taxi drove down Pocahontas, watching him wave and then stand there gazing after her and then wave again, a suburban husband in a striped bathrobe, ordinary and extraordinary both, with a warmth that was absolute and could not be diminished by winter.

Chapter 30

She couldn't concentrate. She was supposed to prepare a presentation on an insurance package for the board of a big new co-op in downtown Hartford, but her mind was all energy and no contents, her eyes kept straying to the windows. She leaped at the interruption when her secretary buzzed and said Mrs. McKay was on the phone. Then she heard Sue's choky voice and she just about stopped breathing.

"Hank?"

"No, not Hank, he's fine. I'm sorry I scared you," Sue sobbed. "It's me. Gar and me. We're splitting."

Margo almost whistled her relief, but that didn't last a minute. "Sue, no!" she shouted, her stomach in her throat, her shoulders drawing in and down. "What happened?"

"He—shit, hang on, I've got to get a cigarette, and don't tell me not to smoke. He does, you know."

"Gar? Smokes?" As if this were all the bad news.

"At home, the two-faced bastard, where none of you people who think he's God can see him. You're probably going to think that's worse than the other thing he does. He's been screwing Ruth Lilley."

"Ruth? Lilley? The nurse?"

"No, Ruth Lilley the quarterback."

"I'm being stupid, I'm sorry," Margo said. "I'm just so shocked."

"How do you think I feel?"

"Like a train ran over you. Don't move. I'm coming to see you."

She scribbled Sue's number on a memo sheet and gave it to her secretary. She drove to the big brick house across from Elizabeth Park—the most solid-looking house in West Hartford, the storybook family house. And Sue was the storybook wife, the one who was supposed to get to live happily ever after. She was that unmistakable entity, a good woman; and a handsome one, with her height and athletic body and all-American friendly face; and an ace mother for the eight-year-old twins; and the tennis and golf, and the Wadsworth Atheneum, and the summer parties in the sloping backyard, and always (though not now) jaunty.

"But it doesn't matter," Sue said, as Margo enumerated her virtues in the McKays' airy green and white living room. "Apparently nothing counts except rubbery lips. I would call the hospital, and some little thing who was laughing up her sleeve would tell me Dr. McKay was having a nap—darling heroic Dr. McKay, so worn out from saving lives—and what she wouldn't tell me was that Ruth Lilley was in there with him. She really knows how to make a man feel like a man, says our eminent cardiologist."

"Oh God, I was just telling Debbie this morning that men are smarter than that."

"Jewish men, maybe—"

"Jewish shmooish," Margo said. "People are people."

"Except when they're animals." Sue shook a Marlboro out of the packet. "I'll open the window," she said, "so you won't yell at me for contaminating your air."

Margo waved away the thought. "Come on. You're allowed. I'm not going to lecture you about smoking—at least until tomorrow—and I didn't bring you soup.

Ruth Lilley!" She tried to remember how the two of them were with each other, but even in retrospect she couldn't pick up any special vibrations. She did remember Gar looking strained, and she said so.

"Strained! Worn out is more like it. What do you bet that Ruth isn't the only one. I'm starting to rethink a lot of late nights that didn't quite add up. Mickie Ross? The fabled Elaine Mancuso, maybe?"

"I can't believe anything could be more important to him than all of you." She looked to the near wall and ornately framed pastels of Emily and Clare McKay at age four, features pretty but vague—the eternal blond children of a certain world. If Andrea had children, they would slip into those gilded frames. "Do the kids know anything yet?"

"That pleasure is yet to come." Sue blew bitter rings up toward the ceiling. "Tell me about Ruth."

"Tough little cookie. Oh, nice enough to me, and terrific with the patients, but she always reminded me of the military. I mean those forties comedies about WACs and WAVEs—do they still call them that? As Skip would say, Ruth Lilley as the other woman just doesn't scan. Are you sure, Sue? That it has to be the end?"

"He's discovered America. He says he loves her." Sue got up and started pacing the room. "Shit, shit, shit. How do I tell the girls?"

"Don't tell them. Yet. Don't make it real before it has to be."

"You could carry that off, but I don't think I can."

"Let me put it differently," Margo said. "If he wanted to stay, would you let him?"

"Oh, please. I can't bear it. I've always had the feeling that when I was about to die I would realize that there had never been any other moment, and that's how I feel now. This is what everything was about. Always. From the night I met him to our wedding day to the

230

kids being born and the kid who didn't make it, all the kisses and fucks and the thousands of meals and millions of words and the big thoughts and the cracker crumbs: everything. It was all leading up to this goddam magazine article moment. If he wants to stay, will I let him? Yes, no, if this, if that, see quiz on page forty-eight, and here's what ten celebs have to say about the day they found out he was cheating." Sue sank dryeyed into an armchair covered in green-striped silk "Sure, I'll let him stay. It's what Ann Landers would tell me to do, isn't it? It's what you would do. Isn't it?"

Margo groaned. "I don't know, and oh God I don't want to have to know. The truth is, I can't really imagine it. Which I suppose is why Debbie informed me this morning that I'm the most naïve woman in the United States. Because if it could happen to you, it could happen to anyone." She started to tell Sue that Andrea had spent the night, but she didn't want to tell her, not then, not with Sue all torn up and strangeness in the air. "If he wanted to stay, I think I'd let him. If he still loved me."

"You see? There we go with the ifs. If he still loves me. If he stops seeing her. Or doesn't it matter what he does as long as he's here? I still like our life, you see. I want to go to the Fullers' party on Saturday and take the kids skating in the park on Sunday — if there's ice, that is — and afterward I want to cuddle up with him. I guess I still love the bastard."

"Sue, you're terrific."

"Sure I am. I'm terrific, you're terrific. But you know something, Margo" — tears started down her cheeks — "I wish we didn't all have to be so terrific. Tell your young feminist that's what liberation is really about. The freedom to be possessive, sloppy, lazy, two-faced, boring, ugly, and still be loved. Because that's what our men have won for themselves, isn't it?"

"Did you know?" Margo asked Hank, after she'd told him the news.

"No, kid, I didn't."

"I still can't quite believe it."

Hank shrugged.

"Oh, Hank, how can you be so casual? Sue's devastated. All those goodies I baked for Ruth Lilley — the little hypocrite."

"Why? She's still one first-rate nurse. I suppose this means we have to choose sides."

"Well, socially, if they split up. No one's saying you should give up Gar as your doctor."

"Please thank the committee for their gracious indulgence."

"I don't understand," Margo said. "When Dave Gratz left Zora for that girl from Palm Springs, you were very upset with him."

"Dave Gratz was a stuffed shirt. Probably still is. He was always going on about how degenerate rock music is, and the things they put in movies nowadays shouldn't be allowed, and when Walter Hirsh was alive, Dave used to make cracks about how nobody better get caught in the showers with him. I felt sorry for Zora and the kids even before he officially gazumped them."

"And you don't feel sorry for Sue? And the twins?"

"I always liked Sue, but what do we know about their private life? Maybe she only wants to do it on Saturday nights with the lights out and he wants it Monday, Wednesday, and Friday with bells on their toes."

"I'm sure she's not cold, if that's what you mean," Margo said. "She has a bidet."

"And you have a Chevy."

"You bet I do, big boy." She reached out and stroked his lower lip.

He winked, but he didn't touch her. "I'm hungry," he said.

"Lunch in ten minutes," she said.

"Vanilla," Hank said.

Her scalp seemed to tighten. "What?" But she knew.

"I have to have something vanilla. Ice cream, pudding"—he was actually digging his nails into the arms of his chair—"a soda. Something. Or I'm going to be sick. I have to."

"Okay, honey. Don't get panicky. Amanda left behind some of her diet cream soda. Ordinarily I wouldn't—"

"Just get it," he said. "Hurry."

She ran into the kitchen, plucked ice cubes out of the freezer, dropped them into a glass. Here was one for the medical journals! As soon as Hank was calm, she'd call Mickie and ask which of the medications provoked a craving for vanilla. Well, it could be worse, right? Imagine a craving for chocolate! She slopped a little soda and she sponged it up, and then she realized she was crying. Because of Sue. Only because of Sue. Never cry over spilled cream, she told herself, hastily fisting away her tears, putting on a smile for her darling.

Chapter 31

She got to the station with ten minutes to spare and went straight to the bank of phones. She pressed O and 212 and then she blanked, she couldn't remember Mark's number. She hung up, looked through her bag for her address book and didn't find it, got out a pen and a scrap of paper (she didn't seem to have a notebook either), dialed Information for 212, got his number, wrote it down, and started again. An operator came on and Andrea said, "This is a credit card call," but she couldn't remember her calling card number. The operator held on while she searched her wallet for her card. She found it and triumphantly reeled off the four digits; the operator told her the digits had to be preceded by her billing number, area code first "It's 212," she said, then stopped. "I'm sorry, I drank decaf this morning. Please make it collect to Mark Feingold. From" — she paused for a moment to tease the operator, who probably thought she was high on drugs or walking around with a stolen wallet — "great news, I remember my name, Andrea Pearce."

Mark got right on. "Andrea? Where the eff are you? Your mother and I have been frantic. I even had Sukie on the phone."

"You and Kitty are buddies now? I should go away more often. I'm in Hartford."

"You could have told someone. Left a message on

your tape."

Oh, but he was being unfair, bringing her down this way. Her shoulders ached toward Pocahontas Drive, and she considered hanging up, forgetting about New York, but that wouldn't help anybody. "I'm sorry, Mark. I didn't know I needed a pass. I'm getting on a train in a couple of minutes. Are you free for lunch?"

"No, but if you need me I will be."

Her resentment fell away. "You're a pal. Veau d'Or okay? At one? You book the table, I'll treat." The public address system crackled, and she said, "My train is coming in. Would you please call Kitty and tell her I'm okay? I'll call her this afternoon."

"I'll call everyone. You really are okay?"

She said she was more okay than he could imagine, which was why she had to see him.

She looked out the window as the train started to move, chugging across a snowy billow of park before getting up to speed, then she closed her eyes and gave herself over to the sweet hot memory of kisses. This car, where the air tasted of newsprint, and a man was chomping peanuts almost in her ear, seemed a better place for making love than that cheerful, tidy house.

The conductor broke the spell. She surrendered her ticket and dozed until she felt a hand on her shoulder and heard a woman saying, "Excuse me, excuse me, we're in New York." She opened her eyes to the rushing darkness of the tunnel into Penn Station and a seatmate who hadn't been there in Hartford, a woman in layers of tweed.

"It must have been a wonderful dream," the woman said. "You didn't want to wake up."

"It was," Andrea said, though she couldn't remember the dream — remembered only how much she'd wanted to stay inside it. Oh, but wasn't it good to be awake now that she had those kisses?

Not much slush in the streets and she decided to walk to the restaurant, on Sixtieth east of Park. She had forty-five minutes, time enough, and she needed to clear her head, figure out how to break the beautiful news.

Mark, hold onto your hat. Or: Mark, a miracle has happened. Some kind of preamble because she didn't want him fainting with joy. Mark, it's about the memorial service. I think you should cancel it. His body is gone, but he's here.

She zigged and zagged, Seventh Avenue to Thirty-ninth Street, across to Sixth and up to Forty-eighth Street, across to Fifth and up to Fifty-seventh Street, an imperfect symmetry but a pattern, proof she was in control. Because, the cucumber side of her warned, Mark might think she'd lost her mind. And, oh God, had she? The question broke her stride, made her lean for a dizzy moment against the rock of Bonwit Teller. Was she a sister to the tabloid crazies—recycled Cleopatras, mothers of Martians? But those kisses, those new old kisses, electrifying kisses, truth-telling kisses, nobody-but-John kisses.

At the restaurant she gratefully checked the Burberry and her overnighter and walked through the flowered curtain to the washroom. She scrubbed her face and did her makeup over from scratch—quickly, in case some other woman needed the room for more urgent business. She might not be as good as Margo (she found herself saying to the mirror), but she did have something of a conscience.

Mark had remembered to reserve her favorite table, right up front. She liked watching the bartender in his striped shirt, hand motions as crisp and swift as those of a sushi chef—two Kirs in goblets for the pretty couple at the small polished bar, a Perrier on the rocks and a beer with a pilsner glass for the tall waiter's tray,

236

and in between taking orders from a mother and daughter who wanted spritzers while they waited for Daddy. John always said this was the true bistro, the way the laughter mingled with desire and the smoke from unfiltered Gauloises. We have endless needs and they will be met exuberantly.

She ordered a Perrier (no ice) for herself. And there was Mark, flinging his coat onto the checkroom counter, hurrying toward her.

He kissed her cheek. "Never fails, does it? One who's further away gets there first. My effing cab got jammed up in traffic." The waiter brought Andrea's Perrier. Mark ordered one for himself.

"We should be drinking champagne," Andrea said. "You can't imagine how wonderful Hank looks."

"That is good news," he said, but he looked at her with the air of someone who knows that more news is coming and maybe not so good.

"He's been working hard on the poem. When he talks about it, wow, does he sound like a writer."

Mark grunted. "We'll see."

"He refused to show it to me. Just like John."

"Or because there's nothing to show."

"Margo," she said determinedly, "thinks the poem is terrific."

"From what I've read and heard of Margo, she even thinks his stools are terrific. Oh Jesus, Andrea," he said, as the goblet in her hand exploded, "are you all right?"

"I'm fine, I'm fine," she said. An army of black and white jackets descended, clucking over her, removing the broken glass, replacing the bread and butter in case splinters had invaded, spreading napkins over the spill. "My Perrier collided with my water," she said. She wasn't in fact sure what had happened. "Sorry about the mess."

237

"It's my fault," he said. "Something about you in Hartford scared me. Deep down scared me. But I shouldn't have said what I said. I'm sorry."

She put her hand on the sleeve of his navy blazer. "Don't be scared. Be happy for me. For him. For us all."

Fresh Perrier appeared, and tiny dishes of mussels in mustard sauce, compliments of the house, and were they ready to order? Monsieur Feingold might want to know there was cassoulet today.

Andrea ordered an artichoke and poached salmon, the sauce on the side. Mark wanted leeks and then cassoulet.

"Of course I'm happy for him," Mark said. "God knows, I hope I get a second chance someday. And of course I'm happy that you're getting—"

"That's not what I meant," Andrea said. "When I said be happy for him. And for me."

Mark picked up a fork and didn't do anything with it. He looked at her.

"I kissed him," she said.

He carefully set the fork down. "No."

"I kissed him and he was there." Mark looked at her uncomprehendingly and she said, "John was there. I tasted him."

"No. Please. No." He rubbed his hands across his face. "Tell me you're kidding."

"Mark, I thought I was telling you something thrilling. Why do you want me to be kidding?"

"Because if you're not kidding me, you're kidding yourself." He gulped Perrier. "We've got to get you some help, Andrea."

She shook her head in disbelief, shoulders rising and falling. "I didn't realize you were so committed to his nonexistence."

"You're going to talk to someone. Today."

"What kind of someone? A shrink you mean?"

238

"A therapist, a minister, a witch, a grandmother. Whoever can help you face the terrible truth. John is in that graveyard in Kent. Henry Corman is Henry Corman and he belongs to somebody else."

"Make me understand," she said. "I know how much you loved him. Why do you need for him to be dead?"

"That's like asking me why I need two and two to make four." He picked at a mussel. "It has nothing to do with me. What is, is."

"Suppose I can prove that what is, isn't."

"I don't even know how to answer that. Some woman—this goes back a zillion years—told me it was mathematically possible to turn an orange inside out without breaking the skin. I tried to imagine it and I got about the worst headache of my life. But if I'd seen an orange do that, I like to think I would have accepted it. Gone on the road with it." He waved at someone emerging from the back room. "Next to you I cared more about John than any other person on earth did. You can ask Annette. I still wake up crying sometimes. So I guess if he were alive—Christ, it really is beyond unimaginable to me—I'd be almost as happy as you."

He stood up and held out his hand to a tall man with a snowy frizz of hair and pale blue eyes. "Andrea, I want you to meet Graham Walsh, one of the last of the gentlemen in publishing. Graham, this is Andrea Pearce, John's wife."

"May I offer my condolences, Mrs. Pearce?"

"No, you may not," Mark said, before she could speak.

She smiled at the white-haired man. "Mark and I don't see eye to eye, Mr. Walsh. I think John is still with us. I know it."

"I understand your sentiments exactly, Mrs. Pearce. I buried my Annie eleven years ago, and I still talk to her every morning while I'm making the tea. Don't let them tell you you're crazy. I'm going to be reunited with Annie someday, and I'm sure you'll be with your John. Take care of this lovely lady, Mark. There aren't many people around who understand the meaning of marriage."

"You wretch," Andrea said, as Graham Walsh headed on toward the door.

Mark tried to look innocent. "Why? It should make you feel good, knowing you're not the only one."

"He believes everything he learned in Sunday school. Souls meeting in heaven and all that. Do you really think that's what I've been saying?"

"Don't be so quick to mock. There's no shame in having faith. Here comes food."

"Faith is fine. But it's not my line. Life after death, resurrection, survival of the spirit, whatever you want to call it — I don't know about those things and I don't need to know." She broke off an artichoke leaf but didn't eat it. "I'm saying John didn't die. Can't you see the difference?"

"I don't think there is a difference."

"Because you've fallen for the received opinion. Well, let's see what we can do about that."

"What are you up to, Andrea?"

"I'm going to find a way to convince you. Something like that inside-out orange. Because I know what I'm up against here. If my friends don't believe me, what will my enemies say? I need an army, Mark, and I want you in it. To help me fight the war to set him free."

Chapter 32

No, she said to John Pluskowski of Hair-Plus, she didn't want the usual today. She wanted a facial with a light peeling, some hair-minus work on her chin, a French manicure, a pedicure, and a whole different look to her head. In fact, if he could consider her a candidate for a head transplant—

"Margo, you're a character." John stood tall and blond behind her, sifting her hair through his fingers, posing them both for the mirror. "Now seriously, darling—"

"I am being serious. Whatever you and Lydia have time to do to me. A bikini waxing. A ruby in my navel. The works. How are you going to do my hair?"

"Oh my. Oh my. Now I could exfoliate. You'd still have the volume"—he always drew out the word, pronouncing it like Valium, which on other days made her smile—"but you'd get away from the artichoke look, be a little more punk."

"Exfoliate, good heavens, isn't that what we did in Vietnam?"

"Shh, the walls have ears. Seriously, what I do is cut the hair different lengths, but none of this boring suburban symmetry, and I actually razor into the hair shaft, peel off layers, and it changes the texture. You get spring all over the place."

Margo said she'd been waiting for spring.

"Wait no longer. You'll love it. Throw away your comb and brush, just ootz it with the towel after you wash it. Freedom now." John put his message into motion, his pointed nose and chin bobbing, his hands rearranging the air.

"What about color?" His enthusiasm was firing her own. "I want to cover up the gray."

He walked around the chair to look her in the actual eyes. "Is that really you, darling?"

"Never more so."

"Well, Margo my love, if we're going to get you out of here before midnight—and if I'm going to have even five minutes for the rest of my clients—"

"John, I'm sorry, this really is nervy of me, booking myself for a cut and then asking for the works. Forget the color."

"I'll tell you what. I'll ask Fern to throw on some henna. If you like it, come back next week and I'll give you the real thing. Now let me look at the book and work some magic." He got the appointment calendar from the front desk and scanned it, running his fingers back and forth across the open pages, humming a melody Margo knew but she couldn't remember the title, exuding nervous energy the way Skip did. "Let's see. Mrs. Linwald can read *Vogue* for fifteen minutes while Lydia does the waxing—she's made Lydia wait often enough. Fern can do your nails—no, we'll let Fern wax Mrs. Linwald and do Helen Thomas's tootsies and Lydia can do everything for you. I know how you feel about Lydia."

Lydia stretched her out on a fresh length of white paper in a little room that smelled of warm honey, shook baby powder onto her thighs, dimmed the light and pitched it away, said the wax was coming now and would hurt but only for a minute and afterward such a clean and beautiful look. She danced around, talking, doing — nurse, beautician, big sister, a dubious head-mistress in some blue movie boarding school for girls.

"So you are abandoning" — zip, zip, zip, Lydia did her work — "this endless winter?" She patted Margo's violated skin to stop the stinging.

"No, nothing so wonderful," Margo said. "Those hairs will all grow back before I get near a bathing suit."

"Ahah, you just want to show off for someone." Lydia's Russian accent heightened the innuendo. "I do the inside now, big ouch coming."

"For my husband," Margo said into the pain. "I don't want any rumors starting, Lydia." Pretty little Lydia liked to talk, no doubt knowing she was much talked about — had married John maybe for love, maybe for a green card, and maybe he was gay (though Margo thought he played at camp to titillate the West Hartford matrons), and maybe she liked Fern —

"No rumors, Mrs. Margo. Not for such a lady. You're so good, I can see it hurts but you lie there and smile, not like the ones who scream."

"I'm not screaming but I just promised myself I'll never ever do this again. Do you believe my feminist daughter is the one who got me here?"

"Everyone promises and everyone comes back, and the feminists they come too. That beautiful blond one in New York, Gloria, she can tell the girls not to wear makeup but they look in the mirror and they don't see Gloria and they come to me. Turn, Mrs. Margo. Now we have the easy side."

Two hours later John proclaimed Margo the make-over of the year, and Fern said they should have taken pictures for *Glamour*, and Lydia talked her into buying a denim outfit, long wide skirt and big blazer, that she would have felt unable to carry off that morning but now was right at home in. (Lydia had thinned her eyebrows and dyed her lashes, and not only did she seem to have enormous eyes, she somehow looked leggier.) Even the smarting of her thighs was positive, more a tingling awareness than a discomfort, and as she assessed her new self in the mirror—a breezy gamine who looked ready for Paris—she had an inspiration born of freshened confidence. Next time Amanda came to clean, she would ask her about getting Elgar to do a bed swap, the twin beds into the guest room and the double bed into the master. She would buy gorgeous new sheets, maybe even satin, in time for Valentine's Day.

In the car she remembered what John had been humming. "Fine and Dandy." She hummed a few bars but the tune went flat on her and she stopped.

Gar's gray Saab was parked in front of the house, and her mood shriveled. She ordered herself to stay calm. Maybe he was just passing by and wanted to say hello. Or he'd found that long missing copy of *Golf in the Kingdom* and had decided to drop it off before he lost it again. At worst (but not a thousandth as awful as something having gone wrong with Hank's heart), he'd come by to give the Cormans his side of the affair with Ruth Lilley.

"Darling?" She got from car to house without being aware of parking, running.

"In the living room," Hank said, not in pain but not in joy, and she knew he was okay and knew at once who wasn't.

"Sam," she said to the two dejected-looking men. They nodded.

"Gone?" She sat down on the red sofa and took Hank's hand.

"An hour ago," Gar said. "I thought you and Hank should hear it from me."

"Are Elaine and the kids okay?" she asked automatically. What she wanted to say was, Tell me dear doctor god that Hank means more to you than your other patients, what happened to Sam can't happen to him.

"They're okay. Mickie's the one who's really distraught. She always thought of Sam as her failure. She couldn't get him to believe in the program, not the way you and Bobby and Mike and the others do."

"Maybe he knew something," Hank said. His voice was tight the way it had been before his surgery. The energy and zest were gone.

"But maybe if he'd believed, the reality would have been different," Gar said. "The more medicine I practice, old boy, the more I believe in the power of the psyche."

"If he'd believed, he might have done a better job of following the rules," Margo said. "Remember when we had dinner at Al Di La with them, honey, and he had that rich hot antipasto and then lasagna. 'After what I've been through, I deserve a little something,' that was his attitude. And Elaine smiled and nodded and said, 'Just this once,' but I think she said it every night. Oh God, listen to me, why am I so angry at them? They wanted life as much as we do." She started to cry.

"It's not enough to want things," Gar said. "You have to be willing to fight for what's important. Make sacrifices."

Margo blew her nose. "I have the feeling we just changed the subject," she said. "I'll tell you right up front, Gar. I love you for what you've done for Hank. But I hate you for what you're doing to Sue."

"Guilty until proven innocent," Hank said. "Come on, Margo."

"I'm guilty, all right," Gar said. "But I still love Sue and I'm glad she has such a good friend. Well, I better go off and break the news to Mike."

"The heart he was supposed to get," Hank said.

"That's right." Gar stood up. "I'll see you at clinic tomorrow. Bobby should be back. Sounds as though he had a great time in Florida."

"We got a postcard," Margo said.

"Your turn to send them soon," Gar said. "I like whatever you did to your hair, Margo."

For a moment she didn't know what he was talking about and she could see that Hank didn't either.

"It's shorter," he finally said.

Of course he hadn't noticed with his thoughts all on Sam. Besides, it meant she still looked like herself, the self he had always loved. A testimony to John's skill! She hoped she had tipped enough.

Chapter 33

How different the apartment on Twelfth Street felt. She looked at a leather couch in the living room and pictured him stretched out the length of it, feet propped up on one arm as he read the *Times,* but he kept putting it down to read her face and confirm the brimming joy he saw. Dandy girl. Didn't I tell you. That we'd do it all before we were finished.

The couch was for his body; the windows offered him views; and on the two-tiered towel rack in the new bathroom that no longer mocked her, she set out green towels and a washcloth for him, yellow for her. She showered and got into a terry robe and was trying to figure out what to say to Kitty—how to hint at the lightness in her heart without causing a commotion—when the telephone rang.

"Mother?" she said.

"Philip Porter here," he said in that formal way of his.

"Hello, Phil." A bit on edge because he never brought great news.

"I'm on my way into New York, and I wondered if you'd join me for a drink."

"Well, yes," she was surprised into saying. "I'd like that." Something to tell Kitty, who approved of him despite his interest in moving hearts from one body to another.

They agreed on the Oak Bar at six.

Black and white, she decided: snowy cashmere cable knit sweater over inky silk shirt, baggy bold checked pants, striped and spotted scarves twisted at her waist. But then the normality of getting dressed stopped her, dizzied her, the way calling Mark from the Hartford railroad station had done, as if such ordinary acts couldn't take place in the world as she now knew it. Was it only that morning she'd been in Hartford? She sat down on the edge of the bed watching kisses swarm around her, hot purple butterflies. And what were the color of his eyes? Gray but they shouldn't be gray, hadn't always been gray. Would he wear brown contact lenses? And Pamela could cut his hair, cut it straight and blond, with those scissors that remembered.

You need help.

So somebody help me.

I better help me.

Pull yourself together, Andrea. We rise above.

White silk knee socks, black ballet flats. Burgundy lipstick to match the leather at the Oak Bar. No jewels. A single spritz of vanilla.

The Oak Room was pleasantly mobbed, but Phil had managed to snare one of the tables of choice at the long banquette by the windows. He stood up as she approached and offered the inside seat; she said thanks but she'd take the view of Central Park. He was wearing a dark suit with a faint bluish pinstripe and a straight face to match. A serious man, Dr. Philip Porter.

He conjured a waiter, ordered the Guinness she wanted, tendered a smile. "I suppose you wonder why I called you."

"I did wonder."

"I wanted to thank you for the good work you've done on behalf of organ donation. Last week we had two accident victims and I didn't have to approach the fami-

248

lies—they came to me with copies of the issue of *People* that had your interview."

"The interviewer asked the right questions," she said.

"You were fine even on that radio show where they asked the wrong questions."

"How on earth did you come to hear Steve Coe?" Her Guinness arrived, and she let the waiter fill the glass halfway up.

Phil raised his glass to her—a vodka gimlet. "I didn't hear it. I heard about it from Mark. I was thinking"— he blinked in the rapid way she remembered—"that you've done far more than your share on behalf of transplantation. Why don't you retire from the PR business? Treat yourself to a vacation. Then get on with rebuilding your life."

Oh, but shouldn't she have guessed the moment she'd heard his voice on the telephone?

"Mark called you, didn't he? After our lunch today? Called you and said I was talking crazy and somebody had to help, maybe you could do it?"

"Maybe I can," Phil said.

He was so cool, so sober, so straight-shouldered, so sure of himself, that just to look at him—look at him knowing they were on opposite sides—filled her with a wild exhaustion. Because she was a pinprick of hope and he was the mass of respectable opinion. For one desperate moment, she wanted to fling herself at him, surrender, beg shelter in his version of the truth. Tell me over and over and over again, until I truly believe: The heart is just a pump and dead is dead. And I will cry in Mark's arms and wear black and be dead myself, but at least I won't feel so tired.

"Don't you think," he said, "I'd have given anything for John to survive? I know I did the best I could, and I don't believe any other doctor could have saved him, but that still doesn't make his death something I can take in stride."

"I don't want to hear about your guilt, doctor." She fiddled with the black lacquer bowl full of salted nibbles, but she didn't take any. "You've managed to stay afloat; you've made your peace with death."

"It's not guilt. I know I'm not God. What gets me is the loss. This glorious creation we call a human being, tuned and refined for millions of years, and some machine goes out of control and just like that"—he snapped his fingers—"the human being is gone. Six, seven years ago I thought I was going to have to get out of medicine because I couldn't handle the loss; then along came cyclosporine, and transplantation became a meaningful reality, and though I grieve when a patient doesn't make it, I have something to hold onto." He touched Andrea's arm, made her look into the glittering darkness of his eyes. "I'm worried about you, and frankly I'm also scared you're going to send out some flaky message that will turn people off being donors. I can't let you do that."

"Excuse me," the hugely pregnant redhaired woman at the next table said to Phil, "I need to squeeze by you."

"Please." He pulled their table closer to the end of the banquette; he smiled to encourage her passage.

"I should have sat on the outside," the woman said. She looked around inquiringly.

"Downstairs by Trader Vic's," Phil said. She laughed her thanks and hurried toward the door.

"You're a father," Andrea said. She knew he was divorced—her mother had let her know—but his ease with that belly told her more.

"Yes. A father and a doctor. That's my story. No other passions. I don't bake bread or grow roses. Don't give a damn who wins the World Series. A father and a doctor. A doctor and a father. Andrea, I didn't mean to lecture at you. I feel desperately sorry for you. Can't

250

you find consolation in knowing that a good man like Hank Corman who would otherwise be dead has been restored to meaningful life thanks to you?"

Over his shoulder and across the street, she saw a young couple arguing with the top-hatted driver of a horse-drawn carriage, the woman's head at an impassioned angle—clearly, it was mostly her fight. If John were there, he'd be weaving them into a story, all the ingredients, the way the dirty white horse kept swishing his tail, and the sullen look on the young man's face, and the way his girlfriend—somehow not his wife— tugged at him: the ordinariness and the specialness of the moment. His reporting had made him famous, but she'd liked the short stories best. And the poems.

"If that's all that had happened, maybe it would be enough. I'm not crazy, Phil. I heard his voice. When I listened to the heart. And Hank used the nickname only John knows."

He smiled sadly. "When I listen to hearts, I hear Beethoven. Good thing I'm not a cardiologist."

And now his sureness—his smugness—was working for her, not wearing her out but spurring her on. Because she had tradition behind her too, didn't she? She was Christopher Columbus trying to tell the sages the world was round.

"I know what I'm saying sounds outrageous. But as a man of science don't you have to consider the outrageous? Or are you saying that you're the culmination of all knowledge? That there's no more to reality—and never will be—than you think there is? What about the myths that have sprung up since the dawn of civilization about good hearts and stout hearts and hard hearts and broken hearts? Maybe hearts are just muscles and maybe they're more and John Malcolm Pearce didn't die."

He grabbed a pen from his pocket, the napkin from

under his drink.

"This," he said, sketching furiously, "is what a heart is about. Right atrium, left atrium, right ventricle, left ventricle. Up here"—the dampness of the napkin blurred the ink, and the drawing took on the look of a swollen butterfly—"we have the aortic arch, and these are the pulmonary arteries, and here is where the donor heart is trimmed to fit the—"

"No." She crumpled the napkin, threw it to the floor. "I don't accept it. It's a partial truth, the most dangerous sort of lie. It doesn't explain anything. It doesn't explain how we got from caves to the Plaza, from cupped hands full of water to frosted bottles of Guinness, from animal skins to . . . that's a Dior tie, isn't it? Doesn't explain anything. Anything. Doesn't explain one minute in the history of the world. And most definitely doesn't explain a blinding miracle called John Malcolm Pearce. So why"—she touched a finger to the back of his hand—"don't you stop thinking the way you think you ought to think and start thinking the way you want to think? Because what you want to think, what they told you was the boyo fantasy useless indulgent part of you, might get you somewhere worth going to."

He gave her the sad smile again. "I really do wish."

"All right," Andrea said, "if all you can do is wish, then wish. Make believe with me. Pretend you heard John's voice. Pretend you know he's there. Now dig back into your medical mind and find an explanation. It can't be, but it is, you know it is, so there's got to be an explanation. A fact you overlooked or read wrong."

"Well, it's true—" He shook his head. "I can't."

"Yes, you can. It's okay. It's just make-believe."

"It's true that in the first days after an organ transplant"—he huffed air, he shook his head again, he signaled every which way that here was folly—"the organ has visitor status. It's doing the work of the old organ,

252

but it hasn't yet become integrated with the rest of the body. So in a very narrow technical sense, it still bears its original chemistry. Of course," he said emphatically, as she began to register excitement, "the situation will change. The first time there's a rejection episode, a shower of white blood cells from the recipient will invade the organ on the mistaken notion that it's a hostile invader. Assuming the organ withstands the attack— and cyclosporine helps the odds enormously—it emerges more closely related to the rest of the body. A blood relation, you might say."

Her heart seemed to leap to her throat She grabbed Phil's arm. "You mean rejection is the end?"

"Not at all. You know that. Minor episodes are normal. And useful. They help the doctors set the level of immunosuppressants."

"You don't understand," she said. "We can't let a rejection happen. It might change everything. The visitor status . . . how can he tell if he's starting to reject? How do we stop it?"

"The patient doesn't feel it," Phil said, "not if it's minor. That's why they go to clinic and get biopsied, every week in the beginning, eventually once a month if all goes well."

"The weekly pain in the neck," she said. She bit her lip. "But can't they give him enough cyclosporine—"

"It's a fine line, you see," Phil said. "You want the immune system to accept the new organ as part of the body. But you don't want it so relaxed that it lets in dangerous invaders. If he gets too big a dose of immunosuppressants, no, he won't reject, but he'll be like someone with AIDS—he'll die of infection."

"So you're telling me we may not have much time."

"I'm not telling you anything. I'm playing make-believe with you."

"What you just said, though, about the heart being a

visitor and then it's not a visitor—that's a fact."

"I've explained it very primitively, but I guess you could call it a fact. But Andrea, you mustn't—"

She grabbed a handful of nibbles from the lacquered bowl, closed her fist around them, opened her fist, and watched the crumbs rain down. She thought about kisses—how had kisses brought her here? And how had this man who'd been sent to dissuade her convinced her more than ever that she alone knew what was what?

The hot sweaty pull of exhaustion tried to claim her again. How kind Phil and the others would be if only she recanted. They would build her a fine white room and bring her soup and dreams. But if it had been the other way around, if she were the one who'd been stolen, would John settle for sleep?

She heard his vibrant voice at their wedding. "To have and to hold, from this day forth, so long as we both shall live."

And so long as we both shall love, we both shall live. I love you forever, my John.

Chapter 34

The day of Sam Mancuso's funeral, the sun came out and the thermometer made it up into the high forties. The trees were still barren, but Margo saw a greenish haze around the branches of the maple in the front yard, and the forsythia were starting to swell — a day heady with promise of spring, though not for poor Sam.

She and Hank sat with Bobby Cline and Mike Weller, Hank and Bobby in their surgical masks, Mike's face almost as white as the masks because the heart that had died in Sam would have been his if his beeper had been working.

The priest's words brought her back to the graveyard in Kent. The crowded chapel was warm, but she shivered with remembered cold. Earlier in the morning Hank had said that one of these days he wanted to go to Kent to pay his respects to John, say hello and goodbye to his old heart. He hadn't mentioned wanting to take her to the Plaza.

Afterward they got into her car and she maneuvered into line behind the hearse and limousines.

"What a wipe-out." Hank took off his mask and dropped it into Margo's black leather purse. "Those kids."

"The little guy can't be more than, what, two and a half? Just a baby," she said with a sigh. "And Sam sick all that time—I don't think Donny ever knew what it was like to have a real father. I hope Elaine finds another man."

Hank gave her a sidelong glance. "You used to be furious when people talked about your next husband."

"Because I knew you were going to live."

"And if I hadn't?"

"Oh, I would have clung to my martyrdom. Spent the rest of my life doing good works."

"A Jewish Sister Theresa," Hank said. "Bringing low-fat cooking to the poor."

Margo giggled, and he did too, and the car filled up with the sound, and then his laughter turned into sobs.

"Are you okay?" she said. "Want me to pull over?"

He got a tissue out of her purse and blew his nose. "I don't want to go to the cemetery. I want to work on my poem. Let's go home. Can we get away with it?"

You've gotten away with everything else, so why not this, she wanted to say, but she swallowed the unkind words, tried to pretend she hadn't thought them. She told Hank he'd been valiant to go to the service and Elaine was no doubt touched to pieces, and later on in the day she'd run over to the Mancuso house, bring a basket of wonderful fruit for the kids.

"Ms. Kovner, where would I be without you?"

She signaled to make a left turn and pulled out of the procession at the light on the corner of Farmington and Broad. "Where Sam is," she said.

"You think so, huh?"

The words had slipped out unbidden, but she wasn't about to recant. "I do think so. Do you resent it?"

"Now you sound like Mickie."

"Do you, Hank? Resent it? Is that why you—" She couldn't finish the sentence.

"Why I what?"

Why you don't touch me. Why you don't talk about

256

our second honeymoon.

Why you've fallen in love with vanilla.

She focused on the traffic; then she burst out, "Like a child."

"Come again?" Hank said.

"When you want to get rid of your mask, where do you put it? In my purse. When you want a tissue, where do you get it? From my purse. I'm not your mother, Hank. You do know that, don't you? I may have saved your life, but I'm not your mother."

"Sure, I know it. If you were my mother, I would have put the tissue back in your purse. After I used it."

She braked, and a car honked at her; a driver yelled as he swerved around her.

"Jesus Christ," Hank said.

She pulled over to the side of the street and turned off the engine. "Are you okay?"

"Oh, I'm fine. If I weren't wearing a seatbelt, I would have gone through the window, but they need more organ donors, right? May I ask what the hell is going on?"

Margo looked at her gloved hands on the wheel, at the placid façade of the *Courant* building across the street, everywhere but at Hank. She would sit there forever, not moving, not talking, until someone scooped her up, made all her decisions for her.

"Margo?"

Remembering her breezy dismissal of Debbie's fears. But hadn't she known even then that Debbie was right?

"Hey, kid. Anybody home?"

Remembering the hot wax ripping out her hair to turn her thighs to silk and Hank hadn't even noticed.

"Margo. For Chrissake."

She licked her lips; she sucked in air. "Are you in love with Andrea?" Still not looking at him for fear she would see the truth before she heard the lie.

257

"How can you ask me that?" he said. Answering her question with a question to postpone the telling of the lie. Indignant the way he got — Skip did too — when he had reason to feel uneasy.

The dull ache inside her got bigger, grew claws. God, how she'd wanted him to explode with laughter, ruffle her exfoliated hair, make her feel a fool but so cherished that she knew on her the foolishness looked good.

"How can I not ask it? You've been mooning around ever since she was here—"

"That's the old prednisone moon face," he said, but the joke didn't work.

"—crying, craving vanilla, being obsessive about your poem."

"She made me want to work. She believes in me as a writer. Is there something immoral in that?"

"I don't know about immoral," Margo said, "but I'm beginning to think there's something wrong with it."

"Because you don't want me to be anything more than an insurance broker — a sick one at that. Did it occur to you to let me drive today?"

"Let you? Listen to yourself, Hank. Is it up to me to let you? As I said, I'm not your — uh oh." The rearview mirror flashed red. A police car was pulling up behind her.

The officer had scrubbed pale skin with freckles on the nose; he looked about Debbie's age. "See that sign there, ma'am? The one that says NO-STANDING ZONE? May I see your license?"

She opened her purse to get her wallet, but there was Hank's surgical mask, and impulsively she took it out and waved it. "Officer, don't be alarmed by the mask. We're not bandits. My husband just had a heart transplant, and he has to wear this when strangers are near."

The officer peered in the window as Hank adjusted the mask. "You the one I saw on TV? Channel Eight?"

"That's right," Margo said. "The six o'clock news a couple of weeks ago." She handed him her license.

He gave it a glance and handed it back. "The heart came from that writer?"

"John Malcolm Pearce," Margo said. "I'm sorry about the no-standing zone, officer. Hank said he didn't feel well, and of course I pulled right over."

"You okay now, Mr. Corman? You need an escort to the hospital?"

Hank's cheeks puffed as he smiled behind the white gauze. "It was just gas, officer. I'll be fine as soon as I get to a john."

Margo started the car, pulled out onto Broad Street, turned left on Asylum. The publicity that had been meant to buy a new heart for Sam had done nothing more important than get them out of a ticket. Oh, Mickie kept saying there had been an increase in donors, but would the benefit come home? If, God forbid, Hank's heart turned out not to work for him, would another heart show up in time? Please, dear heaven, no more funerals!

Hank took off his mask. This time he put it in his pocket. They drove the rest of the way in silence.

At home, Hank said, "I don't mean to be ungrateful."

"I'm not looking for gratitude."

"The hell you're not. And you have a right to it. Thank you, Margo."

"You're welcome," she said stiffly.

"I know it's been a rough few years. I'm sorry. As soon as I'm up to it, we'll start having some fun."

But he didn't say anything about the Plaza, and he didn't say anything about Andrea, and he didn't kiss her or even touch her. He hurried off to his desk to work on his poem.

It seemed right because it was perfectly wrong that Mark Feingold called at three with an invitation.

Would the Cormans please come to the memorial for John? He'd already talked to Dr. McKay, and Dr. McKay would come too. Mark would hire a car for the drive to New York. They would all be his guests at the Plaza.

She knew Hank would be thrilled by the invitation, but she didn't want to tell him. "I didn't want to interrupt your work," she heard herself explaining later; though of course the truth was that she was punishing him by withholding the delicious news.

She was ashamed — all the more because she felt distinctly satisfied as minute after minute passed and Hank, oblivious in the next room, didn't know what she knew.

Oh God, was this what all the waiting and praying and sacrificing had come down to, this sickening blend of satisfaction and shame? Was this what John Malcolm Pearce had died for?

Hank deserved to be punished, but she couldn't bear the insult to John. She pasted a smile on her face and went to break the great news.

Chapter 35

Andrea could hardly believe what Mark was telling her.

"What made you decide to invite him?" she said. "I thought you wanted to pretend he didn't exist."

"No, you're the one who's pretending," he shot back. "I absolutely believe in Hank Corman. I thought you'd be thrilled to have him there."

She looked down at the telephone, at her own hands, at the fine old gold of the wedding band that Grand'Anna had worn for half a century.

"If you believe in him, let him be who he wants to be," she said.

"He doesn't need me to let him be himself. He needs you to do that."

"Please, Mark, if you can't be with me, at least don't be against me. But you might have another chat with Phil Porter before you close the door. He's in my army now."

"I'm sure he likes you—"

"Call him," she insisted, "and call me back."

Mark called back and told her that Phil said he was in her army but she didn't know where the war was—it was inside her own heart.

She tried to forget Phil and Mark. Sukie was coming from London. She would help.

Oh my darling Daddy, you would have helped—this

was what you wanted, but you left the theater too soon.

She was cold all the time. Twice a day she went down to Tortilla Flats on the corner and ordered a bowl of chili. Peppery food was supposed to cool you, but she knew she was running skewed, and the chili helped warm her a little. Kept her mouth feeling purified and ready for married kisses.

Late at night in her JMP-monogrammed shirt, television set propped on the edge of her aching double bed, she found a friend on a late night talk show. A plainsuited midwestern woman, the wife — "Don't you dare call me the widow" — of an American soldier missing in Vietnam eighteen years. She waved a Baggie of bones and declared, "The science doesn't exist that can prove this is my husband. I say he's still alive and I mean to find him."

Andrea grabbed the telephone and called Mark. "I'm sorry, I know you were sleeping, I hope I didn't disturb Annette, but we've got to get a tape of this show, we have to meet this woman, make her a general. She refused to go to the funeral, Mark. His mother went, the kids went, but she wouldn't go. Do you remember that awful day in Kent when Sukie said I would be like an MIA wife if we kept John going on a respirator? I turned out to be an MIA wife anyway. This woman is my sister."

The next day she dialed 999-8888 when the Steve Coe show was on the air. It rang a full four minutes; then the cocky voice was saying, "You're on the line with Steve Coe."

"Hello, Steve, this is Andrea Pearce."

"Hey, Andrea Pearce, my old buddy. So what's your opinion about the mayor? Does he need a morals transplant or what?"

"I have no opinion about that, Steve. I just wanted to tell you and your listeners some wonderful news. My husband isn't dead, he's missing in action, and if all of you will write to your representatives, maybe Washington will wake up."

"Thanks for calling, baby, keep those cards and letters coming."

She listened to the echoing emptiness for a while; then she hung up the telephone and turned the radio on, fiddled with the dial until she hit WKNO. A man with a sandpaper voice was talking about why the mayor wouldn't last the term. As if she didn't exist; as if she hadn't just announced the best news since the dawn of the world.

She lay in the dark reliving kisses, undiminished for being tasted daily. So what if his hair was different, sweet dearest it was you, the thrill that only you, not a single doubt, only stealing what was mine in the first place, we will look back on this winter and laugh.

One more day and he would be there. Desperate to call him but sitting on her hands because if Margo knew what was what she would fill the gas tank with sand.

No longer up to going out. Tortilla Flats delivered.

Yes, Mother, I have something to wear.

But what about John? Nothing right in the closet. Most of his clothes were still on Forty-ninth Street. Because there had been that feeling of hers that many things shouldn't begin until they were married, at which instant the whole world would change.

She got Pete to call her a cab that would take her door to door.

Up the stairs to his flat in a bound. Key trembling in the lock.

Everything inside as it should have been. Foreign agents had not invaded. The walls in the front room, his workroom, still dense with mounted and laquered maps, all the places he had gone and the ones not yet seen, the ones they would visit together. Here, above his word machines, a map of his native Toronto; here, above his collection of dictionaries, the Old Town of Geneva; here the market district of Mexico City; here—with cigarette burns along one edge, he'd never explained those burns—the glory that Lebanon was.

In the back room, the bedroom, hung a map of Andrea painted by Ellen Lampert, a four-foot square acrylic head, all eyes and a blast of bright hair. "I have to have that painting," he'd said, their second night at her place on Jane Street. "Then you have to have it," she had said. Next morning they'd hired a van to cart the painting uptown. He'd taken down the Riopelle print hanging opposite his bed, hammered in a second hook, and fiddled the head into place while Andrea lolled on his bachelor striped blankets and lazily offered instructions. Do you remember sweetie what you said. That when we had to spend a night apart you'd make love to me anyway. Show me, I said, and you did, and afterward you made us omelettes with bacon and Canadian cheddar, omelettes that crunched and yielded, were all and everything.

Same blanket on the bed today. On it almost every sock he owned—four or five dozen pairs. The all-important prenuptial sock sort, she remembered him saying in Kent. He'd started the morning of their wedding as an act of meditation. Had run out of time.

She picked up a kelly green cotton anklet with yellow vertical stripes. Its mate sat atop their dryer in the laundry on Twelfth Street. She kissed it and put it in her pocket. She opened the closet.

The sight of his second best Donegal tweed sports coat made her swoon a little. She rested her cheek against a sleeve.

"Hello, guys," she said, sliding hangers along the pole. She stroked the softness of a navy cashmere blazer. "I've got some good news and some bad news. The good news is Mark Feingold is throwing a party. The bad news"—her voice began to crack and she bit into the cool black silk of a dress of hers that had never made it back downtown—"the bad news is only one of you can come. And it's got to be a suit."

She turned away from the disappointed faces of the sports coats. Suits clamored for her attention. The chalk-striped navy with the unvented jacket, normally the soul of dignity, flapped its arms wildly. The brown-and-tan check, the one that made him look donnish and pubbish and Scotland Yard, tried to grab her around the waist. The suede suit she'd had made for him—golden reddish brown to match his hair—just hung there, though, knowing she knew it was right. And a blue-and-white bold striped shirt; a yellow silk tie with blurted blue octagons on it; socks, a subtle light brown and yellow weave; an unopened tube—he too had bought a trousseau—containing a rolled-up pair of royal blue silk almost-bikini briefs. She carefully packed a brown leather weekend bag. Added the comb and brush she'd bought him in London. A monogrammed handkerchief.

When she got back to her building, Pete said he'd given her friend the keys.

Sukie was waiting in the living room. "Hello, love."

"Hello, sweetie." The women hugged, and Andrea said, "I'm glad you came. It's going to be a swell party. I just picked up some things for John. Come to the kitchen, I'll make you a cuppa. What are you going to wear?"

"I'm wearing a black-and-white checked suit with a mid-calf pleated skirt, a gray silk shirt, and gray kid button-up boots. What I wore," Sukie said firmly, "to George's father's funeral."

"You wouldn't." Andrea filled the flat round glass kettle, got a flame going under it.

"John is dead, Andrea. This is a memorial service. I'm not going to wear purple sequins."

"Not purple. Yellow. For faith. Like Mrs. Aquino. The ribbon on the old oak tree."

Sukie burst into tears.

Andrea put an arm around her. "Don't you want him to be alive?"

"Of course I do. But I know that my wanting it doesn't make it so."

"If you could just consider it. Instead of looking at me in that tragic way."

Sukie snuffled up her tears. "I don't know how to begin to consider it."

"Mark," Andrea said with a nod, "told me the same thing. But you have to admit that the realities of the world aren't limited by the limits of your mind."

"I deserve better than that, dammit," Sukie said. "I just got off a beastly flight, and George has gotten some little girl pregnant, and you're not playing fair."

Andrea looked at her calmy. "Everything is fair except John's being dead. Will you at least wear some yellow diamonds?"

Chapter 36

Skip was on the phone at seven in the morning, sounding like the end of the world. "Mom, there's something you have to know. It looks as though Andrea's flipping out. She went on the radio yesterday, this wild man Steve Coe, and she said John is still alive, he's just missing in action."

"Oh God. Poor Andrea." Margo sank down into a chair. She could hear the sound of Hank's shower upstairs. Debbie would be down any minute. "How did you find out?"

"Sara gets up early and runs, then reads the *Post* while she has her breakfast. There was a story on page six, where they have all the gossip. Maybe you shouldn't come to New York."

"Or maybe more than ever we should." Margo's mind hopped and skipped. If anything would quickly cure Hank of his crush on Andrea, it might be knowing that her feeling for him was grounded in delusion. "I'll call Mark Feingold," she told Skip, "and check things out. If I don't call you back, honey, we're still on for dinner tonight. Meanwhile, let's keep this just between us."

But Debbie didn't need to read the *Post* to know that something was wrong.

"Don't go to New York," she said to her parents at breakfast.

"Why on earth not?" Margo managed to say, pumping light and air into her voice. Did they give Oscars for best supporting mother?

Debbie's mouth crumpled. "I'm scared that Daddy's going to die."

"Oh Debbie. Daddy's going to be fine. Gar wouldn't let him go as far as East Hartford if he hadn't scored perfectly at clinic this week. And Gar's going to be with us every minute in case he so much as breaks a toenail. Not that he's going to."

"He's my father! If he dies, you can have another husband, but I'll never have another father."

Hank started to whistle "Fine and Dandy."

"Go to your room," Margo snapped at Debbie.

Debbie stared in shock. "What did you say?"

"You heard me. Go to your room." Hating her own unfairness but not stopping. "Move it. Now."

"How can you do this?" Tears streamed down Debbie's face. "I don't think you care about our family anymore. Ever since you changed your hair, you've been different. I'll go to my room but don't expect me to come out."

"What's the matter with you?" Hank asked Margo. "You really jumped down her throat."

"She was carrying on, and I couldn't take it. And somehow your whistling just didn't help. I'm sorry," she said stiffly, "if you think I was unfair."

"Maybe"—he reached for the apple butter—"we should bring her with us. Maybe she feels left out because we're going to have dinner with Skip."

"Do you think so?" She leaped to bask in his familial tenderness. "I bet you're right. She's got that big biology test tomorrow, or I'd suggest it. And she's awfully excited about staying at Ginger's again. After a night with that household, I think this one looks normal! But we must plan a family weekend in New York, absolutely." She looked up at the clock. "I'd better get

268

moving."

She hurriedly got down a red plastic tray, spread a pink flowered napkin on it, poured two goblets of skimmed milk, set them on the tray, and added a plate of carob brownies. She carried the tray to Debbie's room and knocked on the door. "Room service."

"Leave me alone," Debbie said.

"I can't. I love you too much. Let me in. Please. I have a special breakfast dessert. Brownies."

Debbie opened the door. "You used to make real brownies. With chocolate chips. They were pure fudge inside. The best brownies in the world."

"They were, weren't they?" Margo set the tray down on Debbie's dresser. "Do you know, I still dream about chocolate? Our wedding cake was marble and I remember perfectly the taste of that chocolate vein running through the white. But it's not worth the dues." She sipped milk. "I'm sorry I snapped. I know the transplant has been hard on you. But look at poor Sam Mancuso, and Mike Weller still waiting. We could be a lot worse off."

Debbie sat on the edge of her bed. "That doesn't mean you have to go to New York. I was thinking—it was Ginger's idea, actually, her mother's new boyfriend is a lawyer: You could get a court order keeping Andrea away from him."

"Why would I want to do that?" Margo wondered if Debbie could see the heat rising behind her eyes. "You're forgetting how much we owe her. Aren't you going to eat anything, honey?"

"Do we owe her Daddy?" Debbie said.

Margo looked out at the falling snow. The longest winter in history. So easy to think of Debbie as a baby, but she was smart enough and brave enough to see a false spring for what it was. A part of Margo wanted to hug her, thank her, congratulate her, offer her the truth of shared dreads. To what good end, though? And the impulse to calm was a habit that couldn't be easily shucked.

"You're blowing this up into a myth. She wants Daddy to write a poem, keep her husband's name alive. Strange, yes, and I won't pretend it thrills me, but hardly a calamity. Keep your fingers crossed, honey. Maybe tomorrow will be the end of it. Maybe she'll say a final goodbye to her husband and she'll find peace and we will too. Good heaven, look at the time. Take a brownie and let's hit the road."

Debbie seemed somewhat convinced, which helped Margo to believe her own words, but at the bus stop the plea came again: "Won't anything make you reconsider going?"

Margo drove straight to West Hartford Center and the Temple on the Green.

The receptionist had the tallest gray beehive she'd seen in years. And a kind smile. "The rabbi is on the telephone, Mrs. Corman, but if you'll wait just a moment. Would you like to sit down?"

Margo said no thanks, she would take another look at those intriguing photographs outside.

"The rabbi took them himself when he hiked the Appalachian Trail. Talented, isn't he?"

She was standing in front of a Depression-style portrait of a hollow-eyed farm family when Rabbi Klein appeared. "Hank is okay?" he said, as he led her toward his study.

"He's recovering beautifully. The doctors are letting him go to New York overnight. We're supposed to leave in a couple of hours."

"The Big Apple. A little holiday?"

"Not exactly a holiday." She settled into a green leather armchair across from his desk. The room had an airy feeling, even with the yards of books and the dark upholstery. A guitar hung from pegs over the desk. There were framed photographs of Justice Brandeis, Bob Dylan, and some whitebearded rabbis she didn't recognize. "There's a memorial service tonight for John Malcolm Pearce. Hank and I were invited. My daughter begged us not to make the trip. She thinks something terrible is going to happen to Hank."

"Something physical or something spiritual?"

Margo considered. "Both, maybe."

"And her fear got to you?" He steepled bony fingers under his long intense face. "You came to me for a spell from the Kabbalah?"

She laughed. "Thank you, Mitchell. I needed that. But —" She spread open her hands to tell him that neither reason nor jokes could make the fear go away.

"Let me ask you a question, Margo. Is this a trip you want to make?"

"Yes. All right, yes and no. Yes because of how much I owe Andrea."

"Ah." The rabbi nodded.

"That's also the no part. I owe her so much, I don't know what I wouldn't do for her."

"Margo, you realize you have given this woman a great deal. You stood in for her at her husband's funeral. You let her into your life. Above all else, you and Hank have given her the consolation of knowing that her husband's heart is still beating." He paused, and then he said, "I read *The New York Post* with my breakfast; I find it more digestible than the *Times*. If that satisfaction has contorted in Andrea's mind, you are not to blame. You are not responsible. You could, with a clear conscience, break the connection."

"No." Margo got up and wandered over to the wall for a closer look at the photograph of Bob Dylan. "Did you take this?"

"I did."

271

"I thought he became a born-again Christian."

"He's still a great musician. Why are you in thrall to Andrea?"

" 'In thrall.' I like that." She sat down. She looked at him; he was waiting. "I owe her more than you know."

He nodded.

"I'm having a hard time telling you."

Smiling slightly: "Evidently. But you came here because you need to tell someone. I guarantee, whatever your secret is, I've heard darker."

"Darker than wishing for someone's death?" She let out a long breath. "No, it's worse than wishing. I prayed to God. For someone to die so Hank could have his heart."

"And the Almighty heard you and reached out and caused John Malcolm Pearce to skid off a snowy road? Margo, Margo. Do you know what you're guilty of? Arrogance. A child's arrogance. The sort of innocent arrogance that makes a little girl believe quite literally that if she steps on a crack she may break her mother's back. Magical thinking, the psychiatrists call it. An arrogance that covers our rage at our real powerlessness. There was no evil in your prayer. You were just telling God how sad you were that you couldn't do more for your husband. I have every confidence that He heard you right."

She closed her eyes. "I feel foolish."

"Which is worse, feeling evil or foolish? Don't be too quick to answer. It's not a simple question. My favorite of Solomon's proverbs — yes, I am sometimes rabbinical enough to quote from the Scriptures — is the one that says: 'Every way of a man is right in his own eyes, but the Lord weigheth the heart.' The wisdom of those words is so wonderful that their obverse is equally true. Sometimes the ways of a man are wrong in his own eyes, and still the Lord weigheth the heart. We are not

272

the best judges of whether we are good or bad. Or clever or foolish. If you want one man's opinion, you are neither bad nor foolish. And you need a vacation. Not just a night in New York."

"We promised ourselves Paris. When Hank has completely convalesced."

"Sounds good to me."

Margo rose and gathered her bag. " 'The Lord weigheth the heart . . .' What is a heart?"

"On one level a mechanism, and on another — the essence, I suppose. Call it soul, psyche, personality, character, what have you."

"Do you think any of the second level gets transplanted?"

"No." Flatly. "I don't."

"There have been moments since the surgery, and now I'm going to sound more than foolish, when Hank has seemed to be someone new. An out-of-character phrase, an unlikely reference. Whistling a tune he never whistled before."

"Serious illness is a watershed for many people, Margo. Underneath he may feel that his old ways brought him to the brink of death. You can't blame him for wanting to change. You may have to allow him" — the rabbi tilted his chair and crossed his legs — "to reinvent himself. Not so easy when there are children involved, I know, but I think yours are old enough and wise enough to understand."

"Am I?"

The rabbi smiled, and she decided she liked him very much and would never again mock the jeans and guitar. "Do you believe he loves you?"

"Yes," she said without hesitation.

"Then you'll manage." He stood. "Come to temple some Friday night or Saturday morning. It would be a joy to see you there. Meanwhile I'll be thinking of you,

Margo."

His words buoyed her, and when she got to her office there was a message from Sue McKay: "Hank needs Gar and you need me. I'm coming along for the ride." New York would be dangerous, but she wouldn't be alone. God was not against her — she would triumph.

She thought of Mitchell Klein thinking of her as they checked in at the Plaza.

A hundred times before, during the darkest hours of Hank's illness, she had pictured Hank filling out the registration form; she'd made an icon of the imagined moment. The reality — Hank nervous and inward and hardly aware of her, and the McKays sniping incessantly at each other (and who needed chaperons, however dear, on a second honeymoon) — was so different from the jolly and tender moment she'd imagined that she wanted to scream.

Only Skip's arrival from downtown saved her. Never mind that he hadn't been part of the original Plaza fantasy. He looked tall and solid and jaunty, with rosy cheeks and a tangy cold-air aroma because he'd walked the fifty blocks from his dormitory. A straight shot up Fifth Avenue, he said, and walking everywhere was the only way to keep your body alive in New York.

He was full of pronouncements. After five months at NYU he owned Manhattan. He'd never before set foot in the Plaza, but he had it on reliable information that Trader Vic's, the Polynesian restaurant a flight down from the Oak Bar, was not the place for dinner — strictly tourist; the Oyster Bar was a better choice. Or if they wanted to be real New Yorkers like him and venture out of the hotel, he would show them some great little places. There was fresh pasta in a West Village hideaway, not yet discovered by the yuppies, and he knew the absolutely best restaurant in Chinatown, Phoenix Garden, in a secret arcade — Sara Simon's older sister had taken them there—

"We're going to have a light meal in our room," Margo said. "The trip was tiring for Daddy. Will you join us, honey? I'm sure you can find some excitements on the menu." He looked wistful, and she said, "Next time we come to New York, we'll do it your way. We'll stay downtown, and we'd like to meet your Sara."

As they walked to the elevator, she had the feeling that everyone around them had read the *Post* that morning. She concentrated on the display cases full of brilliant silk scarves and perfume in cut-glass bottles. The wonderful Plaza.

"The first time in thirteen years that I've had my own hotel room," Sue McKay said in the elevator. "Thank God I won't have to share a bathroom with him. Do you know he never—"

"Stow it, Sue," Gar said.

The Cormans had a corner suite, all pink and earth tones. Their living room had views straight up the middle of Central Park and to the East River and beyond. Hank and Skip stood at the glass trying to one-up each other with their knowledge of New York buildings. Margo went into the bedroom to hang up their clothes for tomorrow. In her Plaza fantasy, Hank came up behind her and kissed her neck while she was unpacking. But, of course, with Skip there, he wouldn't.

Sue and Gar came over, and Margo ordered drinks and salads, dressing on the side.

The doorbell rang.

"I've heard about speedy room service," Skip said. "But this takes the cake."

"Brings the cake," Gar said.

"Not with Margo ordering," Hank said.

Skip opened the door. It was a bellman, not a room service waiter. He held a brown leather overnight bag. For Mr. Henry Corman, he said.

Hank unzipped the bag. He took out an envelope and opened it. "From Andrea," he said. He shrugged, he made funny eyebrows, but nobody laughed. Sue moved closer to Margo. "She says it's something for me to wear tomorrow." Tenderly, almost reverently, he extracted a brown suede suit, a blue-and-white striped shirt, and a blue-and-yellow tie and laid them out on the couch — this man who tossed jackets over chairs and dangled sweaters from hooks.

Margo could see the monogram on the shirt: JMP. She imagined Andrea taking it out of a drawer, carefully putting it in the bag — such a tiny useless move in the face of almighty death that Margo wanted to weep. She went into the bathroom and drank two glasses of cold water. She liked hotel bathrooms, the little soaps in their wrappers, the neat undemanding towels. She and Hank had once made love in a hotel bathroom, the mirror facing the tub had turned them on like crazy. A million years ago. His cousin Sandy's first wedding, in Cleveland, and the daughter born of that marriage had recently gotten married herself.

When she went back into the living room, Hank was wearing the suit coat. Gar was pretending not to be there.

"No," she said.

Everyone looked at her.

"Take it off, Hank. I beg you."

"Isn't it enough you tell me what to eat and when to go to sleep and did I remember to brush my teeth? You're going to tell me what I can and can't wear?"

"I'm not telling you; I'm asking you. For my sake, and for yours. You're Hank Corman and you belong in Hank Corman's clothes. Anyway, I happen to like your gray suit better. Fawn isn't your color."

"I'm wearing his heart. Why can't I wear his suit?"

"I want to go home," Margo said.

"Nuts," Sue said. "I was about to order a bottle of champagne. To toast the madness of life."

"You know you can't handle champagne," Gar said. "You'll get a splitting headache. Did you bring Fiorinal?"

"Well, what kind of headache should I get?" He gave her a blank look, and she said, "We're splitting, aren't we?"

"You can have champagne in the limo," Margo said. "Where's that card with our driver's number?"

"I don't want to go home," Hank said. He pointed to the windows. "Look at those lights. Look at them, Margo. It's five years since I've been in New York. I want to watch the skaters at Rockefeller Plaza. I want to see a show. I want to walk around Washington Square with my son."

"Next time," Margo said softly. "We'll come back soon, and it will be very, very different."

"I want to finish my poem," Hank said. "I know it's not much, but it's mine."

"Then finish it," Margo said. "Nobody's saying you should throw it away."

"Oh, no? You want us to go home and forget all about John Malcolm Pearce. You want me to be what I was before I got sick, just take up where I left off. But there weren't any poems in that life. I'm not saying I wasn't happy. I was probably happier than most people. I love you and Skip and Debbie, there were lots of laughs—I was very happy. But no poems. I think between the laughs I worried too much. About making money, about doing right by everyone. For forty-five years I was a good boy, and where did it get me? Almost dead. Then I had the luck to get a special heart, and you want to pretend I didn't. Business as usual. Is that what I almost died for?"

Sue got up, smoothing her tweed skirt. "Maybe you

277

two could use some privacy."

"Stick around," Hank said. "You'll hear it all on the telephone anyway."

"Hank!" Margo said.

"Hank!" he mimicked. "You make me hate the sound of my own name."

Skip got up, kissed both his parents, and wordlessly walked into the bedroom, shutting the door behind him. Margo was gratefully aware of the absence of musical riffs — Sara had taught him some grace.

"Listen, old boy," Gar was saying to Hank, "I think you're operating under a misapprehension here."

Hank moved to another window and pulled the curtains back all the way. "Is that so?"

"What you're going through has nothing to do with the heart you got. I heard the same speeches from Sam Mancuso when he got his heart: Is this all there is? Is this what life is about? Bobby Cline went through it too, even though he's younger. Talk to his mother sometime if you want an earful. Hell, I've seen men get starry-eyed after bypass surgery, sometimes after one night of chest pains. Quit their jobs and take up painting, leave their wives for younger women, go off to India, the whole bit. You're turning fifty in, what, three months?"

"May Day," Margo said. "Two and a half months."

"So you didn't need ticker problems to make you start asking questions. But you had the ticker problems. Big ones. Four shitty years, if you'll pardon the technical jargon. And then the transplantation surgery and a lot of post-op drama. For much of which, I take the blame. All in all, my good friend Henry, it was just about guaranteed that you'd want to make a right-angle turn in your life."

"Interesting," Sue murmured. "About men turning fifty. You always were a year or two ahead of your class."

Gar flushed and Hank roared.

"Sue," Margo said, "I just had a marvelous idea. Let's go to Paris."

"You and me?" Sue said.

"You and me and who knows," Margo said. She felt definitely giddy.

"Now that's interesting," Sue said.

"I used to pot," Margo said, "did you know that? Bowls and plates and what-have-you. My teacher said I was promising"—she shrugged—"and then I got married. Would I love to put my hand to the wheel again. In some little Left Bank studio."

"Paris," Sue said. "Clothes. I'm so damn tired of tweed."

"They're funny, aren't they?" Gar said to Hank.

"Funny?" Sue said. "I wasn't being funny, Margo, were you?"

"Not that I was aware of."

"What about the kids?" Gar said.

"Yes indeed, Daddy dear," Sue said. "What about them?"

"I want to stay in New York long enough to see a show," Hank said. "How did we get from that to Paris?"

"Just lucky, I guess," Margo said.

"You can't do this"—Hank put his hand over his chest—"to a sick man."

"You're not a sick man. You're a healthy man with a healthy young heart. Isn't that right, Gar?"

"I think we should all get some sleep," Gar said. "We've come this far. We might as well wrap things up tomorrow. But, for Chrissake, Hank, don't wear those clothes. Doctor's orders."

Room service arrived. Margo got Skip from the bedroom. To her amazement, she was hungry. Everyone was.

279

Skip went downtown to study. Or maybe to escape. Gar told Sue it was time for them to go.

"What about my champagne?"

"We can have it downstairs. Or in our room."

"Our room? Our room?"

Margo got a pale blue nightgown out of their suitcase — she'd also tucked in a brand-new nightie, a heavy ivory satin edged with ivory lace, but she knew she'd be inviting disappointment to put it on — and she went to wash her face and brush her teeth. She turned on the table lamp between the two double beds and got into the bed farther from the bathroom, the way she did every night at home.

Hank put on the blue-and-white striped pajamas she'd packed for him. "Are my medicines all here?"

"Yes, darling. There's your kit, on the desk."

"I guess I've been an idiot. I'm going to concentrate on being the best damned transplant patient they ever had."

"It thrills me to hear that," she said. "Yes."

"I'm going to beat the record. I owe it to Hank."

She looked at him. "You mean you owe it to John."

"That's what I said. I owe it to John."

"You're going to double the record," she said. "Take your prednisone and persantine and do your teeth, and let's go to sleep."

"Did you remember the fluoride rinse?"

"It's on the bathroom sink."

He did what he had to do and then got into bed with her and encircled her from behind. "I'm bushed."

"Me, too." Though it was lovely to have him in her bed and she wasn't absolutely bushed.

"I wish I didn't need sleep. There's so much to do."

"And so much time to do it," Margo said. "You feel nice."

"I guess this isn't exactly the way you pictured the

280

Plaza, huh, kid? The McKays are having the champagne, and I'm thirty seconds from sleep. You think one sip of champagne would hurt me?"

"Who's going to be the world champion transplant patient? Anyway, we don't need alcohol. For anything."

He touched her breast, then slid his hand down to rest on her belly. "Well, tonight it's no alcohol and no anything."

"There's always the morning," Margo said.

But she stayed awake long after Hank fell asleep, the prisoner of his hand and the mocking sweetness of unanswered desire—prisoner of his self-centeredness and her own fears.

"Enough!" she finally cried out inside her head, exhausted from listening to her thoughts chase each other. She would see him through the memorial service, let him play it however he chose; and then the game was over. She wasn't going to collaborate in his undoing. That wasn't what love was about. She would rather be alone than live a lie. "But please, dear God, don't make me choose!" she prayed, as she tumbled into fitful sleep.

Sudden
Death

The ball may be deemed unfit for play when it is visibly cut or out of shape or so cracked, pierced or otherwise damaged as to interfere with its true flight or true roll or its normal behavior when struck . . . . If a ball break into pieces as a result of a stroke, a ball shall be placed where the original ball lay and the stroke shall be replayed, without penalty.

—THE RULES OF GOLF

Chapter 37

She couldn't sleep because he was so near and yet so far away. She left a note for Sukie, who was on Greenwich time and couldn't stay awake, and she went to Tortilla Flats to lose her mind in the din — Wall Street kids with slick haircuts shouting for frothy drinks over the rock 'n' roll. A table would have been nice, but she didn't want to eat, might never eat again, not even chili; and anyway the tall guy in the black T-shirt with the scribbled-on notepad was making it clear to others that no tables were to be had. She pressed her way toward the bar. A group of people cocooned in laughter, trailing corn chips, detached themselves from the mass and headed toward the door, and a single stool miraculously floated free. She sat down, put a ten-dollar bill on the bar, and ordered a Noches Buenos, the dark thick sweet spicy beer that reminded her of Indian pudding. See, Mom, I'm eating after all.

She was halfway down the bottle, shoulders easing and the small of her back warming, relaxed enough to survey the crowd without worrying who thought what about her, when a young man in jeans and a denim jacket came in from the outside, looking for someone or trying to look as if he were looking for someone, and she knew she knew him (or did she know that looking-for-someone look?). He saw her. Waved. Started toward her.

Skip Corman.

Her heart tripped crazily. A whir of illogical thoughts fought for center stage. He was here as an emissary? But she couldn't imagine who was less likely to send him, Margo or what's-his-name. He was wild about the local margaritas? Too nifty a coincidence.

"I'm glad you knew where to find me," she said brightly as he approached because she had to say something.

He tried for a grin. "Your doorman gave you up. Just like that." He chirped his fingers and the effortful gesture hung in the air between them.

She nodded. Cliff the night doorman had a standing order for chili whenever she headed this way, and she'd let him know he could count on it tonight.

"Buy you a drink?" she said.

He blushed. "I guess it better be a Coke. I've got a fake I.D. but I'm scared to use it." So young, so natural that she felt full of warmth for him even though she knew his being there had to mean trouble.

She ordered a Coke and another beer and moved the basket of tortilla chips so he could reach. "Everyone should have a fake I.D. Just for a change of pace. Sometimes when I go out I pretend I'm Leonora Whittlesey, my great-great-great-aunt. She was a wonderful feminist who used to dress like a man to get into forbidden places. Like bars."

"You told us about her," Skip said. "The night you came to West Hartford. It must be interesting to pretend to be a pretender."

"Well, yes. I never thought about it that way, but you're right. Though we're all pretenders, aren't we? I'm Andrea Sprague Olinger Pearce, but I'm not. Because whatever that means to whoever hears it, I'm more and less and different."

He pushed a tortilla chip through a dish of salsa. "The

286

big question in my family these days is: Who is Henry Corman?" He flapped his eyebrows the way Hank did to signal that he was being funny, but she heard an undercurrent of panic.

Her breath caught. "Oh God."

"Guess you don't want to think about that part of it. The wife and kiddies and all." The chip hovered; then he ate it.

Her throat went absolutely dry, and she guzzled beer, but it didn't touch the dryness. The more he strained to sound the jaunty cynic, the softer he seemed.

"Does it matter," she said, "if I tell you that I'd give almost anything not to hurt you?"

" 'Almost.' " He leaned into the word as if it were the very slip he'd been waiting for; he fixed reproachful eyes on her. "My mother wrote you a letter once — one of her sappy but sweet letters. 'My dear friend . . . 'Ring a bell? I seem to remember she said she'd give anything to heal your broken heart. There wasn't any 'almost' in there." His Coke came and he looked at it and then picked up the fresh bottle of beer and drank half of it down in a gulp.

"Your mother's a better person than I am. I won't dispute that for a minute." She touched his hand. "That's not what this is about, though."

"What is it about?" he burst out. "Geez, he's almost fifty years old. You can probably have any guy in New York" — his arm swung a wide arc to show her the possibilities on the very premises — "so what do you need my dad for? What's so great about him, anyway?" He started to cry but seemed not to notice. "Sometimes I wish he'd just died and gotten it over with. Do you know what it feels like to almost have gotten him back and then to lose him again?"

"Oh God, oh God, when you say that you make me wish that if John had to drive off that bridge he'd been

287

smashed to bits, burned up, ashes, nothing left over, not a cell." She looked at him, shaking her head for helplessness, her whole body shaking, and she gave a single dry sob and said, "But that's not what happened."

He didn't say anything, and she didn't either, and in the vacuum they heard the man next to them say, "Why don't we use your frequent flyer miles and go to Hawaii?" and the woman with him say, "Why don't you take a flying fluck?"

"Come on," Andrea said, leaving two dollars on the bar and taking Skip by the wrist, "let's get out of here."

Outside they gulped the cold, quiet air, as though all they had needed was to escape the place they'd been in.

"Take me home with you," Skip said. He burped beer.

"For milk and cookies?"

"I want to fluck you," he said.

She threw back her head and roared, then flung her arms around him, and they danced a mad dance on the corner of Washington and Twelfth. A passing cabbie saluted them with his horn.

"Skip, I love you. I really love you. And your mother and your sister — you're the best family I ever had, the only family. Oh God, I wish, I wish, I really do wish . . ."

He pulled free of her. "I wasn't kidding. I want you."

"But why?" She put her hand to her heaving chest, truly perplexed. "You probably have all the girls at NYU knocking on your door."

"Hey, you're not the only one with a right to strange tastes." He gave her a bold look — heart-stabbing boldness. "You'd be my first. I have a girlfriend but she draws the line. Or maybe I do. Because she's terrific but only terrific."

Andrea didn't move. She couldn't ever remember wanting so much not to say the wrong word, make the wrong gesture. This brave bull, unlikeliest of suitors.

288

How to give him whatever he needed to wake up the next morning ready to face the mirror?

"It wouldn't be fair to you," she finally said. "You deserve someone new."

"You're only ten years older than I am." He waved away a decade of her life.

"Yes, but I'm old, old—older than your mother, believe me. You don't want to get too close to me. I know things that maybe you'll never have to know."

"And my father knows them too?"

She nodded. "Even if I disappeared, it wouldn't undo the strange and wondrous thing that happened—it wouldn't make him the man he used to be."

"If I could cut out that heart and throw it back at you, I would."

She reeled. "No. Please. Stop. You don't see."

"I see what you're doing to my mother, and I hate you."

"Lucky Margo to have such loyalty."

"Don't condescend to me, dammit!"

Two men laden with shopping bags from D'Agostino's around the corner stopped and looked at her, and she shook her head to tell them she was okay, at least deserved what she was getting.

"I'm not condescending." Her voice begged him to believe her. "She really is the lucky one. No matter what happens. And I think she knows it even if you don't. I wish so so much that you wouldn't hate me."

"You want to have everything, but you can't."

"Some kind of everything." She jammed her hands into her pockets and hunched against the wind off the river and looked at the opaque sky. It didn't crack a smile. Alone, alone, and no hints to help her, just a roller-coaster momentum that swept and bumped her along—dizzying to the core but she was stuck with a book of tickets.

"I refuse to feel sorry for you," Skip said.

"I'm not asking you to. Just don't hate me. Maybe you think it would be disloyal not to, but I wish you could find a way."

"I don't have your knack for doing the impossible. Goodbye, Andrea." He stood there for a minute and then gave a little nod, a final nod, and moved on down Twelfth Street.

She stood watching him until he reached the light up at Hudson Street, hoping he would turn around and come back — but what would she do if he did?

She was almost at her building when she remembered Cliff's chili. She turned around because she couldn't bear to let anyone else down, not even a bowl's worth.

She fell asleep on her couch, still in her jeans and sweater and sneakers, her jacket on the floor. Dreams of flashing, whirling blackness — some infernal bar — grated her to the surface every time she went under. At something after seven she gave up on this tainted sleep and sought clarity in the angular whiteness of the double shower, adjusting one nozzle to blast her skin with steam, the other with ice, trying to wash off the night and Skip's hatred and make herself ready for yellow.

At high noon they were going to hang him, but she would dress to match the sun — she would blind them and he would escape. And someday Skip would understand, everyone would understand.

"Andrea love?" Sukie was knocking at the bathroom door, telling her the coffee was ready. Do you remember, oh do you remember the morning you dropped the filter and coffee sludge smeared the counter and you said, Well I've given you grounds.

Thank you but we only drink it yellow.

She blew her hair just so. She took her time with her makeup, adding apricot to the lime around her eyes, dusting her cheeks with peach.

She wasn't hungry, but Sukie had gotten sticky buns from Priscilla's and the crunchy sweetness lured her. A trap—the moment she put a piece in her mouth, hummed her satisfaction, Sukie set down her mug of tea and pounced.

"All right now, love, what's the scenario for today? Hank arrives at Frank E. Campbell's and you line everyone up to listen to his heart? And a gasp goes up from the crowd as one and all realize he's John?"

Andrea swallowed what was in her mouth, licked sweetness from her fingers.

"Then, let's see," Sukie went on, "Margo says, 'Take him, he's yours?' The two of you hug in the best American tradition—applause and cheers in the background—and she takes her runner-up trophy and heads for Hartford? And you and John come back here—no, scratch that, you head for Kent and the honeymoon goes on as though nothing had ever happened? Do I have it right?"

"Oh boy," Andrea said. "Talk about open-minded. You've set a new standard."

"I was thinking about that," Sukie said. "Yes, I went to Sarah Lawrence, my liberalism is pure, but I've learned a thing or two from George. Being open-minded doesn't mean you give up the right to make value judgments, to be just plain commonsensical. I'm afraid we've got a case of the emperor's new clothes here, my love. I've looked from every angle and I still say he's naked."

Andrea got up and paced the dining alcove. She felt little bubbles of energy exploding inside her, infusing her. This wasn't the path she'd meant to take, but wasn't destiny ever full of surprises? A heartbeat overheard, kisses that knew her name—tiny gossamer treasures, she'd thought them, scarcely more than hopes; but her challengers had offered a different mirror. Mark, Phil, and now Sukie had made her know the grandeur of her vision. She might have to endure Skip's hatred, but it wouldn't be for nothing.

"Well, I guess I'm part of a noble tradition — people bringing freedom from received opinions and being stoned for their trouble."

Sukie seemed to burst out of her chair. She grabbed Andrea by the shoulders. "He's dead! Dead, dead, dead! He died, and someday you're going to die, and I am, and the baby who was just born this second — nobody escapes. And you know what happens if you don't face that? You spend your whole bloody life dodging phantoms; you don't have a life. Face death and then forget it, or death owns you every minute, not just at the end. For the sake of everything that matters, stop denying!"

"But a part of Hank is dead and buried and no one's mourning him," Andrea said. "No one's telling Margo to stop denying."

"Can you really equate —" Sukie said, then shook her head and groaned. "There's no point in talking, is there?" She cupped her face with her hands, smiling sadly. "I miss you, Andrea."

Andrea touched her friend's shining hair. "I miss you too."

Sukie didn't say anything, and then the intercom buzzed, and Andrea nodded knowingly.

"Enter the men in white coats. This is where I say, 'Ah have always depended on the kindness of strangers.' " She lifted the receiver. "Good morning, Pete."

"Morning, Andrea. Gary Hodges is here."

"Right on time," she said gaily. "Please send him up."

Sukie's shoulders sagged. "I suppose it figures. The one person who'll do anything you ask. Is he going to witness for you today?"

"Actually, I had no idea he was coming. But it's a good thing he's here. Since I seem to be short of friends."

"Damn you, Andrea, you have fabulous friends. A

friend is not necessarily someone who agrees with you. Sometimes a friend has to save you from yourself."

"Not to be ungrateful, but the Crusades were fought by right-minded folk saving people from themselves. It's a pretty bloody tradition. I wouldn't sign on too quickly."

The doorbell rang.

Gary stood there in the hooded parka that made him look bald, trying for a casual smile. He thrust a brown paper bag at Andrea. "I thought you might need cheering up today. I brought a few of your favorites from the store. That homemade baked ham and some potato salad, and I got one of Mrs. Goode's cranberry breads."

"How really nice of you, Gary. All the places around here put rosemary in the potato salad. I like to taste the mayonnaise. Sukie, Gary, you remember each other, don't you?"

Sukie and Gary said they did.

"We were just having breakfast," Andrea said. "Will you join us?"

Gary eased down his hood but didn't open his jacket. "I ate breakfast before I left home. Wouldn't say no to a cup of coffee, though. Heater was out in the pickup, and it got kind of breezy on the highway." He took in the big open space. "Is this what they call a loft?"

She knew he read *Architectural Digest,* but she let him play the rube. "I think 'loft' is a bit much when you have a doorman. It's just an open apartment."

Sukie said she was dying to get out of her running clothes and jump into a shower — would they excuse her please. Andrea took down a mug and asked Gary how he wanted his coffee. He said the same way as always — said it as though challenging her not to remember or to pretend not to remember.

She got cream, not milk, out of the refrigerator, and sat down across from him at the pale oak dining table.

"I like your dress," he said. He warmed his hands on

293

the mug before he stirred in the cream and sugar. "I never thought of you in yellow, but it works."

"It better work. I need help, Gary. Can I count on you?"

"Of course you can." His eyes glittered. "You know that. That's why I came."

"I'm surrounded by people who claim to love me, who think they know better than I do what's right for me, but they're wrong and they're making me crazy. I know John is alive. And they just won't listen to me."

"All your life people have thought they knew what you should do," Gary said.

"You mean my grandmother. About you."

He nodded.

"This is different," she said. "This is bigger, Gary. Bigger than you, me, John, Hank—bigger than anything."

"I read the story in the *Post*. I know what you said on that show. What do you want me to do? I've got the pickup in a lot—I can kidnap him if you like. Though I guess we'd have to be careful he doesn't have a heart attack. Make sure he doesn't think it's a stickup or anything."

"You'd do that for me?" she said.

"I'd do anything for you."

"Why? I'm curious. What's in it for you?"

He gave her a long look. "Your grandmother once said to me that everyone had a moment in life and I should be glad I'd had mine with you. Maybe I want a second moment."

"My God"—a bubble of laughter breaking on her lips—"it's a super joke, isn't it? All these people who pride themselves on being so high-minded and wide-minded and you're the only one who can hear what I'm saying. My grandmother was right about us, but she was wrong about you, and she'd be the first to say so. We've all been wrong about you. Tell me you're glad he didn't really die."

"Come on, Andrea." He slid his hands across the table, palms up, but he didn't seem to mind that she didn't offer hers. "It's me, Gary. I've known you all your life. I'm offering to risk my butt for you. The least you can do is level with me. It's just an excuse, isn't it?"

"Gary—"

"Like with me. You couldn't admit that you were just plain hot for the grocer's son so you worked up an— elaborateness, is that a word? All about how I was your rebellion and stuff like that. And now it's embarrassing that you've fallen for this ordinary married insurance agent—"

Her hands tightened on her mug. "Don't say another word. Don't you dare say another word. You're as bad as the rest of them."

"The funny thing is, it doesn't change anything for me. I still love you and I always will. I really would kidnap that guy for you. I'll cut out the heart and bring it to you if you want to play your game. I can't do it for nothing, though. Give me a crumb."

"Go," she said.

"What do you see in him? Will you just tell me that? What's so special about him that you'd bury the whole world in bullshit just to get your hands on him?"

She had never before felt so tired. "Please, Gary. Please. Go away."

He got up. "Thanks for the coffee. Nice and hot. Comfort never gets the coffee hot enough. My offer stands if you change your mind."

She thought she might burst for loneliness.

"Andrea, I can't bear to see you looking like that." He looked ready to cry himself. "I didn't mean to hurt you. We could always say anything to each other. You used to tell me I knew you better than you knew yourself."

"Everything is different now," she said dully.

"Look—did you ever stop to consider that John's heart went somewhere else?" He pulled a newspaper clipping out of his pocket. "The *New Haven Register.* January eighth. I didn't show it to you before because you seemed to need to think what you were thinking, but now I don't know any more."

She read the clipping.

Heart Recipient Dies

Harold J. Kallukalan, Jr., 22, died at Yale— New Haven Hospital last night, four hours after receiving a human heart in "uneventful" surgery. Gail Arnheim, spokesperson for the transplantation team, said that death was caused by massive rejection of the donor heart.

"No," Andrea said. "No."

"I'm sorry," Gary said.

"You're sorry! What are you sorry about! I said no! His heart didn't go to New Haven. No."

"Are you sure?"

"No, no, no, no!" she yelled.

"Andrea, I'm only trying to help."

"I don't need anyone's help! I'm the army, and I'm going to free him!"

She grabbed her shoulder bag and a coat, skibbled down the stairs to the lobby, waved at Pete, and burst out onto Twelfth Street, caught a cab coming up Greenwich, told the driver to take her to the Plaza.

296

Chapter 38

Margo woke to the sound of Hank in the shower whistling "Fine and Dandy." She'd been dreaming of morning kisses, and she wanted to fall back asleep, get back to those silky feelings, blot out the strangely disturbing tune. She closed her eyes, and the image came clear again: Hank with hair still wet, smelling of soap and water, a towel around his waist and then no towel, pressing his lips to her, wanting her. Oh, but so long ago, and maybe it hadn't happened, never would. She surfaced out of the tantalizing dream. She'd resolved something last night, but what was it? She missed the children.

The shower went on and on. She got up and used the powder room off the living room, making herself focus on the luxurious details — the professional makeup lights around the mirror, the little basket on the sink with foil packets of hand cream — and not quite succeeding. She put on slacks and a sweater; she would have plenty of time to shower and change into her dark green ultrasuede suit before they left for Frank E. Campbell's.

She sat down in the living room and placed a call to Debbie at Ginger's house. Debbie sounded surprised to hear from her. Who, me need reassurance? Gotta run, Mom, I said I'd make pancakes.

Children! When you were desperate for them to

stand on their own, they wrapped themselves around you. When you needed to be needed, they barely acknowledged you.

The shower finally stopped. As she dialed Skip's number, she watched Hank move around the bedroom.

"I'm in the living room, darling," she called, but he didn't hear her or maybe he thought she was talking to Skip.

No answer at Skip's. She called information and asked for a listing for Sara Simon on Washington Place, wrote the number down, then stopped herself in the act of dialing. Skip was a big boy—he had a right to some privacy. And what if he'd spent the night with Mary Margaret!

In the bedroom, Hank had laid John's suitcase on the bed and was taking out his clothes. Margo watched, incapable of speech, as he opened a plastic tube and unfurled a pair of blue briefs. Stepped into them. Smoothed them over his hips. Flexed a little.

She was in a foreign country and didn't know the language. Was this what life came down to? You thought you knew people, thought you'd bound them to you, but in the end they were only strangers. She'd laughed at Debbie when Debbie had said there were too many illusions in family life, but the laugh was on her, wasn't it?

Well, whatever else was or wasn't true, she knew this: Anything would be better than sitting in that elegant pink chair watching her husband dress in a dead man's clothes.

"Darling," she called out, "I'm going downstairs for breakfast. Join me if you like." Then she fled so she wouldn't have to witness his polite indifference.

Chapter 39

She tapped gently on the door.

"Who's there?" she heard him ask from the other side.

She swallowed mirth. "It's the troops."

She heard the cautious turning of a bolt. The door opened.

He was wearing his own true clothes and her heart leaped though his hair was still so wrong.

"Liberation is at hand," she said.

He didn't seem to know what to make of her. "Margo's downstairs having breakfast," he said — said it as though she might be disappointed. "We could join her."

"I'll make you breakfast. Do you need to bring anything with you?"

"You're serious, aren't you?"

"Never more so. Hurry, please. We've got to get out of here. I thought I could share you, I thought we had time, and I was wrong. Everyone wants you dead."

"I can't just go off and not tell Margo. She'll panic."

"Leave her a note. Tell her you've gone to work on your poem and we'll meet her at Campbell's."

He didn't move, and she pressed herself against him and reached up to put her arms around his neck.

"Have you forgotten everything?" she murmured into his neck. Her lips teased the corners of his mouth.

"Andrea."

"Sweetie. Sweetie."

The purifying heat of their kisses was the one and only truth.

"I've been so silly," she said. "Thinking I needed to convince the world as if we couldn't decide for ourselves. An elaborateness, Gary would say. But I am the army and you are free." She heard an elevator door open and shut. "Don't worry about a coat. I have a taxi waiting."

It was forever and no time at all until their mouths met again in the backseat of the Checker. Words kissing words kissing kisses as they drank up the gliding city.

"It's so—"

"I know—"

"I've been—"

"Me too."

Hands on his soft suede arms inside her coat, her yellow silky breasts.

"Andrea. Andrea."

"Sweetie."

"Let's never ever ever—"

"We won't."

The driver cleared his throat. She looked up and told him they wanted the far corner on the right.

The cold air was a shock as they got out. The everyday faces of those who didn't know.

He looked up and down the row of brownstones. "Is this the Village?" he said.

"Forty-ninth Street. Your old place. Because Sukie's staying in mine. Don't strain to remember, sweetie. It will all come back before you know it." She put a key in the door and let them in.

He glanced at the front hall table, the way he always did, and she smiled.

"I got the mail when I came for the suit," she said. "Come on."

He followed her up the stairs. She unlocked another door.

He took in the books, the maps, the paintings, the computer. Reverent finger on the keyboard though he didn't press a button. "I dreamed about this room."

"Yes," she said.

"I never even learned how to type, but I bet I could work at this thing."

She pretended to fake a pout. "Is work what's really on your mind right now?"

"If I don't work"—he gave her a long slow smile— "you won't believe in me."

He sat down at the computer and she heard the dark gods laughing. She was dancing in eight worlds at once.

"I'll make coffee," she said. "I went to that Cuban place this morning and got them to sell me some beans. And I bet you're dying for eggs and sausage."

He found a toggle switch and flipped it and the computer came to life. "Peppermint tea for me, if you have it," he said. He pressed a couple of keys. "Or juice would be fine. Any kind. And some cereal."

She poured orange juice into big green Mexican goblets.

"Rice Krispies, Corn Flakes, or Cheerios?" she asked from the cupboard.

"Look," he said.

She walked around the kitchen counter and leaned over him to read. Green letters bright on a midnight screen.

Henry Corman came to town
In a limousine. He
Stuck a feather in his cap

301

And called it cappellini.

She turned off the machine.

"Why did you do that?" he said.

"I didn't like it. It wasn't—you."

"I thought it was cute," he said. "The kind of rhyme Skip does." He made piano fingers on the keyboard. Started to sing: "Henry Corman came to town—"

She put a finger over his lips. "Please."

He seemed to change his focus, to realize she was there and what that meant. He pulled her onto his lap—he breathed her skin. "Please, what?"

"Please let's just be ourselves." She wound a finger around a curl, tried to tug it straight but it bounced right back. "Our most amazing selves." She kissed his lips. "This kind of amazing." His eyelids. "And this kind."

"Andrea."

"Call me Dandy."

"I'm still not sure."

"You said we had a right and we do. Don't be scared. It's not like you."

"I don't know what's like me," he said.

"Well, sure. After what you've been through. But everything will come back."

"I can't hurt Margo." He was stroking her hair, her back. "She's the nicest woman who ever lived. She saved my life."

She clenched her fists in exasperation. "But if you don't live it what good is it? Do you want me?"

"Yes. You know I do. You're the most—"

"Don't tell me. Show me," she said.

He stood up, not letting go, and carried her into the bedroom. They tumbled onto the bed, pulling at each other's clothes. His shirt came open, and she saw the bright red scar bisecting his chest and she just about stopped breathing.

"Does it hurt?" She put the most tentative of fingertips to it.

"A kind of pulling feeling sometimes," he said. "Itches, mostly."

"I've got a cure for itches," she said. She worked her way from his throat to his navel, now feathering with her tongue, now huffing little puffs of breeze, now making butterflies of her eyelashes: teasing, tasting, healing, loving.

He said her name on a long moan of pleasure. "If I'd known what a scar could feel like, I'd have done this years ago."

"I can make you feel good everywhere. Here. And here. And here."

"Dandy. Dandy."

"I wanted to be naked with you."

The yellow dress got tossed to the floor; all their things. He held her and kissed her and their hands went everywhere.

Nothing happened.

"I don't understand—"

"Shh, relax—"

"My medicine—"

"Just let me—"

Nothing.

"I love you, John."

Less than nothing.

She kissed him on the cheek and padded off to get their orange juice. Came back into the bedroom. Found him snoring.

Well, honeymoons were like that, weren't they? All the magazines said so. Even the darlingest couples.

She got into bed. Raised her glass to the big bold portrait of herself hanging on the opposite wall. Do you remember, oh do you remember the weekend in

Kent when we decided to hallow every bed in the house. Carting that old striped towel around with us, laughing like a couple of loons.

She turned out the light and the snoring stopped.

Sweetie. Dearest. Alone at last. Tell me you love me.

She put her ear to his heart.

Dan-dy. Dan-dy. Hardly. Hear you. Don't feel. Near you.

Her frantic lips moved over his breast. She fastened on his nipple, trying to urge life from him.

Below she felt the sacred stirring. "Margo?" he mumbled. "Want you."

Her mind was a panicky jumble, but Phil Porter's words filtered through and she knew what was happening. Hank's body was trying to drive out John. Even if the heart survived, John would drown in the shower of foreign blood cells.

"No!" she screamed. "No!"

She grabbed the telephone, dialed 911. Send an ambulance, send it now—we have a transplant recipient rejecting.

"Oh God, let him live, let him live," she sobbed, crawling around the bed, clawing at the heap of crumpled clothing. She got the blue silk briefs on him, but they looked so terribly wrong that she gave up on clothes for him and made him warm with the sheet and blanket. A siren muddled the air and she realized she was naked. She started dressing herself.

The yellow dress, her shining badge of hope, seemed to melt in her hands, and she crushed it, bit it, wept into it, finally flung it away. Her chest opened then, as though she too had been bound by stitches and now the stitches were torn, and the sound of her wailing filled the room, tears flooded up and out.

As a child she had imagined bombs falling, billions dying, and a panoramic grief seized her now, as though evil gods had designated her the only survivor, mourning for life itself.

She cried out for her mother and father to tell her it was only a dream, to offer her warmth and comforting words. They didn't come and didn't come, and the dream got bigger and darker, swallowing tables and chairs and the rug and finally her. Hank might live but John was dead. Her love, her only love, her always and ever John, was truly gone.

She stumbled through the emptiness to his closet, took her old black dress off the hanger, and put it on. A fresh wave of desolateness swept over her. "I am a widow," she thought, touching the dark silk, the badge of ultimate failure. She remembered Sukie saying, so long ago, "Today is the bottom of the pit. You will probably never again in your life have a day as awful as this one." Sukie had been wrong. The most awful day was now.

But as she kneeled down next to his body, a thin little ray of comfort stole into her heart. At least there was nothing to fear because everything that mattered was over.

Chapter 40

She paced the sunless solarium down the hall from Hank's bed in the Columbia-Presbyterian surgical cardiac unit, as wired as a beast snatched from green freedom and shut up behind cold metal. She kicked the faded orange imitation leather chairs and slapped the left-behind magazines. Wouldn't they love to see her anger, Mickie Ross and the others who thought she was a goody goody blob of marshmallow fluff. Oh, but she was angry, damn angry, fucking angry. The waste of it. The damn fucking waste of it. They should have given John's heart to Sam Mancuso except that he was too small — no I didn't mean it God, not even for half a second, I tasted the thought but I spat it out, thank you for giving Hank the heart, please make it okay for him, I am grateful and I love you God, and I'll never make another muffin —

A nurse came in and smiled at her. Margo didn't know her name, but they recognized one another. Soon she would know the pattern of the curtains, the smells of the cafeteria, the stories of the other patients. She'd only imagined that she and Hank had escaped the hospital world for a minute or two.

She went into a washroom and did her best to scrub the grief and fear and anger off her face because her son would be arriving any minute. "Hang in there," said another kind nurse, as she headed back to the solarium.

And there were Skip and Gar, Skip holding open his arms for a bear hug, announcing that he'd coincided with Gar in the hallway as though this might make the wonderful difference.

"I was just telling him, Margo," Gar said, "that rejection is part of the process. It's when they go too long without an episode that the doctors start getting worried. I wish it had happened at home, but New York's not a bad second choice."

"If I hear one more version of that speech, I'll scream!" Margo said. "Give it to us without the parsley. How severely is he rejecting?"

"There's been a slight decrease in ventricular compliance," Gar said crisply. "That's why we picked up the abnormal diastolic gallop rhythm, but we've shot him full of prednisone and we hope to turn him around within hours. Why don't you have a minute with him and then stretch out—you look like hell. They'll give you a bed here. Or I'll take you back down to the Plaza. Sue says she'll meet you wherever you want."

"I'll stay with you, Mom," Skip said.

"Thank you, honey, but I'll be fine. I don't need—" The lie froze in her mouth. She'd been lying to her children, to herself, ever since Hank's surgery, and where had it gotten them all? "Yes, I do," she said to Skip. "I need you very much. You go see Daddy, and then I'll have a turn, and then we'll follow doctor's orders"—she didn't try to disguise her bitterness—"and get some sleep."

Gar waited until Skip was out of hearing and then he sat down and crossed his legs and clasped his hands behind his head. "Okay," he said. "Let me have it."

Her eyes sought the safety of the window, but something clicked and she looked at Gar. "I just realized—this isn't what you expected me to say but it's

307

important — that Debbie's been trying to tell me about windows, about women looking out of windows. That's what I've been doing for years, and Sue too, checking the trees, the sky, what people are wearing, sometimes just letting our eyes get lost in the middle distance, because anything was better than seeing what was right in front of us."

Gar didn't answer, just nodded a little, not enough of a nod to show agreement but enough to let her know he had heard. "Get on with it," he seemed to be saying. "Let me have it between the ears." So she did.

"You two fabulous studs must have a lot to say to each other. Did you compare notes on your — pieces?"

"Margo —"

"Is that why you pushed him to do all that so-called publicity, so he would end up in Andrea's bed and you'd have company? Or was it his reward for pain and suffering — is that how you saw it? Tell me, goddam it. Of course you miscalculated a little, didn't you? It's one thing to throw away your wife and kids, another to throw away your life. You heard your own baloney so many times you started to believe it. You're not a sick man, Hank. You're a healthy guy with a healthy young heart. Not healthy and young enough to handle Andrea, though. God, what a waste. All that effort to end up dying in the saddle. What a humiliating waste."

"You're really something," Gar said.

The quiet voice stopped her. "What do you mean?"

"I always thought you had wonderful values. The real true liberal, the woman who absolutely loved life. I guess I was wrong. Capital punishment is too cruel for murderers — how many times have I heard that argument from you? — but not for husbands who cheat. You really think Hank is supposed to die because he wanted Andrea for a moment."

"No. That's not fair. No."

"He loves you, Margo. Nobody but you. And he needs your love more than ever."

"He has brilliant doctors like you. The miracle of modern chemistry. Oh, don't worry, Gar. I'll do what I have to do. He won't guess what I'm feeling."

He shook his head. "That's not good enough. I want you straight in your heart."

"Since when do cardiologists care about that part of the heart?"

"The good ones always have. You used to think I was just talking when I said you were the one who kept him alive. I wasn't."

"You want me to forgive Hank because you want Sue to forgive you. That's it, isn't it?"

"I don't know what I want from Sue. I'm very mixed up at the moment. This trip has been strange for us. Wonderful in a way. I don't know what I want to have happen. But I know what I want for Hank. As his friend and as his doctor."

A nurse came hurrying in. She wasn't smiling. "Dr. McKay. Quickly."

Hank's bed was surrounded by medical people. His bright red face was oozing sweat. He was clutching Skip's hand but staring into space. A doctor snapped out an order for a respirator. Margo's guts seemed to liquify.

"His damn blood pressure," Gar said.

"Dearest," Margo said to Hank.

He conjured the start of a smile. "Hi, kid."

"You're going to be fine," she said.

"Doesn't feel that way," he said.

"You are. I've been thinking—I don't want to go to Paris with anybody else but you. Can you set that to music, Skip?"

Skip managed a nod. "Absolutely."

A technician wheeled in a breathing machine.

"Pot," Hank said.

"Bedpan?" a nurse said.

"Pot in Paris," he said.

"That's right," Margo said. "I'll pot and you'll write poetry. We'll eat in little cafés every night. The children can support us."

"Henry Corman came to town in a limousine. He." His eyes closed.

Gar took her arm. "Let's give him a chance to sleep."

Margo leaned against him as they walked down the corridor. The floor beneath her feet seemed to wobble. "He's status six again, isn't he?"

Chapter 41

March at the churchyard in Kent, and pale splinters of grass pushed through the patches of old snow. Andrea, clutching Mark, stepped carefully, keeping to the flagstone path, because the grass looked fragile enough to perish from the weight of a single tread. She'd been attentive to such details lately. She'd seen a spider in the bathtub and she'd taken great care to get it out of there alive, murmuring reassuring words as she cornered it, carrying it down to the cellar on a piece of cardboard because shooing it out the window might have meant that it would die.

"Are you all right?" Mark asked.

"Yes." She craned anxiously, though, and she said, "I wish they'd get here."

She'd tracked Hank's journey toward death and back again through daily calls to Phil Porter, so many calls that she'd needed only to say "Hello, Mary Jo" for his secretary to know who was calling and why; but she hadn't seen him since the ambulance had taken him away from John's apartment. Hadn't talked to Margo because Gar had told Phil to tell her that Margo needed time to recover from the wildness of New York.

Then she'd woken up one morning knowing that she had business in the churchyard, the saddest business in the world, only to be borne if everyone who mattered were there to help her, Hank and Margo most of all. She'd asked her mother to invite them and they'd accepted. Someday when she felt absolutely strong she'd ask Kitty how she'd done it.

"They'll come, dear," her mother said now. "Margo promised to call if there were any problem, and she didn't call, did she?"

"We should have met at the house," Andrea said. She'd been afraid to have her mother make the suggestion to Margo because that might be one request too many and Margo would change her mind about the day altogether.

The Reverend Peter J. Taft said everyone was welcome to wait inside the church.

"No, here they are," Sukie said. "A blue car, didn't you say?"

"A Chevrolet," Andrea said. She watched Margo maneuver the car into a parking space, and she remembered the day in Hartford when the car had been waiting for her at the train station, and at three o'clock in the morning Hank had offered her Familia and John had called her Dandy and kissed her. Such craziness it seemed now, and she knew that this judgment meant she was healing; and then she remembered another day when she'd known — screaming and ripping John's bathrobe — that healing was the very thing to dread. That judgment had been right too. Maybe denial was noble and a sickness both.

In the end you had no choice. Life made you want to be well. A message in your cells or something. Better to be ordinary than dead. Her father's programming had been screwed up, he hadn't gotten the message, he hadn't survived. Kitty, less wondrous, had. So Andrea was more like her mother than her father in that important respect, and now, here, among the pale tombstones, she was glad.

She still had so many questions. And no John to help her find answers. Well, she would just have to find them herself. Maybe somewhere in the book about Leonora Whittlesey—she was halfway there now—she would find an unexpected mirror and understand what had happened and what it meant. Writers don't know what they know until they write it, John had once told her. She would never hear his heartbeat again, but she could listen to those words every working day.

And, oh, it was Hank getting out of the driver's side, Margo getting out of the passenger's side. She wasn't the only one who had changed.

"Look at that bounce," Mark said. "You'd never know he'd been through surgery again, would you, Phil?"

"Gar McKay says it's been a textbook recovery," Phil said.

"You all keep going," Andrea said, meaning to the grave. "I want a minute alone with them."

"Dear, do you think—" her mother said.

"Come on, Kitty," Mark said. He put an arm around her, and the group moved on down the path.

Andrea stood motionless in the thawing air, watching the Cormans come toward her—and, God, wasn't it something that her mind had made the leap, that she had looked at these two people and actually thought "the Cormans?" As they made their way down the path, a band of light seemed to wrap itself around them, blur the edges between them. Marry them, as she and John had been married. She cautiously tested her own feelings, looking for pain. But her grief this day was centered on the coffin fifty yards away. It wasn't Hank whom she had lost or Margo to whom she had lost him.

"Hello, Andrea," Margo said. Not warm but not wintry either.

313

"Hello, Margo. Thank you for coming. You look glorious, Hank." The words seemed to bounce off the air, and she realized that they were the words she had uttered in the hospital room the day John had been buried without her to witness the unbearable deed. And was she now ready to concede in the final judgment chamber of her mind that, yes, it was truly John who had been buried that day? Was it Hank, for sure and certain, to whom she'd said those words? Looking at the man before her, no one but Henry Corman, she still found herself unable—or maybe unwilling—to pass judgment on who he had been six weeks before. Maybe she would never know.

If Hank remembered her words, he didn't show it; he didn't echo himself (because it hadn't been himself that other time?).

"I'm feeling pretty good," he said cautiously. Then Margo squeezed his hand, seemed to give him the okay, and the words started coming out the way Andrea remembered (but which man was she remembering?): warm and bouncy and a little rushed in their eagerness to be heard. "Margo wouldn't let me feel bad. I was carrying on about having gone under the knife again, I wasn't cooperating with the docs, but she zapped me with oatcakes until I realized how lucky I was to be around at all. Store-bought oatcakes," he added, in a voice that mingled affection and pride. He carried Margo's gloved hand to his heart; he held it there. "When I was coming out of anesthesia, I had this terrific revelation. Why"—he lifted his shoulders—"had Margo become a compulsive baker?"

Margo was wearing the half-smile of someone who'd heard a story too many times but didn't mind hearing it once more.

"I give up," Andrea said. "Why?"

"Because she was supposed to be baking pottery!"

Hank said triumphantly. "So I told her to order a kiln for the backyard and unplug the oven in the kitchen."

"He really did," Margo said, face warming in pleasure. "And I drove right over to Wethersfield and ordered everything I needed." She and Hank turned to each other at the same moment and exchanged small conspiratorial smiles. Then she seemed to remember where she was, and she gave an apologetic gasp and said: "Forgive us, Andrea. It's hardly the moment to talk about pots. You must want to get this sad business over with." She gestured toward the gravesite, where Andrea's people stood waiting. "Shall we join the others?"

"I have to tell you something first," Andrea said to Margo. "About that morning in New York."

"Really, you don't," Margo said quickly. "I know as much as I want to know. Maybe more. I'd rather not hear the details, frankly." Hank gave her a small hug. Andrea didn't know if the hug signaled pride or the desire to comfort, but with some small grief she recognized its other name. It was "husband." Hank was Margo's husband.

Margo gave Hank a reassuring look, a look to tell him he didn't have to worry for himself or for her, but Andrea wasn't sure she believed it. Even with that husbandly arm around her, Margo still needed something more, and she, Andrea, was the only one who could give it to her.

"Details! I'm not telling you details!" She got the words out fast and urgently, before tears could come or Margo could move away and a golden chance with her. "I was gorgeous, I was wondrous, I was desperate for him, and it didn't matter. He couldn't, he wouldn't make love to anyone but you. That's how I knew he was rejecting. You see, he wasn't John any more. He was Hank. And there was only one woman ever for

Hank."

Margo didn't say anything, but Hank shot Andrea a grateful look. "We came here to offer comfort to you, and you're worrying about us."

"I'm doing it for myself," Andrea said. "This is my day for setting things right. This morning I told my mother that I love her. Even if she can't cook chicken."

"Andrea, we need you," Mark called.

They started down the path, Andrea alone, Hank and Margo just behind, and then Margo said, "Did you really, really believe that Hank was John?"

"I thought you didn't want details," Hank said. "Let's leave well enough alone."

"No," Margo said firmly, "we've started this conversation and we might as well finish it. Andrea's right. That's what funerals are for."

Andrea stopped and turned around to look at them. "The truth is that I don't know," she said. "I remember one day telling Mark that I was somewhere between wanting to believe but not believing and not wanting to believe but believing. Does that make any sense to you?"

"Oh, but it does!" Margo said. "I never put it into those words for myself, but I think that's how I feel about God. Because if you believe, really believe, that should be the most important fact in your life, that should dominate every moment. Which is a terrible burden as well as a joy. And if you don't believe, there's a kind of freedom, but what loneliness!"

"Yes," Andrea said softly. Her eyes filled with tears.

Margo opened her arms and put them around Andrea and said, "You poor baby. Nobody ever told you that life was going to be like this."

"My father told me, but he didn't tell me what to do. I guess he didn't know himself."

"Nobody knows," Hank says. "You just live. And if

you're very lucky, you get to love some people who love you." He linked arms with both the women, and they moved on down toward the grave. "I only hope John knew how lucky he was to have you, Andrea."

"He knew," Margo said softly. "If anyone can be sure of that, it's you."

Andrea went very still, not quite daring to believe that she'd finally heard the message of acceptance she'd been so desperate to hear. "Thank you, Margo," she said fervently. "Thank you."

"Oh no," Margo said. "We're still the ones who have to thank you. Because you saved Hank's life that second time, too. I didn't see it before, but I do now. You're the only one who could have known he was rejecting. Because that heart really did belong to you."

Andrea's body seemed to lighten, as though Margo had taken the burden of their shared belief on herself, leaving her—even today—with the joy. She kneeled down next to the fresh mound of dirt and let her fingertips carry a kiss from her lips to the coffin. "Goodbye, my sweetie," she said. Tears slid down her cheeks. "We only had twenty minutes, but what a twenty minutes."

The Reverend Taft cleared his throat. Andrea stood up and faced him, let his words burn into her skin, become a part of her, the way the words of her wedding had done.

"For as much as it hath pleased almighty God to take out of the world the soul of our brother John departed, we therefore recommit his body to the ground; earth to earth, ashes to ashes, dust to dust, remembering that if our earthly house of this tabernacle be dissolved, we have a building of God, a house not made with hands, eternal in the heavens." He turned to Phil Porter. "You have the heart?"

Phil carried the small wooden box to the edge of the

grave.

"Let me do it," Hank said, though he was trembling. He took the box and laid it atop the coffin next to the box that held his own heart. "From *The Rules of Golf*," he announced, in a defiant voice that made Andrea think, with a sad inward smile, of Skip on the dark and windy corner of Washington and Twelfth. Hank Corman, husband and father and his own absolute self. " 'The ball may be deemed unfit for play when it is visibly cut or out of shape or so cracked, pierced or otherwise damaged as to interfere with its true flight —' " He shook his head and looked at Andrea to tell her he couldn't go on, and she nodded her understanding and more, and he went back to Margo's side.

"May the Lord grant peace to all who are here," the minister said. "Amen."

Later, at the house on Sprague Road, Andrea heard her mother (who'd had two bourbons) ask Mark, "Whose heart does he have this time?"

"He told the doctors he didn't want to know," Mark said.

"Maybe he needed a Jewish heart for it to work," Kitty said.

Mark patted her cheek. "Everyone needs a Jewish heart, Kitty."

"I hope not, Mark, because last week I had to renew my driver's license and I told them I would be an organ donor." She folded her cashmere arms across her thin chest. "What do you think of that?"

Andrea wandered into Papa Sam's library to take a moment away from the muchness of the day, collect herself; but when she turned on the light she saw that she wasn't alone. Hank was there.

"I'm sitting in the dark," he said, as though she'd asked for an explanation, "because I can't bear thinking about all the books I'm not going to have time to read. Even with two lives, you don't get to do everything."

"It's true," she said softly. "There's no such thing as enough life."

His eyes took in the rows and rows of burgundy bindings, and then he said to her, "You and I must have the strangest relationship of any man and woman around."

She nodded without saying anything.

"I'm very grateful for what you said to Margo, but I have to admit in my heart of hearts I'm not sure it was only John who wanted you. Wasn't there maybe one half a second when it wasn't just John you wanted?"

She smiled. "You're a very sweet man, Hank. You don't have to worry about me. I'm going to be all right. How's the poem coming?"

"I sent a dozen verses to Linda Ammiccare. She says I have a genuine voice. Whatever that means."

"It means she wants you for yourself. Not because you sound like John. You should be pleased."

"I guess so," he said. He put a finger to her hair, then let it drop. "Will you answer my question?"

"But I don't know the answer," she said. "If I find it I'll tell you. I promise. Give my love to the children." Then she went upstairs to the honeymoon bedroom to weep one last time for what might have been.

Acknowledgments

Joanne Lamb, R.N., supplied facts that nourished my fantasies. Lance Dworkin, M.D., commented on draft after draft. Jesse Manlapaz, M.D., offered information on brain injury. Nancy Weinstein, M.D., cheered me on. Saul Weber and Caroline Fox Weber taught me about the heart. John Abrahms was my insurance guru. Tom Watson's book made me see the poetry in *The Rules of Golf.* Jim Wyllie and Donald D. Williams were my technical angels. Elzbieta Czyzewska tempered bran muffins with espresso. Diana Horton and Susan Shweisky were encouraging critics. Copylot did great work in no time at all. Katharine Weber saved my manuscript from Mr. Death. Joyce Engelson saved my manuscript from me. Jane Berkey saved me from my manuscript. Sharifa Hamid saved my family.

Isaac Epstein put my first novel in his bookshop window eighteen years ago. I wish he were here for this one.